Cry Baby

King Benjamin

Cry Baby

Acknowledgments

First and foremost I have to thank God for the talent, and opportunity to develop it. This was by far the hardest thing I've ever set out to accomplish but I knew when I set out to do it that I was following God's lead to a new beginning. I have to thank my number one fan Destiny Horne for pushing me to get this project into the hands of readers. My sister Melanie Thomas. Words can't describe it so I won't try. Tisha Landrum, Joe Jackson Donald Washington, Duke, Lakelia Deloach-Lucus, India Norfleet-Lewis, and Sharon Stanley Hillman. You have all played such a pivotal part in this process and I can't thank you enough. Last but not least my mom Alberta and my daughter Dalejah. I hope I'm making you both proud.

Chapter 1

1989

"Chris Johnson Sr. if you put your hands on me I'm gonna kill you. And after that, I'm gonna call the police and tell them to come get your dead ass!"

Chris Sr. didn't take kindly to the threat and he was at the end of his rope with Sheila. Pow! He cocked back and slapped the dog shit out of her. He slapped her so hard that it split her lip and blood came pouring out. The second blow was a backhand and it sent Sheila crashing to the ground. Sheila did a drop-and-roll and was back on her feet before Chris could kick her like he planned. She ran to the bathroom and locked the door. Breathing hard and trying to think as fast as she could, Sheila grabbed the bottle of alcohol from the cabinet. Chris kicked the door in on the first try and Sheila splashed the bottle of alcohol in his face then pushed him down in the tub.

"Aahhh! Aahhh!" he screamed as she ran out of the bathroom scared for her own life.

At this very moment, Sheila wasn't a Christian, but a woman in fear for her safety. She made it to the kitchen and went straight for the knife drawer. She heard Chris coming fast. The sound of his heavy feet stomping towards her made Sheila's heart jump out of her chest. If it was going down then fuck it. She backed into a corner as Chris came charging into the room.

"Come on muthafucka! Come on!" she yelled.

Chris stopped dead in his tracks when he peeped the butcher knife Sheila was clutching tight.

"Bitch you really think I'ma let you stab me with that knife? That knife going in your ass bitch!"

Chris charged at Sheila full force and as she lunged forward with the knife in her hand, she spotted her ten-year-old son in the doorway.

"Mama noooooo!" Chris Jr. yelled, but it was too late and the knife plunged into his father's stomach as he screamed at the top of his lungs. He watched as his father fell to the ground and grew silent. His eyes were open but he wasn't moving. Sheila didn't move either. She stood over her husband's body watching him die with a deranged look in her eyes.

Chris Jr. woke up dripping with sweat and breathing heavily. He sat straight up and looked around his bedroom. The realization crept in that he was only dreaming, and that his mom and dad were still alive. It was so real because it was something that had been on his mind almost every day for the past month. Since his father had been out of work, the tension between his parents was growing thicker and thicker. His father had become a bitter alcoholic who was looking for any reason to scream and yell like a five-year-old. His mother just wanted her husband to get out in the streets and look for a job. She was tired of carrying the load and she was becoming more vocal about it on a daily basis. But the screaming matches had become so intense lately, Chris Jr. was almost sure it would escalate to violence. In the meantime, there was nothing he could do so he got up and got dressed for school.

In school, Chris always sat in the back of the class and kept a low profile. He didn't want the teacher calling on him to answer questions. He didn't need the attention. A lot of students took advantage of the first-hour teacher who happened to be a real softie. The girls chewed gum in class while the boys chose to make some sucker the butt of their jokes. The bad thing about the back of the class is that's where all the class clowns posted up at. This way, nobody really knew who the culprit was when dirt was done.

"Rabbit ears, rabbit ears! What's up doc?" Chris heard someone say.

He knew the joke was supposed to be on him being he had the biggest ears of everyone in the class. He tried to ignore it.

"That nigga look like Doctor Spock on Star Trek," another dude joined in.

Chris started to get that horrible feeling in his stomach he got whenever he felt embarrassed. He knew it was Dink's punk ass being the follower that he was. Chris was so young and impressionable; he was still trying to figure out how to handle these types of situations. He had never confronted anybody about anything in school. Never had a fist fight and never had a real incident that had the potential to lead up to a fist fight. Only thing he was really sure about was that Dink was a pussy. As the jokes continued, the targets shifted but always seemed to boomerang back around to Chris. All the negative attention caused him to perspire and he could feel his heart rate increasing. He began bouncing his left foot on the floor nervously.

If he was a joker type, he could have come back with a jab of his own. But he wasn't, and there was no need to add fuel to the fire.

"Silly rabbit, tricks are for kids!" someone shouted.

That one got the whole class in an uproar. That one even got the girl he secretly had a crush on laughing at him. He could feel the lump in his throat now. His eyes were getting all glassy. He tried his best to hold back the tears. Tears would only make matters worse. But sadly, it wouldn't be the first time he'd boo-hooed in class. Fifth graders could be such cruel little people. Hopefully, this verbal assault wouldn't last much longer and they'd move on to the next victim. But why don't the goddamn teacher ever say anything? he thought.

"Y'all better chill out. Y'all know Chris can hear y'all talking with them big bionic ears. Aye, I bet he can hear his mama call him from around the corner and up the block."

That was it. He laid his head down on his desk between his folded arms to conceal his tears. He cursed the teacher for letting the assault continue. In reality, he knew it wasn't anybody's fault. It was just his day to get made fun of. Tomorrow it would be somebody else. Hopefully, tomorrow it would be somebody who could stand up for themselves and had some skills in clapping back. Better yet, whip some ass. He wished he could be that somebody.

By lunchtime, Chris had recovered from the ordeal and just wanted the day to be over so he could go home. He stood in the line waiting for his lunch tray, excited because it was pizza day. He scoped out Evelyn Turner sitting at the far end of the cafeteria. Even though he knew he'd never have the nerve to speak to her, he wanted a seat nearby so he could admire her while he ate. He moved quickly so not to be spotted by Randy the prankster who started to whole mess in English class.

He kept a stiff neck, not trying to make eye contact but kept an eye on Evelyn. All of a sudden, he felt a leg being swept out from under him. His lunch tray went flying in the air and he went crashing to the ground. It was like a belly flop with no water to cushion the fall. His palms were stinging from attempting to break his fall and he felt a sharp pain in his stomach. He could hear roars of laughter throughout the cafeteria. He saw all teeth and tongues as the crowd of people became a blur. Someone was pulling him up from the ground. He glanced up to see that it was his big burly gym teacher lifting him to his feet.

"You okay Chris?" he asked.

"Naw, I wanna go home."

"Are you hurt?"

"Yeah, I wanna go home."

Chris sat in the chair being examined by the school nurse. He was fine but exaggerated his pain so he wouldn't have to return to class.

"Aaw, ouch," he complained.

"Is this where it hurts?" the nurse asked.

"Yeah, I wanna go home."

"It's not swollen," she informed, rubbing her fingers across his ribcage.

"But it hurts."

"Well, we can call your mother and see if she's able to come and pick you up."

He knew she would. His mother would come running at the thought of her baby being injured. She'd be pissed that she had to leave work for this so he'd have to play this thing out for the remainder of the day. Give her the old hound dog eyes when she showed up.

"What did you do, trip over your own feet?" the nurse asked.

That was the second time he'd been asked that. Apparently, nobody had seen that punk Randy stick his big foot out and purposely trip him.

"Yeah, that's what happened," he agreed.

"Well, you gotta be more careful; you could have chipped a tooth or worse."

He was thinking about Randy's stupid ass.

"Yes, ma'am."

"Now let's go see if we can get in touch with your mother."

It was music to his young ears. On the ride home, Sheila stopped at McDonald's. She had concern in her voice as she questioned him about what happened.

"Did you trip over your own feet baby?"

"Yeah," he lied for the third time.

No sense in snitching on Randy. That would only make him more of an outcast than he already was.

"I wanna go to another school Ma."

"Is somebody messing with you in school boy?"

"Naw, I just wanna go to another school."

His mother sighed.

"Son, let me tell you something. Kids can be cruel no matter what school you go to. You're a smart, handsome, young man and you have nothing to feel ashamed about."

There was no outsmarting Sheila. She always knew how to read her one and only child. She was right about all the things she'd said about Chris, but he couldn't see it. Besides his flawed ears, he was becoming quite a handsome young man. He had almond colored skin with beautifully crafted eyes and his mother's good hair. As they pulled into the driveway, Chris let out a sigh of relief. It was definitely good to be home.

He jumped out of the car in a hurry but had to slow his pace. He'd forgotten he was supposed to be hurt. He wiped the smile off his face and dragged up the steps.

"Hey Dad," he said as he saw his father on the couch dusting off a forty ounce of Old English.

"Hey son," his father replied.

"Did you look for a job today?" she asked annoyed.

"Look woman, don't start that bullshit with me!"

It was a repeat of the same argument over and over. Sheila was just plain old tired.

"What bullshit? You gonna have to do something or get the fuck out of my house. I'm tired of this."

"Since when did this become your house?"

"When I started paying all the damn bills."

It was on already and this wasn't a good sign. They had decided to skip all the pleasantries and get right to it. His mother was fed up and Chris could hear it in her voice. Now that he was home, he wished he was back at school. He grew nervous as the confrontation grew louder. Chris sat in his room thinking the whole thing was his fault for faking hurt to get out of class. From the sound of it, the commotion was getting closer.

"I'm packing yo' shit today!" Sheila threatened.

He heard footsteps fly past his bedroom and down the hall to his parents' room. He heard his father stomping up the stairs and his voice was so loud Chris was startled by it.

"You better not touch my clothes bitch!" he yelled.

He heard his parents' bedroom door being kicked on. Kicked in. This was definitely about to turn violent. His heart was pounding as he rushed to the closet fumbling through the mess until he found his bat. He knew he was no match for his father but he had to do something. He could hear the rumbling now. Appliances breaking and glass shattering.

"Get the fuck off me!" Sheila screamed.

Chris ran into the hallway clutching his baseball bat.

Bang, bang, bang.

The sound of gunfire made him drop the bat and curl up on the floor in the hallway. Silence…then footsteps. Chris remained in a fetal position until someone pulled him up by his arm.

"Let's go," his mother said with a trembling voice.

"Mama—"

"Let's go!"

In a state of shock, he went back to the dream the night before and for a second he thought his mom might turn the gun in her hand on him. Sheila dragged him downstairs gripping a .38 snub-nose revolver. They hurried next door to the neighbor's house and banged on the door. The neighbor's son Sergio opened the door and was stunned to see Chris and his mother standing there, petrified. Sheila had the gun in her hand and blood on her shirt.

"I need to use your phone," she said, pushing her way past Sergio and dragging Chris inside. Sergio stood in the door for a second in disbelief before coming in and closing the door. "Sergio, can you take him up the stairs with you for a minute?"

"Come on Chris."

Once upstairs, Chris sat on Sergio's bed wiping tears from his eyes. He was still in shock from the gunshots, the seeing blood all over his mom, the fact that his father never came out of the bedroom. Slowly, the realization of what had just happened began to sink in. The sirens grew louder and closer. Something in the back of Chris's mind told him he'd never see his father again.

Chapter 2

1992

Years later Chris would still have nightmares about the night his mom killed his dad. It wasn't until now that he realized how much he needed a dad around as he began to have all kinds of questions about life. At age fourteen, he didn't know of too many dudes that had fathers at home.

Chris sat in church next to his mother with a Bible in his lap, clapping and singing old Christian hymns. He sang, not because he was really in the spirit, but because he'd get smacked upside the head if he didn't participate and show some enthusiasm. His mother had become a devout Christian since the horrible afternoon she'd shot and killed her husband. No charges were ever brought against her although she was detained for a short period. The shooting was ultimately ruled an act of self-defense. All of Sheila's neighbors, as well as the Detroit Police Department, were aware of the verbal and physical abuse she'd withstood over the past couple of years.

Sheila loved her husband and was still trying to find forgiveness. Chris was taking it hard not having his father around. He had more memories of this father as a decent man than the person he had become before his death. They moved out of the old house trying to get past the memory of that afternoon that changed their lives forever. Unfortunately, they didn't move far away and every time Chris rode or walked by the old house, he got a little teary eyed thinking about how much he missed his dad.

Once Chris was old enough to take it all in and analyze the situation, he understood that his mom did what she had to do under those circumstances. He vowed to never become abusive to women.

"Stand up," his mother nudged him as the pastor ended service with a final prayer. Chris bowed his head and repeated after the pastor word for word. He peeked up at his mother just to see if she still had her eyes closed. She did. He began to get a stiff neck from all the bowing his head over the past two hours.

"Amen," came from the congregation.

****

One the ride home, Cece Winans blasted through the speakers of Sheila's Thunderbird. She sang along and did a little dance move every time she stopped at a red light.

"Sing it with me, Chris," she nudged him as he refused.

She turned the music down and glanced over at Chris. "Everyone keeps asking me when you're going to join the choir."

"I can't sing Ma."

"You can sing good enough to be in that choir, anybody can."

"No, I can't."

"If Sister Jackson's son can be in the choir, you sure as hell can. That boy can't sing a lick."

Chris didn't want to talk about this. It just wasn't on his agenda to be getting all holy and sanctified. The only reason he even agreed to church is that it was forced on him.

"I don't wanna."

"Well, I don't care what you want. Friday, you're going to choir rehearsal."

He didn't try to argue any longer. Resistance was useless. In his mind, he still couldn't see it happening. Next, she'd be trying to get him in one of those Bible study meetings and all kind of shit. At home Chris went straight to his room to change clothes so he could go to the park. If his mom saw what he'd put on she'd make him change clothes again and put on his so-called play clothes. Play clothes were the clothes he could still fit but weren't in good enough shape to wear to school. Chris felt he was getting too old for his mother to be the one who still decided what he wore. His voice was transforming into something close to a baritone.

He moved swiftly past his mother who was in the kitchen. Once he was at the front door with the door half cracked, he called out to her.

"I'm going to the park Ma."

"Be back before dinner," Sheila said.

"I will."

He shut the door behind him and jingled his keys merrily as he walked to the park. He passed by his old block but didn't look down the street at the old house as he usually did. He could hear Sharky, his mutt puppy nemesis, all grown up still selling wolf tickets behind the fence. Chris was expecting to see Sergio at the park playing basketball. Since his father's death, Sergio had become like a big brother to him, teaching Chris how to slap-box. Once when Chris was eleven, Sergio hit Chris a little too hard and he burst into tears. They didn't do much slap-boxing after that. 0

He spotted Sergio's Monte Carlo on Daytons sitting in front of the park. Scanning the park, he found Sergio in the middle of a three-on-three. Sergio always played aggressively and popped shit the entire time. He wasn't a big dude but he was in great shape. At 5'11, dark brown skin and cut with plenty of definition to his frame, he could dunk on a lot of dudes bigger and taller.

"Let me get that ball," he taunted while playing defense. "I said let me get that ball."

Sergio reached out and yanked the ball away from the dude he was defending. After about thirty seconds of fancy dribbling, Sergio crossed him and went all the way to the hoop with ease, finishing with an around the back lay-up.

"Oooh," the spectators moaned.

Chris took a seat on the bench and spotted Evelyn, his ongoing crush. She was standing on the opposite side of the court watching the game with three friends. Two of Evelyn's friends were not much to look at, but if he had to choose between her and her best friend Charlotta, it would be a toss-up. Luckily, he didn't think he'd have to choose anytime soon.

"Check up sucka!" he heard Sergio taunting, and his attention went back to the game. Sergio was taking dudes to school and all eyes were on him.

"Oooh," the crowd of spectators sounded as he dunked on some cat while holding his dick with his free hand.

Chris couldn't help but laugh out loud at the guy who'd just gotten posterized. He'd glance up at Evelyn once in a while just to see if she was still there. The game, Evelyn, the game, Evelyn, back to the game.

"What's up Cry Baby?" a voice called out.

Chris turned to see some dudes he knew from school taking seats at the bleachers.

"What up?" he replied.

He'd gotten used to the nickname Randy had given him now. Not everybody called him Cry Baby, just the kids who remembered his episodes in elementary school. Right now he was just glad to be acknowledged by the cool kids no matter what they called him.

"You mad nigga?"

Sergio was now checking the same dude's nuts he'd been serving all day on the court. Sergio loved to get under people's skin when he was balling.

"Shut the fuck up," the guy responded.

"You mad nigga? 'Cause you keep throwing that ball at me like you mad."

"Shut the fuck up and play ball."

"Okay, throw that ball at me again like that and see what happen."

Sergio was about to finish the game now that he'd spoken his piece but this dude just had to have the last word.

"Man fuck you!" he lashed.

Sergio had his back turned walking away but he pumped his brakes and came back.

"Who you think you talking to?"

"I'm talking to you nigga; ain't no punks here."

The trash talk had quickly escalated into something else. Chris watched on growing nervous.

"What's up then? We ain't even gotta talk about it no more."

Sergio threw the ball down as he approached his target. Dude wasn't so tough now. He was expecting this thing to stay at an argument level but it was obvious Sergio wanted to fight.

Smack!

Sergio gave him an open-handed blow to the face and jumped into his fight stance. "What nigga?" Sergio barked as the man backed up staring in shock.

"Game over man," he finally said then turned to walk off the court, head down, shoulders slumped. Defeated.

****

Chris was proud to call Sergio his big brother. Proud of the way he handled himself. Wished he had the guts to be that combative. After all the commotion nobody really wanted to ball anymore. Everyone started to leave the court. Sergio was headed to his car when he spotted Chris and detoured.

"What's up lil' bro?"

"Chilling," Chris said.

"How long you been up here?"

"Not that long."

"Did you see me about to smash that fool?"

"Yeah, he was scared," Chris said, and he and Sergio laughed.

As Sergio reenacted one of the dunks that had gotten the crowd into the game, Chris tuned him out for a second as Evelyn and her girls came strolling by.

"Hey Sergio," Charlotta said waving her fingers.

"What up?" Sergio replied.

Chris was straining his neck trying to watch them all the way out of the park.

"Which one of them lil' hoodies you want?" Sergio asked.

"Huh?"

"You heard me, which one you feeling?"

"Oh, I like Evelyn."

"You holla at her?"

"Naw," Chris said shaking his head.

"Why not?"

"Man, she ain't gonna talk to me."

"Chris, stop acting like a sucker. How you know she ain't gonna talk to you? You ain't even tried yet."

Chris knew Sergio's words were harsh but true. He was acting like a sucker about the situation. Chris didn't need Sergio to tell him that. It appeared Sergio was about to finish telling him anyway.

"Let me tell you something lil' bro, nice guys finish last and bad guys always get the girl. You wanna get the girl, get out that nice box. Come off that shy shit. Don't just stare at her like she from another planet or some shit. Next time she walks by and don't acknowledge you, just be like 'damn you can't speak with yo' fine ass?' After that, she'll speak every time she sees you."

"How you know?" Chris asked.

"Put it this way, you don't see no girls walking past me without speaking do you?"

Chris was skeptical but Sergio had a point.

"I'll try it."

"That's what I'm talking about, and let me put you up on something else. When you ain't playing ball or some shit, you gotta stay fresh. I mean your gear tight but look at your shoes," Sergio finished with a look of disgust written all over his face.

"What's wrong with 'em?"

"They dirty as hell, that's what's wrong with 'em."

"I was about to ball doe," Chris explained.

"Okay, but look how many girls was just up here. You could have come with 'em clean and left with 'em dirty. You could have made a better entrance. You gotta give girls something to look at. Get you brush waves or something, iron your clothes so they stay creased up; that way a girl don't mind telling her friends she gave you her phone number."

Chris nodded and took it all in even though he had no plans on going anywhere near Evelyn. He was too afraid of rejection. At best, he could start small and work his way up. He'd try his hand with one of the less attractive girls and see what happened.

Sergio dropped Chris off that evening and sped off before his mom could get to the door. Chris knew he might catch some flak for being late for dinner, but it was worth it. He had a chance to ride around and listen to music he had to sneak and listen to at home. The Monte Carlo was a real attention getter; white with a flip-flop paint and Sergio loved every minute of the attention he got from it. Chris knew Sergio was a hustler, but until today he'd never seen him involved in any illegal activity. Chris had never witnessed transactions between him and other dudes.

"Hey Ma," Chris said coming downstairs after washing his hands.

"Don't 'Hey Ma' me! Where the hell you been?"

"It's only seven o'clock."

"Before dinner means before six o'clock, and what were you doing with Sergio anyway?"

His mother didn't have anything against Sergio and she appreciated him taking the time to teach Chris how to play sports and things of that nature. She also knew Sergio was no angel and felt Chris needed to be with kids his own age.

"He just gave me a ride home," he lied.

Chris had been trying to find a way to tell his mother he had no plans on attending choir rehearsal. He'd just started to gain an ounce of respect from being affiliated with Sergio. He was sure the choir boy thing would kill his baby buzz of popularity he had generated. Thing was, he had to choose his words carefully because sticking his chest out would surely get him popped in the mouth.

"I really don't think the choir is for me Ma."

"And why is that?" Sheila asked with a brow raised.

"I just don't."

"You think you too cool to sing in the choir huh?"

"No, but I wanna try out for the basketball team."

"Don't give me that, 'cause I ain't heard nothing about no basketball team until now. I ain't telling you not to try out, but if and when you do make the team we'll cross that bridge when we get there."

"I don't wanna go Ma," Chris complained.

"Well you going and that's that."

"No, I'm not!" The words spilled out before he could catch them.

Smack.

"Don't you ever tell me what you ain't gonna do! You hear me?"

The stinging. Oh, the stinging. No question about who was the boss here. Chris sat rubbing his cheek and a lone tear came streaming down his face. He never bothered wiping away the tear because at that moment it best represented what he was feeling.

Chapter 3

Chris had been home each night scrubbing his shoes, brushing his hair and ironing his clothes to perfection. He hadn't talked to any girls yet. He was still too nervous. The bell rang and kids spilled out into the hallways. Chris maneuvered through the crowd trying to get to his locker. He had to make his first move on Myiesha, a girl whose locker happened to be right next to his. Myiesha was cute, but she wasn't as fine as Evelyn. As he waited for her by the locker he spotted Sergio bopping down the hallway with Tamiko. Sergio had a gangsta strut that would lead you to believe he was the baddest muthafucka in the school. One top of that, he had the baddest chick in the school on his arm.

"What up lil' bro?" Sergio spoke without stopping his stride. He was too involved in his conversation with Tamiko to even hear Chris when he spoke back. Then Chris heard his voice call out to him again. "Did you do that yet?" Sergio said.

Chris knew exactly what he was talking about but he stood there looking confused for a moment.

"Not yet," he finally answered.

"Quit bullshitting lil' nigga!" Sergio commanded, walking backward up the hallway.

"You right."

"Do it today," Sergio pressed as he turned around and gave Tamiko his undivided attention again.

Chris felt like he couldn't let Sergio down. He had to make a move. Myiesha walked up to her locker barely giving Chris a glance before spinning the combination on her lock. He swallowed the lump in his throat and went for it.

"Damn girl, you can't speak with your fine ass?"

His voice cracked in mid-sentence. He didn't sound confident at all.

"What?" Myiesha said, looking stunned but blushing.

"You heard me," he said going for aggression.

"You don't ever speak to me," Myiesha said.

"I'm speaking now."

"Hey Chris," she finally greeted. She was still smiling at him too.

"Why don't you let me call you sometime?" he managed.

"I can't do that. I have a boyfriend Chris, sorry."

Damn. Why didn't she just say that in the first place, he thought, instead of giving him those bedroom eyes like he was on to something? Bitch.

"Alright then," he mumbled weakly, closing his locker and taking the walk of shame.

He tried to tell himself that Myiesha was just a practice run anyway so she didn't matter. The truth was, rejection still hurt. At least now he could tell Sergio he tried.

"Fight! Fight!"

Kids were yelling and rushing down the hall toward the commotion. Chris followed the crowd around the corner, pushing his way to the front. He saw two big burly dudes hammering away on some dude with loud thunderous punches.

"Fuck him up!" one of the big fellas barked. Then the dude threw a flurry of punches that backed up both of the big fellas for a second. That's when Chris realized it was Sergio being attacked. Sergio's back was against the wall and he was on offense now. Chris had gotten a good look at the other two guys and recognized their faces now.

It was Melonhead and Nutty, two of the most notorious niggas in the school. Melonhead grabbed Sergio in a headlock while Nutty pounded on his ribcage. Chris wanted to help but feared he'd be knocked unconscious if he tried to interfere. All of sudden, Melonhead was screaming and losing his grip on Sergio. It seemed Sergio was biting his way out of the headlock. It worked.

He came up on the attack again but with every punch he connected with, he got blasted in the face with several. The crowd began to open up as security came rushing through to break up the fight. Chris was relieved to see them; Sergio was still trying to break free and finish the fight.

"Whassup hoe ass nigga!" he yelled as he went at Nutty who was the closest to him.

It took a few minutes for security to get them restrained and handcuffed, then another five minutes to disperse the crowd to their classrooms. Chris was reeling from the shock of what just happened. First of all; he couldn't believe he just stood by while Sergio got jumped. But more than that, he couldn't believe how well Sergio defended himself. From the looks of things, Sergio wasn't even bleeding, but he was sure Melonhead had a busted lip.

****

Chris went through the rest of the day thinking about Sergio and staring at his textbooks. He couldn't wait for the final bell so he could leave school and go straight to Sergio's house to make sure he was okay. It was the least he could do. Outside the school, he noticed Evelyn and Charlotta walking towards the bus stop together. He wanted to say something but still didn't want to risk rejection. He decided he would speak but that was all.

"Hey Chris," Charlotta beat him to the punch surprisingly.

"Hey Charlotta," he responded.

"You wanna come to my birthday party this weekend?"

"Yeah, I do."

"Okay…here." She handed him an envelope.

"What's this?"

"That's your invite; all the information you need is inside."

"Okay."

"And tell Sergio I said fuck them punk ass niggas; he still my dog!"

"Okay."

"If you have any questions my number is on the back."

"Okay."

"Bye."

"Bye."

Damn, he felt like a lame. Okay, okay, okay. Like those were the only fucking words in his vocabulary. He was glad to be invited by Charlotta, one of the most beautiful and popular girls in Pershing High, but felt unworthy because of his inability to socialize with her type. He kicked an empty juice bottle from the grass out onto Seven Mile Road. A car rode by and crushed the bottle, shattering glass all over the street. He didn't care, wasn't his problem. As he stood at the bus stop, he pondered the questions of how and why he was so lame; fourteen and still afraid of girls. Three grimy looking cats came walking up the street, staring hard at Chris's shoes. He tried to match their intimidating scowls for few seconds but his mean-mug had no effect. They came straight at him.

"Check it in punk!"

"Check what in?"

Chris said nervously.

Bam.

The big one punched Chris in the mouth, making him drop to one knee.

"Them shoes nigga; you know what's up."

He quickly began to loosen up his laces to remove his patent leather Nikes, but not quickly enough for the young thugs.

Bam.

Another punch by the same dude and Chris was on the ground. They beat him, kicked him, stomped him, and took the shoes off themselves. Chris covered his face from the flurry of kicks that caught him in the ribs and stomach. Then all of sudden it was over as quick as it began. He heard sounds of numerous gym shoes scraping the concrete running away. Chris was dizzy and confused. He rose to his feet and tried to pull himself back to present time. In his mind, he was still getting beat unmercifully.

"You alright dog?" a kid from gym class asked.

Chris didn't reply; he just took off running down the street barefoot and cold. He passed a few more familiar faces as the first tears started to leak from his eyes. He didn't care at the moment about people seeing him crying. The people that just saw him getting his ass kicked would know exactly why he was whimpering. The pain in his ribs was bad but the unpleasantness in his stomach was that of an anxiety knot. The kind you get when crying just isn't enough.

The more pain he felt the harder he ran. The harder he ran the more pain he felt. Chris ran all the way home and was shocked to see his mother's Thunderbird not in the driveway. He sat on the porch wiping tears from his eyes and trying to catch his breath. He had a cramp in his stomach from running thirty blocks to get home. He was glad his mother was gone because she was the last person in the world he wanted to see. Chris patted his pocket for his house keys.

He pulled them out, turned the key, and shoved the door open with his shoulder. He went to the kitchen to see if his mom had left a note. She did. It read: Be home late, had to work a double shift.

He flopped down at the kitchen table, relieved he wouldn't have to deal with that choir rehearsal bullshit. The sharp pain his ribs made him think of the time he got tripped in the cafeteria. He went to the bathroom mirror to view the damage. It didn't look that bad, he told himself as he spat blood mixed with saliva into the sink. His only cut was on the inside of his mouth on his upper lip. He played the incident over in his head and began to tear up. Why didn't he fight back like Sergio did? Why didn't he at least try?

He punched the bathroom wall as hard as he could. A million thoughts ran through his mind. He wondered who saw him get his ass kicked. Why didn't anybody help him? What made the thugs choose him? He sat down on the toilet and took a deep breath. His feet were dirty, his clothes were drenched with sweat, and his face was full of dried up tears. He felt like…dying.

After sitting in the bathroom for over an hour completely numb, Chris's emotional pit had bottomed out. He had traveled to a dark corridor in his mind he didn't know existed. Drained, he finally decided to take off his wet clothes and take a shower. He let the hot water massage away some of his tension and soreness. He contemplated telling Sergio what happened. Part of him was too embarrassed, but the other half of him knew he would find out through someone else anyway. He felt like Sergio on some level might be able to relate to what he was going through.

Maybe he was at home right now feeling frustrated about his ordeal with Melonhead and Nutty. He got out of the shower, put on some fresh clothes and the only pair of shoes he had left. He walked the long way to Sergio's house, still thinking if he should tell him what happened. When he arrived at the house he had to knock on the door several times before Sergio finally opened the door.

"What up lil' bro?"

"Nothing. You okay?" Chris asked.

"Of course, why wouldn't I be? Come in nigga."

Chris stepped in sniffing at the weed aroma in the air. N.W.A's classic jam "Real Niggaz Don't Die" blasted through the entire house. Sergio sat down at the dining room table and began to pull the weed out of a garbage bag and dump it on the table. Then he tore the buds away from the branches and tossed the branches onto a Nike shoe box lid. "So what's up with you?" Sergio asked.

"Maaaaan, I got rushed today."

"What?" Sergio yelled as he jumped up and shot to the stereo to turn the music down. "By who?"

"I don't know 'em; they took my shoes."

Sergio sat down with a jarred scowl.

"They took your shoes?" he repeated.

"Yeah."

"Did you fight back?"

"It was three of them!" Chris explained.

"I don't give a fuck if it was ten of 'em. You always supposed to fight back no matter what!" Sergio yelled.

"You right."

"I know I'm right."

Sergio reached for his pack of Newports, tapped the pack, pulled one out, and lit it with his other hand, blocking imaginary wind. "You alright doe? You hurt?"

"Naw, I'm alright."

Chris felt like he had to make it seem as if he wasn't really fazed by the incident because it seemed Sergio had forgotten all about his altercation. Sergio disappeared into the back bedroom and came back with a black pistol with the color worn from the barrel giving it a grayish tone.

"Take this two-five."

Chris took the gun and flipped it over to read the engravings.

"Is it loaded?"

"Yeah, you know how to use it?"

"Not really," Chris admitted.

Sergio took the gun and pulled the rack back until the bullet popped in the chamber. He ejected the clip from the gun.

"Pay attention."

He showed Chris how to hold a gun and how to shoot it. He showed him how to aim at certain body parts. "This ain't for you to go out and try to play big bad ass neither. This is to keep niggas off yo' ass. If you got a problem with a nigga, you beat his ass first. If he go get his friends, that's when you get your little friend involved, you understand?"

"Un-huh."

"Don't forget what I said, and if things get too funky for you, you can always call me."

"Alright."

They slapped fives and Sergio got back to pulling the weed apart. The gun was still in Chris's hand. He sat admiring it for another two minutes before tucking it away in his jacket pocket.

"I got invited to a party," Chris said jumping to a lighter subject.

"Oh yeah, by who?"

"Charlotta, it's her birthday party."

"You talking 'bout lil' Evelyn's best friend?"

"Yeah her."

"Shiiid, you gotta be on point at that party dog."

"What you mean?"

"I mean you gotta go up in that bitch looking like a star. You gotta make it a Kodak moment baby. You know it's gonna be a bunch of dime pieces up in there, not to mention lil' Ev."

"Yeah, I'm shooting for Evelyn," Chris said, not really believing himself.

"If you shooting at Evelyn, you gonna have to come right. She got cats my age trying to get at her."

Sergio went back to breaking the weed down. Chris wanted to ask him about the fight. He wanted to know what the whole beef was about. He knew enough to know it was some street shit and therefore none of his business. If Sergio wanted to tell him about it, he would, eventually.

"So what should I do about the party?"

Sergio was headed towards the kitchen and he didn't respond to the question. Chris noticed the big tattoo on Sergio's bare back for the first time. It read Hustler. He wondered to himself if Sergio's mom had seen the tattoo and if so, what she thought about it. Far as he knew it could have been her idea. Sergio had the kind of mother that was more like a big sister. They smoked weed together, drank together, and sometimes partied together. When Sergio came back he was holding two cans of Old English 800.

"Want one?" he offered, cigarette dangling from his lip.

"Yeah," Chris answered before he had time to think it over. Sergio had never offered him any drinks, guns, or drugs before today. Now he was holding out a can of beer like it was normal for them to toss a couple of cans back.

"To answer your question, I can only tell you what works for me," Sergio said.

Chris took a big gulp of Old English and it burned his throat terribly. He tried to hide his displeasure from Sergio but wasn't doing a good job. Sergio had a devilish grin smeared across his face as if he was enjoying himself. "Right now you just need to work on your presentation and work on giving bitches a reason they should fuck with you instead of the other dude."

"Like what?" Chris asked.

This would be harder than Sergio expected.

"You know, like confidence, humor, style, all that shit. They gotta feel like they'd be missing out on something, you feel me?"

Chris nodded and took another hard swallow from his can. Sergio ran some more stuff down about being aggressive versus playing uninterested. Chris took it all in and tried to imagine being more like Sergio. He sought to match his charm with the ladies. Slowly, the buzz kicked in and the events of the day didn't weigh so heavy on Chris's mind. He really liked the buzz. He really, really liked the buzz.

Chapter 4

Charlotta stood in the middle of the clothing store glancing around at the other customers to make sure she wasn't being watched. She dipped into the dressing room with three outfits she'd grabbed from a rack located in an unattended area. She wore a size nine but made each size a little bigger so she could fit each pair of pants over the other. Two pairs of the blue jean pants went on with ease, but when she went for the third it was obvious it just wasn't going to work.

She'd definitely get swooped on trying to get out of there looking like that. Charlotta flung the third outfit under the bench, figuring there wasn't enough time to take it back. She came out of the dressing room looking natural and inconspicuous. Then she realized she didn't have any clothes and that was suspicious in itself.

"Shit!"

She quickly dipped back into the dressing room and gathered the discarded clothes then placed them back on the rack. After putting the clothes back she moved at a snail's pace towards the exit. She was trying to give the appearance of a girl still browsing, not quite ready to give up on the store. She was almost out of the store when the squeaky voice came from behind her.

"Didn't see anything you liked?"

Her heart skipped a beat but her body language was cool.

"Umm, I think I'm gonna look at some shoes then I'll come back."

"Oh okay, well I'm Teri and you can come see me and I'll make sure you get the right outfit for those shoes."

"Okay, Teri."

"See you later."

"Bye...bitch if you don't go head 'bout your business," she mumbled as she sped out of the store.

Charlotta made it to out to the parking lot where her cousin Tamiko was waiting in a black Ford Taurus. She hopped in and they sped off. Tamiko glanced over at the girl that looked more like her sister than her first cousin. Both had bright skin, yellow like the sun, and cat-like eyes along with shapely figures. Tamiko was the thicker of the two, being three years older, but her protégé was gaining on her quickly.

"What did you get?" Tamiko asked.

"Just two Coach Purses and two outfits."

"That's it?"

"Hell yeah, them muthafuckas was on me," she lied.

The truth was this was her first time boosting and her nerves got the best of her after she was stopped by the sales attendant. Charlotta still felt she'd done good for her first time. Tamiko did a good job at showing her how to maximize her thievery and minimize her risk.

"What you gonna do with that shit, sell it or keep it?"

"Hell naw, I'm selling this shit. I got my outfit for the party; I just need some money for more drinks."

When Charlotta got home she quickly called her crew and began networking the purses. She wanted to make sure everything was perfect for her party. This would be the one thing to catapult her popularity through the roof. She was already considered one of the prettiest girls in her school along with her cousin Tamiko. But Charlotta wasn't the type to ride another girl's coattail. She needed her very own spotlight and this party was just the thing to jumpstart her movement. She couldn't believe her mother had given her one hundred dollars to throw what was sure to be the party of the year. At least that's how she felt about it.

Not only had she invited dozens of freshman, but she also had Tamiko invite a bunch of sophomores, juniors, and seniors. At the moment, she was on the phone with Evelyn trying to drive a hard bargain for the last purse.

"Listen Ev, you know you my girl and all, but I gotta get seventy-five dollars for this purse."

"I don't have it; all I have is fifty dollars to my name."

"Girl this purse cost one fifty, and if you think I'm 'bout to give it to you for fifty dollars, you crazy."

"It's only twenty-five dollars, Charlotta, dang."

"Okay, that's twenty-five dollars I could buy some more music or some drinks with. Hell, I could use that for gas money to pay some of these people that been running me around everywhere. I could use that twenty-five dollars to get some shit at the beauty supply that need. I could use that…"

"I'll call you back bitch!" Evelyn hung up.

Charlotta knew that she'd be calling back soon with the rest of the money. She knew Evelyn loved designer purses just like she did, but if her friend couldn't afford the purse she'd make her way down her Rolodex to the next girl with a dream. She had the clothes sold already and had put Tamiko's cut to the side. This party was going to bang out of control. Everything was going perfectly. Her phone rang and she was sure it was Evelyn calling to say she had the rest of the money. Perfect. All she had to do now was make her birthday wish come true.

****

Chris was never what you would call a bum or dusty nigga; his mom made sure of that. But he was never that fresh to death nigga either, except for today. It was the day of the party and he'd been getting tips from Sergio all week on how to mack. Sergio made it a point to stress that Chris didn't have to stay focused on Evelyn all night. He told Chris if she wasn't talking his language he should move on to the next girl. There would be ample girls at the party to choose from. The goal was to knock as many as he could but for Chris, that just meant to try and get a lot of phone numbers. Sergio had bought Chris an outfit, or at least that's what Chris thought. In reality, Tamiko had stolen the outfit while boosting clothes so Sergio didn't have to pay a dime for it.

He rocked blue jean Guess pants and the matching jacket with white Adidas and a chain from Sergio. He was ready.

"I wish you was coming to the party," Chris said.

"I told you man, if Tamiko gonna be there I'm not. What's the point in me going if I can't get on no freaks?" Sergio asked but wasn't looking for an answer.

"So that's like, like really yo' main girl, huh?"

"You know it. Every real nigga gotta have a real bitch on his side. Kinda like the president and the first lady."

"You think I need a first lady?" Chris wanted to know.

"You just get a lady first and then we'll worry 'bout the rest."

"I guess."

"Right now you got a fresh fade and your gear is tight; it's time to play ball."

They pulled up at Charlotta's house at nine o'clock sharp. The party had started an hour ago. Chris jumped out the Monte Carlo feeling more confident with each second that passed. He had been drinking already so his buzz was a major factor in his boost of self-esteem. Sergio blew his horn and slowly pulled off. As he headed toward the steps he could hear the music blasting from inside Charlotta's house. The door was cracked open and Tamiko was standing in the doorway waving him in. Tamiko did a thorough shakedown to make sure Chris wasn't carrying a gun, and he got a slight hard on.

There was something about Tamiko that demanded respect. He doubted anyone would start trouble while she was there. Tamiko was a female gangsta. From the cars lined up and down both sides of the street Chris could tell the party was jumping but now that he was inside, he couldn't believe his eyes. It was like half the school was at the party.

Sergio would regret he missed this. There were big birthday banners that read "Happy Birthday Charlotta" all around the house. Balloons covered the dining room and living room ceilings. Cleary there was no parental supervision going on. Marijuana smoke consumed the air and everywhere you turned someone had a beer or a cup of liquor. Old English, Colt 45, Long Island Ice Tea, Cisco, everything.

A classic song by rap group Whodini rumbled through the speakers and Chris could feel the bass travel through his body. Everyone began throwing their hands up and reciting the words to the song.

/I'm a hoe you know I'm a hoe/

/I rock three different freaks after every show/

/'Cause I'm a hoe you know I'm a hoe/

/How do you know because I told you so/

Chris knew right then he needed to get hype for this party. He made his way to the kitchen where a variety of drinks covered the table. Chris still hadn't tried liquor yet but tonight he needed the strongest shit this party had to offer. He grabbed a red plastic cup and poured a stiff one.

"Hey boy!" Charlotta said sneaking up behind him

"Hey, happy birthday."

Charlotta propped her hands on her hips profiling the tens and twenties pinned to her shirt. She looked gorgeously dressed to sweat, but her tight jeans and tube top still amplified her figure and exaggerated her hips. Good thing Sergio had given him a few dollars for his pocket because now was his chance to floss. He went into his pocket and pulled out a stack of ones with a fifty on top. It appeared he had a big bankroll but it was actually a hundred and twenty-five dollars. He peeled off the fifty quickly without thinking and stuffed the rest in his pocket. He tried to pin the money on Charlotta but got stuck with the safety pin.

"Shit!" he exaggerated his pain.

"Damn nigga, is you bleeding?"

"Naw, I'm alright."

"Give it here, I'll do it. 'Bout to kill yourself with a damn safety pin."

She snatched the money and pinned it on her shirt.

"You ain't gonna say thank you at least?"

"Of course I'm gonna thank you."

Charlotta reached out for a hug and Chris embraced her, taking in the mesmerizing scent of her perfume and the feeling of her body against his. "Thank you so much; you gave me more money than anybody here so far. I'm so shocked. Now if you'll excuse me my bankroll getting kinda thick so I think I'ma go hide it. I'll be back."

She darted out of the kitchen as quickly as she came. Chris took a big gulp of Cisco and gasped for air after he swallowed. He couldn't believe how strong it was. He was pretty sure he'd be hugging the same cup all night. He stepped back into the party and noticed Tamiko was looking him over. He was wondering what she was thinking as he took another sip. He thought she might have been admiring his swag but she was really admiring the outfit she'd stolen. Tamiko liked Chris but felt he needed to toughen up a bit. He spotted Dink with Randy, his elementary school nemesis.

Chris didn't really want to see them. They'd find a way to ruin his night. He tried to dip past without being noticed.

"What up Cry Baby?" Dink shouted over the music.

"What up? Stop calling me that," Chris said, slapping fives hesitatingly.

Dink and Randy moved through the crowd. Maybe they wouldn't be a problem after all. But it was that kind of night. Everybody came to party. Even he was starting to loosen up after the Cisco took control. When he finally spotted Evelyn she was on the dance floor with Charlotta and their crew doing a dance to Boyz 2 Men's "Motown Philly." Their gyrating moves caught everyone's attention and the whole party surrounded to watch. The crowd chanted.

"Go, go, go, go!"

Chris didn't wanna play the wall like a sucker so he stood in the middle of the floor encouraging the girls with everybody else. He'd seen a lot of guys playing the wall since he walked in, but he refused. Not tonight. As soon as this little routine was over he was going to push up on Evelyn. The song ended and just as he was about to make his move, Evelyn dipped into the crowd. He didn't chase after her but he didn't want to stand there and look stupid while everyone went back to dancing. He moved his way through the crowd getting brushed and bumped all the way. It seemed Evelyn was headed for the stairs…maybe the bathroom.

He tried to catch up with her before she reached the steps but as soon as he got within a few feet, some sophomore dude with curly hair grabbed her by the arm. She stopped and smiled. Now they were engaged in some giggly conversation. Dude propped one leg up on the bottom step and kneeled down elbow to knee. He had her. She wasn't going anywhere for the moment.

Chris remembered what Sergio had said about moving on and headed back to the dance floor.

"Chris!" he heard a female voice call out.

He peered through the crowd to see Charlotta waving him over with one finger. She wore a sexy grin as he approached.

"You gonna dance with me or what?" she asked.

"What?" Chris yelled over the music.

"You owe me a dance!"

"Oh okay…wait 'til a slow jam."

"Alright, you better not try to play me."

"I'm not, I promise."

Charlotta danced off and was stopped by some pretty boy that Chris only knew by face. He watched as they started to dance, showing off skills on the dance floor that Chris knew he would never possess. Charlotta was the best and sexiest dancer at her party. She moved like a belly dancer far beyond her fifteen years of age. She had her back against pretty boy now and proceeded to gyrate her hips and rub on his ears. The whole scene was making Chris jealous as hell. If only he had taken her up on her offer to dance he'd be the one bumping and grinding right now.

The last straw came when she bent over and backed all up on pretty boy. Chris was heated. He took a big gulp from his cup as he watched Charlotta's ponytail shaking wildly on the dance floor. She was the only girl that had shown him any attention all night and he was letting his chance slip away. He knew he had to get out there and do something, the hell with Evelyn. The song ended followed by a slow jam from R Kelly. In a gutsy attempt that Chris would've never expected from his sober self, he decided to aggressively remove pretty boy from his spot on the dance floor.

Chris strolled through the crowd passing several girls until he reached Charlotta. She was just about to lock up with her present dance partner when Chris appeared and stepped in.

"Ain't this my dance?"

Charlotta seemed surprised but happy to see him.

"Oh yeah, that's right," Charlotta said as she glanced back and forth at the two of them. "I'm sorry Jason but I did promise this dance to Chris."

Jason was the one heated now as he walked off and tried to recover quickly by asking another girl to dance. "I was gonna tell him he could have the next dance but he walked off so quick, fuck it."

"He can't have the next dance anyway," Chris heard himself say.

Charlotta was shocked at his aggressiveness but it was a turn on.

"Why he can't?"

"'Cause I want the next dance and the one after that."

"Hmmm, you sure about that Chris?"

"Yeah, I'm your dance partner for the rest of the night."

His arms were around her waist and hers around his neck. Still gripping his cup of Cisco that was almost gone, Chris couldn't believe how all the right words just rolled off his tongue tonight. Charlotta took the cup from his hand and finished his drink. Her face was contorted as she passed the cup to a random girl walking by.

"Why you just drink my stuff?"

"I wish I didn't," Charlotta said, still trying to recover from the burning going on inside.

"But you did," Chris smiled.

"I didn't want you to spill it on me."

"I wouldn't do that," Chris said looking into her eyes.

Even with all the dancing and sweating, Charlotta still smelled delightful. He wanted to kiss her. Her breast mashed against his ribcage making his heart rate increase and sweat beads stream down his armpits. She stroked the back of his head and rubbed his ears. Young seduction at its best. The living room dance floor was filled to capacity with people tongue kissing and squeezing things. Maybe it was the Cisco, maybe he got caught up in the moment. Whatever it was, something drove Chris to kiss Charlotta's neck.

She didn't complain so he did it again. Still nothing. He moved his hand from around her waist to palm her ass. As he squeezed her cheeks she finally lifted her head to look in his eyes. This moment seemed magical. Charlotta kissed Chris softly on the lips…then another one. On the third kiss he eased his tongue into her mouth and she willingly accepted. His penis was rock hard and he expected to wake up from the dream any second. But it wasn't a dream. It was reality and Chris was experiencing the best day of his young life.

When the song ended, Charlotta grabbed Chris by the hand and led him through the crowd. He followed behind her clueless as to where he was going and why. The next thing he knew, he was upstairs and turning right into the first bedroom.

"Don't say nothing," she whispered in a sexy, low tone.

Charlotta led Chris to the bed, pushed him down, and climbed on top of him. Pulling her shirt over her head, he kissed between her breasts. "Yeah," she moaned as he fumbled to loosen her bra then flung it on the floor.

She grabbed his belt to unbuckle it. He helped her out to speed up the process. By the time he was undressed she was lying on her back, completely naked. Chris didn't savor the moment; he lay on top of her and guided his dick inside of her. He struggled with her tightness until he was able to slide the rest of his shaft into her warm, wet pussy. He bounced awkwardly on top of her while she moaned until his body went numb. He stiffened and she clung to him until he collapsed on top of her. For the next few minutes, they laid side by side staring at the ceiling.

Chris was thinking, what the hell just happened? Charlotta was thinking Chris was better than she had expected, but still an amateur.

"What now?" Chris finally said.

"Nothing, now we clean up and take our asses back to the party."

Chris thought she was being pretty nonchalant about the whole damn thing. He knew this could not have been her first time.

"Was this your first time Chris?" she asked as if reading his mind.

"No," he lied.

"Yeah right."

"It wasn't," he said louder than he intended.

He was offended by the fact she just assumed he was a virgin, even though he was.

"Tell me who else you been with?"

Chris was caught off guard by the interrogation. Didn't have a name for her.

"You don't know her."

"Oh my God, Chris we know all the same people; why are you lying?"

"Whatever, it don't matter."

"It does matter. It matters to me."

"Why?"

"Because I thought I was your first and that's the way I wanted it to be, so thanks for ruining it for me."

"Okay then, you were my first."

"Right."

"Right," he echoed.

He didn't bother asking her if he was her first. He knew the answer but it didn't matter. The only thing that mattered was that he was having the most amazing night ever, and it had to mean that things were about to change for him. It had to mean that he was about to start living the life a teenage boy could be proud of.

Chapter 5

"Oh-my-God!" Evelyn squealed into the phone.

"What? It ain't like I didn't tell you I was gonna do it. Remember when you asked me what I wanted for my birthday? I said a virgin."

"Girl you know I thought you was just bullshittin'. I can't believe you, oh my God."

They both giggled.

"Stop saying that. You acting like I robbed a bank or something. I think you jealous 'cause you ain't think of it first."

"Pish, Chris? Girl please."

"He wasn't that bad though."

"Don't tell me he hanging?"

"I mean…yeah…he alright."

"So you gonna kick it with him since you broke him in?"

"I don't know," she said pausing. "I don't know. I don't think he can keep up with me."

"He might surprise you. You know Sergio is his cousin or something."

Charlotta heard a horn blow and she jumped up to peek out of her blinds. It was Sergio outside. He was probably there to pick up Tamiko, she thought. She walked away but then turned and went back to the blinds to peek out again.

"Let me call you back Ev."

"Alright."

"Peace."

Chalotta hung up from Evelyn then sashayed outside in her robe and slippers. She stood by Sergio's car and waited for him to turn the music down.

"What up doe?" Sergio said, still bobbing his head to the low volume bass.

"Is Chris yo' cousin?" she asked.

"Naw, me and Chris ain't blood. But he like a brother to me."

"Oh."

"Whassup, you tryna get at him or something?"

She stood with her hands on her hips looking appalled.

"Now you know, Charlotta ain't gotta try and get at nobody, niggas get at me."

"My bad, don't beat me up," Sergio said throwing his hands up in surrender.

"No foreal though, he didn't ask you anything about me?"

"I ain't seen him."

"Didn't you pick him up from the party?"

"Yeah but that nigga was drunk; he fell asleep as soon as he got in the car."

"Oh, alright."

She wanted to inquire more but didn't want to seem tacky about it. "Don't tell him I asked about him."

"It's our little secret. Now tell Tamiko to bring her ass up out of there."

"Okay."

Charlotta walked back to her house looking at her situation from an outsider's perspective. She liked the idea of having a guy nobody had been with but her. She saw potential in Chris. He was cute and by the time she was finished with him, girls would be trying to steal him away from her. Just then she made up her mind that he would be her own personal project and she would be in total control of him. She would use him to make all the other girls jealous like she'd done with her other boy toys in the past. Only this time, she was taking basically a nobody and turning him into somebody. Only thing was, Charlottta didn't really want a boyfriend, just another boy toy.

She hated the feeling of being tied down to one person. That's why it was extremely important that she could do as she damn well pleased.

****

Chris was on punishment for coming home way too late from the party. Luckily, his mother was asleep when he came home and never found out about his drinking, in which case he would have been grounded indefinitely. It would've been well worth any punishment that came afterward. After sitting in church with a major hangover Chris went home and lay in his bed daydreaming of Charlotta. He loved her outgoing personality, her soft skin, her smell, and the way she smiled at him. He was sure he was falling in love even though he wasn't sure what love felt like.

After a few hours had passed and his hangover came down, he finally got the nerve to call her. He found the invitation she had given him before with her number on it. He dialed her number and the phone rang a few times. He was just about to hang up on the fourth ring.

"Who is this?" a voice demanded.

"This Chris, is Charlotta home?"

"It is I the one and only speaking."

"What up doe?"

"Nothing, still got a hangover from drinking too damn much last night."

Chris didn't remember her drinking that much but he figured it wasn't something to lie about. As the conversation went on, Chris realized that without the alcohol in his system he went right back to his same shy and self. He couldn't find anything of interest to talk about. He had no game, played very little sports, and felt really out of his league. The good thing was it didn't even matter with a girl like Charlotta; she had enough conversation for the both of them.

41

She went on about everything from fashion to school to gossip to music. When the conversation was over he felt like he knew everything there was to know about Charlotta. He also felt like she didn't know or want to know much about him. That was good because there wasn't much to tell. But from that day forward, Chris and Charlotta started out strong. They were always seen walking the halls together. Chris always carried her books to class. Charlotta would check Randy on a regular basis about calling Chris Cry Baby, but never seemed to be curious as to where the name originated from.

After only a few short weeks the fire seemed to be dying out. It appeared as if Charlotta didn't have time for him all of a sudden. Twice this week he'd spotted her playing around with her ex-boyfriend. Now here she was talking to him again, all smiles and flirty with it. He laid low and watched from a distance. When it was over the dude slapped Charlotta on her butt as she walked away smiling. Chris's blood was boiling hot. He couldn't believe she would disrespect him like that. He charged after her, stomping through the hallways. He caught up with her and grabbed her arm forcefully.

"What the fuck you doing!" she snapped.

"What? Whachu mean? Why you just let him hit you on your ass like that?"

"Boy, he was just playing. Let me go!"

"He ain't supposed to be playing with you like that!"

"Tell him that!" she screamed while yanking her arm away.

Chris was stunned by her unwillingness to accept any responsibility on her part. She had basically given this guy a green light to be overly flirtatious. His whole body was warm.

"You know what? Fuck you!" he shouted, after not being able to think of anything else.

"Fuck you, nigga! Matter of fact, don't call me no more." Charlotta stormed off, leaving Chris standing in the hallway amongst the spectators.

"Charlotta!" he called out to no avail.

It was like bursting a big pimple in the middle of class; he was only making things worse. He could feel a few dozen eyes gawking at him. He wanted to crawl beneath the floor or dive into the nearest locker and hide. He'd just been dumped in front of what felt like millions of witnesses. His books and folders were scattered on the floor from struggling with Charlotta. His heart pounded and his hands were shaking as he gathered his things from the floor. As he felt the tears swelling in his eyes he flew into the boy's bathroom before they began to fall. He slung his books at the bathroom sink out of frustration.

He kicked the urinal a good three times before he hurt his foot and couldn't continue. Right now he hated himself because he seemed to have all the bad luck. He wondered why he always seemed to be on the losing end of things.

"Fuck this," he whined while leaning against the sink.

He began to wipe away the tears, knowing someone would be walking into the bathroom any second. He gathered his books once again and tried to put on a brave face. He could only hope that the word hadn't traveled through the school that quickly. Maybe the people in his algebra class hadn't heard of his public humiliation yet.

****

At home, Chris cried more when he thought about Charlotta. He tried calling her but she kept hanging up on him. He was in physical pain as he lay in his bed mourning his loss. Charlotta had changed his whole world for the better and in one sad day, she'd thrown it all in reverse. His mom had been working so much it was hard for her to keep up with Chris, even though he was still on punishment. He could sneak out as long as he was back before she came home from work. He decided to walk to Sergio's house to get his mind off things. As he walked he continued to think about the same thing he'd been dwelling on all day; the break-up.

Charlotta, Charlotta, and more Charlotta. Maybe he should have gone after Evelyn like he started to in the beginning. Maybe he should smack the shit out of Charlotta the next time he saw her for disrespecting him in front of the entire school. He knew he could never really do that. Not after watching his mom getting punched on by his dad. He just couldn't get over the way Charlotta had done him. Like…like all of a sudden, he meant nothing. Maybe they were never even serious about each other in the first place. Well, maybe she wasn't because he knew damn well he was.

Chris spotted a dark Bronco bending the corner. The bass from the truck could be heard for blocks. He glanced at the truck coming towards him and saw the dark-skinned man with thick eyebrows and a matching goatee. He knew it was Dana Dane. He didn't know a lot about Dana but what he did know is Double D, as some called him, didn't like people saying his name in the hood. He wanted to remain mysterious like a ghost; now you see him now you don't. Cross him once, twice you won't. He drove past giving mean stares to Chris and everyone else who just happened to be moving around the block at the time. Just staring in Dana's face made Chris a little nervous, so he didn't. After the truck had long passed Chris could still hear the lyrics to the song he was playing clearly.

/Rata tat tattattatat like that/

Doctor Dre rapped over a hypnotizing beat. It was a song from his new album titled The Chronic.

That shit beating, Chris thought to himself.

****

Finally, he arrived at Sergio's home to find his Monte Carlo gone, which meant Sergio was too. Sergio's mom had her car parked in the usual spot. She didn't leave the house that much. He thought about knocking on the door just because it was cold outside and he had no place else to go but home. He decided to just walk back home and take a nap or something. On his way home he spotted Randy and Dink on the corner drinking a forty-ounce. They waved him over. He really wasn't in the mood for them right now but he was so bored, sad, and confused, he found himself headed in their direction.

"What up Cry Baby?" Randy said.

"What's up?" They slapped fives.

"We heard about yo' bitch dumping you at school today," Dink informed.

"Fuck that bitch!" Chris spat.

Dink slapped him lightly on the back.

"I sure will, I'm glad you don't mind."

"I don't give a fuck," Chris lied as he grimaced from the cold hawk smacking him in the face.

"Want some?" Randy said offering the forty-ounce.

Chris accepted the beer and took a big gulp from the bottle as he noticed Dana's Bronco blocks away, headed in their direction. The trio passed the bottle back and forth as the Bronco approached slowly with the driver's side window rolled down.

"Aye... what's my name?" Dana said mean-mugging.

"Double D," Dink said thinking he had played it smart by not saying his actual name.

Bang!

Dana fired one shot dropping Dink to the pavement.

"You don't know my name muthafucka, period."

Dana pulled off slowly as if he hadn't just shot a young teenager in broad daylight. Randy and Chris took off at the first sound of gunfire. After not hearing a second shot, Randy stopped and went back to check on his friend. Chris ran until he couldn't run anymore and once he stopped, he was only six houses away from where he lived. He caught his breathe as he searched for his keys. Once inside he sat down at the first available support, the arm of the sofa. He couldn't believe what had just happened.

Dink had just been shot for saying Double D. One thing was clear to him, and that was the fact that Dana was crazy as hell. He wondered if Dink was dead. He had to tell somebody what happened, but whom? Sergio was gone and Charlotta wasn't talking to him. But wait…if he had something this big to tell her she would definitely want to talk. Charlotta loved to gossip about what was going on in the hood. He was about to use a tragic situation for his own selfish benefit. He grabbed the phone, dialed her number, and got a quick pick up.

"Helloooo, Miss America speaking."

He didn't waste any time with small talk,

"Dink just got shot," he said still excited and in disbelief.

"What? Who this?"

"It Chris, Dink just got shot."

"Are you serious?"

"Hell yeah, I was right there."

"Oh my God, what happened?"

Chris ran down all the details just the way it happened, without mentioning Dana.

"Who was it?" Charlotta inquired.

"I can't tell you his name; that's how Dink got shot."

"Is he dead?"

"I don't know. I took off as soon as I seen a gun and heard the first shot."

"Ha, yo' scary ass."

"What was I supposed to do, stand there and get shot?"

"I'm just playing. I can't believe this. I gotta call Ev and tell her about this shit. Let me call you back."

She hung up before Chris could even agree. He didn't complain. He was just glad to have her talking to him again. Maybe all she needed was some time to calm down. He'd wait about a half hour to see if she'd call back and if not, he'd call her. He was thinking about apologizing and asking for her forgiveness until he remembered he hadn't done anything wrong. He thought about Dink, wondering what condition he was in right now. Was he dying? He had stopped carrying the twenty-five automatic pistol Sergio had given him, but he was about to start packing it daily. It was crazy in the hood.

☐

King Benjamin's Perspective:

This nigga's a broad. I'll be glad when he get some balls and stop acting like Charlotta is the only fish in the sea. See, when you place a welcome mat over your forehead, don't be surprised when muthafuckas start to walk all over you. If it was me, Charlotta would have been the invisible girl after she pulled that stunt at school. But what the hell made him think she would make a good girlfriend anyway? He banged her at the party after one good slow dance. Oh well, let's just hope Sergio can lace him up a little better in the future.

Chapter 6

Charlotta came hightailing out to the mall parking lot at the speed of light. The wind was so high on this day that no one paid her running any attention because everyone was in a rush to get to their cars. Tamiko hit the auto locks and popped the trunk when she saw the multiple shopping bags Charlotta was carrying. Charlotta hopped in the car on a straight adrenaline rush.

"Bitch, I got not one, but two leather jackets."

"Swear to God?"

"I swear to God."

"How the fuck—what kind?"

"Marc Buchanan."

"Pelle's?" Tamiko questioned.

"Naw, some other slick shit. Cost nine hundred."

Tamiko was in a dazed and confused state. She'd never taught Charlotta how to steal thousand dollar coats at the mall. She couldn't have if she wanted to because she had never learned herself.

"How the hell did you get 'em out without sounding the alarm?"

"'Cause I'm a gangsta, that's how," Chalotta said pounding her fist in her palm as she continued to brag. "I hit they asses up for two outfits, a purse, two leather jackets, and some hair care products."

"Damn bitch, how many stores you hit?"

"I went in five but I only hit four."

Never in her wildest dreams had Tamiko imagined that her baby cousin would wind up being a better thief than she was. At this point, Sergio was providing good for Tamiko and she only boosted now because it was in her nature, and she just knew she would never get caught.

"Well, we ain't going back to that bitch for a minute," Tamiko said as they drove down the entrance ramp to the Chrysler Freeway.

"I know, I know, we gotta chill for a minute. I'ma give it 'bout a month and I'll be right back at 'em."

They laughed loudly and high-fived.

"You wanna go out with me tonight?" Tamiko asked.

"Where?"

"The Dancery."

"Hell yeah girl, you know I been waiting to hit the club."

"Well, we up in there tonight."

"You think they gonna let my young ass in?"

"Hell yeah, girl I know all the bouncers."

"Cool."

Charlotta sold one of the jackets for five hundred dollars to one of Tamiko's friends and kept the rest of the stuff for herself. One of the outfits she'd stolen she planned to give Chris for his birthday. It was a blue jean Guess fit. She thought he'd look cute in a Detroit Tigers fitted cap too, but she couldn't find one his size. A month had passed since they'd broken up and made up in the same day. The time passed without incident as Charlotta kept her dudes on the side at a distance.

She still wasn't feeling the couple thing but Chris was sweet and he took every dime he came up with and spent it on Charlotta. Sergio giveth and Charlotta taketh away. The bottom line was she knew the other dudes just wanted sex and Chris really cared about her. She stood in the mirror profiling a lavender Guess tube top with a matching miniskirt. She figured her mom would be drunk by eight and sleep by ten, so she'd just sneak out. Her mother had always been a binge drinker before her father was killed in a freeway collision. After his death, the drinking worsened and the gap in their relationship increased. Charlotta cupped her breast in the mirror.

"Damn my titties getting big."

She posed for a side view while sucking in her already flat stomach. Her hair was cut like Tamiko's now; long on the right side and back but short and curled on the left side. It was something straight out of a Salt-n-Pepa video. Her phone rang and she answered quickly.

"Who this?"

"Jason."

"Let me call you back Jason."

"Alright."

Click.

She hung up and two minutes later her phone rang again.

"Who this?"

"It's me," Chris said.

"Hey baby, let me call you right back in a minute."

"Alright."

She didn't feel like yapping at the moment. She was still trying to decide on what to wear. After trying on several outfits, she ended up going with the first one. The phone rang again.

"Goddamn!" she yelled before answering. "Who is this?"

"It's your mentor bitch," Tamiko answered.

"Oh, hey girl, I thought you was one of these niggas who act like they addicted to dialing my number."

"Stop giving all them niggas your number, or better yet stop giving all them niggas some pussy."

"Girl please, I ain't fucking nobody but Chris. I was about to fuck Jason though until he went all stalker on me before we could even hook up."

"Better to know now. Besides, Chris is a good dude. I think you should treat him right."

"I'm trying to do right by Chris but I'm just way too young to be tied down, you feel me?"

"Did you tell him that?" Tamiko asked

"Naw, but maybe I should."

"Duuuuh bitch."

"Anyway, what time you coming to pick me up?"

"I'll be there in about an hour so be on the lookout for me."

"Alright."

"Peace."

****

Evelyn stood in the front of her bathroom mirror staring at her almost flawless skin. Almost flawless, because at the moment she was peering at a pimple on her right cheek. It wasn't the end of the world but it definitely made her a little self-conscious. It was the kind of thing she'd have on her mind at school when she should be focused on the task in front of her. From the outside looking in, you would never know Evelyn wasn't like the rest of her girls. She was cool with being popular through association and felt no need to become infamous before she graduated.

She reached into the medicine cabinet and grabbed the Noxzema from the top shelf. She rarely ever had a pimple but used the Noxzema as a precautionary measure. The phone rang but she didn't move to answer it. Her mom would get it and yell out her name if it was for her. She closed the cabinet.

"Evelynnn!" her mom called out.

"Okay Ma."

She ran downstairs and picked up the phone in the bedroom.

"What's up hoodie?" Charoltta said.

"Nothing, what's up with you?"

"Did you find a way to maneuver?"

"Naw, I can't go."

"Girl that shit about to be off the hook. I know you can find a way to get out the house."

"No, I can't. Plus, like I said, I really gotta get up early tomorrow for church."

"Church? Girl y'all always at church. I ain't tripping though 'cause you need Jesus."

Evelyn laughed but couldn't help but think that Charlotta was the one that really needed Jesus. The thing was, Charlotta wasn't off into a lot of the things that Evelyn liked to do. She actually liked going to church and did things like write poetry in her spare time. Charlotta, on the other hand, was becoming a party animal and a professional thief. She thought about telling her best friend to slow down but she knew Charlotta was going to do what Charlotta wanted to do.

"Anyway, I got this big pimple on my face girl I can't do nothing."

"Ev, ain't nobody gonna be looking at no pimple in no dark ass club. But I can see you don't really wanna go so I'm not gonna twist your fucking arm about it. Peace ooooout!"

Click.

She hung up before Evelyn could tell her to be careful tonight. If she didn't say it she'd be worried all night. She called Charlotta back and she answered on the first ring.

"Swanson Funeral Home," she answered.

"Be careful tonight."

"You called me back for that bitch?"

Click.

They always hung up in each other's faces, hardly ever leaving room for goodbyes. They were opposites but somehow their friendship worked. They both secretly admired things about each other while accepting the things they didn't like. Evelyn liked Charlotta's fashion sense and her outgoing personality. Charlotta liked Evelyn's confidence and respected her intelligence. The rest of their friends took on the habit of following behind Charlotta and doing whatever she told them to do. Evelyn was always her own person and always used better judgment than Charlotta. She changed into her pajamas and kicked back with Maya Angelo's classic, I Know Why the Caged Bird Sings.

****

Sergio had a Corvette engine gunning in his Monte Carlo. The dual exhaust roared down East Warren. He was banging the latest Scarface album while choking on sticky green weed. He had this habit of waiting until the song ended and then freestyling over the instrumental. Today was no different.

/Smoking on chronic weed bumping that Face/

/Blunt after blunt and my shit ain't laced/

/Standing too close you can feel the bass/

/My hooptie is my deuce and my gun is my ace/

The feeling was good. Smoking the best of weed, a pocket full of cash, and plenty of freaks on deck. What could be better? he thought. But as soon as he turned right on Buckingham towards his father's house, he lost some of that liveliness for a moment. He kept thinking about how it was every time they met up. Uncomfortable. He turned down the music as he pulled in the driveway behind his father's Chrysler LeBaron. As he rang the doorbell he stood there waiting and wondering if the weed scent was strong on his clothes. It was.

His father always moved slowly when the doorbell rang. He was in great shape for his age but he never felt the need to rush for anybody. He finally opened the door for his son then turned and headed back to his recliner without saying a word. Sergio didn't take it personally; his father just wasn't a man of many words.

"Hey Pop," Sergio greeted.

"Hey…hey son."

His father took a seat in his recliner that put him directly in front of the television. Sergio Senior kept a nice, clean house and all the plants that sat in each corner of the room were real. The smell of freshly brewed coffee filled the air. His father turned up the television and stared intensely at the baseball game in progress. It was always up to Sergio to make conversation with his dad.

"So you been alright?" Sergio asked.

"Yeah," his dad replied.

"Who's winning the game?"

"Tigers up right now."

Silence.

Sergio sat with his head down staring at the floor. His dad was blowing his high with the silent treatment, like he always did. He searched his brain for more small talk.

"You talk to my mom lately?"

"Nope."

Sergio was ready to leave. Being at his father's house was just too uncomfortable. They had absolutely nothing in common even though their features were almost identical. His father was a retired Chrysler worker who believed in playing it straight to get what you wanted in life. He had accepted the fact that he couldn't change his son or make him see things his way. Sergio was old enough to make his own decisions and he chose the streets. Sergio always felt the need to stop by and show his face to the man who helped raise him, although his parents never lived together or even had a real relationship.

He respected his dad just for being there and not just cutting out and never looking back. He had so many friends who were fatherless; he knew things could have been a lot worse for him growing up. Sometimes it made him wish he would've tried harder to make his dad proud. He watched the game for another five minutes then stood to leave.

"You need anything Pop?"

"Nope. Got everything I need right here."

Sergio handed him the brown paper bag he'd been holding the whole time. His father took the bag without inspecting the contents.

Sergio got all the way to the door and was about to turn the knob when his father called out to him. "Son."

"Yeah."

"You do understand that you can have too much of a good thing?"

It wasn't something Sergio wanted to hear, whatever it meant. He just nodded his head and opened the door to leave.

"Love you Pop."

☐

Chapter 7

The line outside the club was ferocious. In fact, it wasn't a line at all, just a bunch of people trying to buffalo herd their way to the front before the line got shut down. Tamiko had managed to maneuver her clique past the rowdiness in record time. She gave the bouncer a hug and pointed out the other girls she was with. Technically, none of them were old enough to get into the twenty-one and up club, but Tamiko was connected.

As they moved inside to pay the attendant, they were searched by a butch looking female bouncer before being permitted to enter the club. Inside, the music was hypnotizing. As soon as the girls walked in they found a table then seized the dance floor. Charlotta got things popping with some new moves she'd been waiting for the perfect time to unveil. Some of the rowdy cats ran through the crowd throwing up their hoods making the crowd divided, thus giving them the attention they were seeking. The Cross Conners Crew and Lynnhurst Lynchmob were both in the building throwing up their hoods and showing out. Tamiko and the girls had to laugh at it all, but knew things would eventually escalate.

Away from the dance floor, the lounge area was reminiscent of the Copa Cabana Club that Tony Montana just couldn't get enough of in the movie Scarface. Red crush velvet sectionals were spread out diagonally from the back wall to the tip of the dance floor. Sergio was posted up with a few bottles of Pipers champagne and his entourage. He never played the dance floor just to prevent having to bust a head or two. Then again, sometimes in a place like the Dancery, it just couldn't be avoided. It was the type of club the scared niggas labeled a death trap so they wouldn't be asked if they wanted to come. But if you were thorough it was all good. As Sergio scoped out the scene keeping an eye on his girl, he wondered to himself should he make himself known to her.

He decided to fall back and let her enjoy herself and he would do the same. He spotted a lot of dudes from his hood. Melonhead and Nutty were there. Randy and Dink were also there. Dink, who'd just gotten off his crutches after being shot in the leg, was moving around good. Even Dana, who rarely showed his face in a club, was posted up on the other side of the room with his goons. Sergio made eye contact with Melonhead and Nutty, and they gave each other a mutual head nod of respect to let it be known there was no bad blood between them. Time had passed and things blew over like the leaves in the fall.

Sergio came to grips with the fact that it was disrespectful of him to take their weed customers by having his workers short stopping them for sales. But that was all in the past now.

****

Charlotta had to take a breather from the dance floor so she took a seat at the bar and waved, trying to get the bartenders attention. There were two bartenders and they both seemed to be moving at the speed of light to Charlotta. She kept waving and flagging and signaling but it was like she was invisible. She finally got fed up and positioned her knees on top of the bar stool so she could bang on the bartender's side of the counter top.

"Hey!" she shouted at the female bartender.

"Can I help you?"

"Yeah, I been trying to order a drink for ten minutes."

"Well, as you can see we are pretty busy tonight, so what can I get for you sweetie?"

Sarcastic bitch, Charlotta thought to herself.

"I'll have a Long Island Iced Tea."

"You got ID sweetie?"

"What?" Charlotta said scowling.

"Do-you-have-ID?"

"I'm in here, ain't I?" Charlotta snapped.

She was about to go off but before the bartender could respond a young man intervened.

"She with me Sherrie."

Charlotta turned to see a familiar face but a man she didn't know by name. He was tall, dark, and handsome. Not in the traditional sense of the word handsome, but as seen through Charlotta's thug craved eyes.

"How you doing gorgeous?" the man said.

"I'm fine and you?" Charlotta responded.

"I'm tight, what's your name?"

"I'm Charlotta, what's yours?"

Before he could answer, the bartender came and sat Charlotta's drink down in front of Dana. He waived Charlotta's hand off when she reached for her money.

"I got it," he said, pulling out a big wad of cash that made Charlotta's eyes buck.

He handed the bartender a lot more than what the drink cost and Charlotta was a bit confused.

"Take care of her tonight a'ight?"

"Gotchew," the bartender assured.

"Thank you stranger."

"Call me D."

"Okay D...I seen you around my hood before."

She began flirting with her eyes. It was her favorite thing to do when she first met a guy.

"I'm sure you have."

"You probably know my cousin Tamiko."

"Sergio's girl Tamiko?"

"Yeah, that's my peeps," she said proudly.

"Yeah, I saw her up in here tonight. Is that who you with?"

"Yup, there she go right there." Charlotta pointed to Tamiko who was in the crowd brushing off some sucker trying to run game.

"Yeah, Tamiko is cool. Good people," Dana acknowledged.

As their conversation flowed, Charlotta tried not to reveal her age by saying anything goofy or immature. If he asked she would say she was the same age as Tamiko, who was seventeen. He couldn't have been more than a few years older than Tamiko, and so what if he was.

"So you not gonna have a drink with me?" she asked.

"I don't drink."

"Hmpt. So what do you do for fun?"

"I make money for fun."

His facial expression was an indicator that he was dead serious.

"Besides that?"

"I come here once and a while. What about you?"

"I party and then I party some more. You like party girls?"

He was just about to answer, but then Dink and Randy came walking in his direction. Charlotta noticed his face turn to stone as the two walked by. They made sure not to make eye contact with Dana.

"What's wrong?" Charlotta asked.

"Nothing."

Dana turned his attention back to the project at hand.

"Anyway, I'm glad I decided to step out tonight."

"And why is that?"

"Why you think? 'Cause your fine ass was here."

She began to blush and finally became a bit shy in the company of an older man. She finished her drink and Dana quickly signaled for another.

****

Sergio had seen enough. This same dude had been aggressively pushing up on Tamiko for a while now. It seemed he just didn't want to take no for an answer. Sergio knew his girl could handle herself in the most threatening situations, but even so, he headed to the dance floor. He could tell by her body language and hand gestures that the dude was beginning to piss her off. Her crew stood behind her as if they were ready for whatever jumped off. The dude just stood there grinning as if they were all one big joke.

"Y'all hoes tough huh?"

"Bitch ass nigga, whatchu say?" Tamiko moved closer.

Just then, Sergio stepped in front of Tamiko.

"Man back the fuck up!" Sergio ordered.

"Oh my bad homey, I-I didn't know she was with somebody."

"Man just get the fuck on before you get hurt," Tamiko said, calmer now that Sergio had arrived.

She didn't dare mention how the dude had just gotten disrespectful. She wasn't trying to ruin her night out. The dude quickly bounced off as they gave each other a peck on the lips.

"Why you ain't tell me you was going out?" Sergio asked.

Tamiko answered with a question of her own.

"Why you ain't tell me you was going out?"

"It was spur of the moment."

"Yeah right, you just didn't want me cramping your style."

"Never dat. You can only compliment my style; that's the reason you the First Lady."

He wrapped his arms around her from behind and kissed her cheek. He wanted her to know the other women in the club didn't mean a thing to him when she was in the building.

"Why don't y'all come join us up top?"

"A'ight…where is Charlotta?"

Tamiko and her friends all looked around, but couldn't see Charlotta with all the movement going on.

"I think I seen her at the bar talking to Dana," Tamiko's friend said.

Sergio's eyes widened along with Tamiko's.

"Dana?" Sergio clarified with alarm in his voice.

They all headed toward the bar.

Charlotta was finishing up her second drink and her buzz was definitely kicking in. As she started to loosen up, she stared into Dana's eyes seductively. Dana was her type of man.

"So I guess you don't smoke weed neither huh?" she asked.

"Naw, but I got some in my truck if you wanna smoke something."

"Why you got weed if you don't smoke?"

"Because all my homeboys smoke."

That was only half the reason. The other reason was for situations exactly like this one. "So you wanna go smoke?"

"Yeah but…are we gonna be able to get back in?"

"Yeah of course. You with me."

Charlotta looked around the club with a devilish grin on her face. She was trying to locate Tamiko. She spotted her cousin headed her way.

"Okay, come on."

Dana was headed directly for Tamiko, but Charlotta stopped him and detoured to another route.

"Let's go this way," she coaxed.

They went all the way around the dance floor to avoid being spotted by Tamiko and her friends. Dana's eyes were locked on Charlotta's butt and would have followed it over a cliff at that moment. When they approached the exit they saw Randy and Dink hurrying themselves out the door. Charlotta slowed her pace not wanting to be spotted by those knuckleheads that might put her business in the street. Randy and Dink weren't looking back at anything or anybody. They moved like two Cheetahs that had just spotted prey. Dana and Charlotta made it outside just in time to see the rear end of Randy's car and hear the screeching tires bailing out of the parking lot. Dana grabbed Charlotta's hand and walked briskly to his Bronco parked in the back.

He opened her door and made sure she made it all the way in safely like a gentleman. Once inside, Dana opened his glove compartment and pulled out a fat sack of marijuana and a box of Philly's.

"You know how to roll?" he asked.

"Not really, I was hoping you did."

"Okay, I'm 'bout to show you how to do this."

Dana had been in this situation plenty of times. A young girl, weed, alcohol; he knew what to do. He took some of the weed and laid it out on the book that read Real Estate for Dummies. Then he split the cigar with his thumbnail and dumped the contents out the window.

"Now this is the part you need to watch closely."

He lined the weed along the inside of the cigar, making sure it was spread out evenly. He licked and rolled it. "Viola!"

He handed her the blunt and she handed it back.

"Now take that back apart and let me try it."

He searched her eyes for the truth, not knowing if this was just her brand of humor. She burst into laughter and he smiled, almost giggling himself. He handed her the blunt for the second time.

"You got a nice smile. You need to smile more often," Charlotta said.

"Don't think so."

She lit the blunt while he popped in R. Kelly's tape. She puffed away, wondering if Randy and Dink saw her leaving out behind them. So what if they did? She tried to convince herself. One thing she knew for sure; Dana had sparked her curiosity and once that happened, there was no turning back.

Inside the club, Tamiko and her crew searched the crowd on the dance floor, while Sergio went to talk to Dana's homeboys. He had already figured out what had happened, but went along with the search for Tamiko's sake. He knew Charlotta was just the type to get caught up and seduced by a thugged out hustler like Dana. Hell, she even flirted with him a few times but it was always innocent. But Dana was free game and she'd fuck him just to be able to say she did it. Sergio always felt that Charlotta wasn't what Chris needed but seeing that he was happy with her, he decided to stay out of it. He was having a second thought about that now as Tamiko approached him.

"Did you find 'em?"

"Naw, his homeboys say they seen him at the bar last."

"Shit!" Tamiko spat. "This girl is always trying to be fucking grown. Don't nobody know where she at or what she doing."

"Look, I know Dana. He crazy but he ain't that crazy. He ain't gonna do nothing she don't wanna do. Now you know your cousin and if she left up out of here, then she must want to be where she at."

"All that don't matter Sergio; she's only fifteen."

Tamiko let out a frustrated sigh, running her fingers through her hair. She signaled for her crew. "Let's get out of here."

In the backseat of Dana's Bronco, he sat wondering had he coaxed Charlotta into the backseat or had he been coaxed. As she undressed him and sucked his neck he fondled her ample breast. She unbuttoned and slid off her jeans, anticipating his touch. As she lay on her backside completely naked, he pulled his pants down around his ankles. He plunged inside of her.

"Ummm!" she moaned.

Tamiko led the way down the hall to the exit door while Sergio and his crew trailed closely behind. Sergio figured Charlotta was probably at a hotel about to get her freak on by now. He was half right. Tamiko shoved the exit door open and they all piled into the parking lot. She was headed for her Taurus until she spotted Dana's Bronco parked in the back. She stormed in the direction of the Bronco before Sergio could stop her. The closer she got, she could see the Bronco was rocking from side to side. Sergio caught up with her and grabbed Tamiko by the arm.

"Let me handle this."

The truck was foggy inside with zero visibility. Tamiko yanked away from him.

"Fuck that!" She charged up to the Bronco and banged on the quarter panel. "Charlotta, get yo' ass out that muthafucking truck right now!"

Inside the truck, Dana paused in mid-stroke and reached for his pistol under the seat. When Charlotta heard Tamiko's voice, she grew terrified. She grabbed Dana by the arm before he could retrieve his weapon under the seat.

"That's Tamiko," she whispered, as if there was still something to hide.

Dana scowled and pulled away from her.

"I don't give a fuck who it is; you better tell her to stop beating on my truck."

"Charlotta!" she heard Tamiko scream again.

She couldn't think straight. Then she heard Sergio's voice.

"Aye man, this Sergio. We 'bout to cut out and we need to get lil' cuz up outta there."

"Hold on!" Dana shouted back.

Charlotta was beyond embarrassed as Dana got dressed and prepared to release her to what felt like an angry mob outside. Neither one of them spoke as she got dressed and tried to fix her hair. She could tell he was upset that he didn't get a chance to finish. He pushed the passenger side door open and Charlotta appeared through a thick cloud of smoke. If only she could rewind time and erase this moment. If only she could just take the last hour of her life back.

The ride home was a cold one. Tamiko scolded her young cousin to the point where she felt like she was ten years old again. The verbal beat down about Charlotta's ignorant choice lasted a solid fifteen minutes. She sat in the backseat, smooshed between two other girls, staring into space. Only the alcohol and weed kept her brave enough not to cry. Even at her lowest moment, it was still all about her. She never once considered how all this would affect Chris.

Chapter 8

Chris arrived at home from church around two o'clock. He thought his mom was in an unusually good mood for someone who couldn't afford to buy her son anything for his fifteenth birthday. As they walked into the house, Chris suspected his mom had a trick up her sleeve.

"Mama gonna cook your favorite today, okay son?"

"Okay."

He watched her disappear into the bedroom. He knew something was up. If he wasn't getting a present, she would at least took him out to eat somewhere nice. We aren't that damn poor, he thought. Just then she came out carrying a shopping bag with looped handles. Her grin was from ear to ear. This had to be good.

"Let me stop playing with you. Happy Birthday!"

She handed him the bag and he could hear the joy in his mother's voice as he eagerly ripped the gift wrapping off the box. He couldn't believe it. It was a Sega Genesis with three games. For him it was about the best present he could imagine receiving.

"Maaaan...thanks Mama!"

He reached out to give her a hug.

Beep, beep.

A horn blew right outside the house. He reached over to the window and peeked out the blinds. Sergio was parked out front. Chris wasn't surprised to see him since Sergio had bought him gifts his last two birthdays.

"It's Sergio; I'm going outside to the car."

"Okay, tell him I said hello."

Chris ran down the walkway and jumped in the car with Sergio. The car was full of weed smoke.

"Happy Birthday my nigga!" Sergio said as he reached in the back seat and retrieved a Nike shoe box. He handed the box to Chris and he quickly removed the lid from the box.

"Jordans! Damn how much these cost?"

"Don't worry about all that. What your moms get you?"

"A Sega."

"Oh yeah? I got some games and shit at my house if you wanna check 'em out. I don't ever play my shit no more."

"Well, she got me three new games so I'm cool for now."

Chris saw his mother come walking out of the house jingling her car keys in her hand.

"I'm going to the grocery store. I'll be right back."

She emphasized the words right back and Chris knew that was his cue to stay put.

"How you doing Ms. Johnson?" Sergio greeted.

"I'm fine and you?"

"I'm good."

"That's good. Tell your mother I said hello."

"Okay, I will."

The pair reclined in the seats of the Monte Carlo as Sheila pulled out of the driveway. Chris could tell there was something on Sergio's mind but he didn't want to be nosey.

"So what's up for the day birthday boy?"

"Nothing really," Chris replied.

This was the part Sergio had been dreading. Now he had to break the lil' homey's heart on his birthday. This was the kind of thing that couldn't wait. Waiting would only make it worse. He rationalized by telling himself if it was him, he would want to know. He took a deep breath and released it. Chris noticed, wondering what was troubling him.

"Charlotta not the girl for you bro."

The words caught Chris off guard. He never expected that whatever was on his mind would have anything to do with him. His mind began to race.

"Why you say that?"

"'Cause she a hoe," Sergio said bluntly.

Chris was heated. He couldn't believe Sergio would talk about his girl to his face like that. He'd better have an explanation for such harsh words and a damn good one too. "Did you talk to her at all last night?" Sergio continued.

"No."

"Did she tell you she was going out with Tamiko?"

"No."

"So you don't know anything about what happened last night?"

"Naw." Chris shook his head.

He really didn't like where this was going. The longer Sergio stalled, the worst Chris felt. Sergio fell silent.

"What happened?"

Sergio sat behind the wheel scratching his eyebrow, wishing there was a better way to say it, but there wasn't.

"Listen, bro, I hate to be the one to have to ruin your birthday like this, but if it was me, I would wanna know that somebody was out there running around making me look like a fool."

Chris adjusted himself in the seat, now preparing for the worst. "Last night I went to the club too. I saw Tamiko and her girls on the floor. Charlotta had gone off to the bar and started talking to Dana. By the time I went down on the floor to get some lame out of her face, we couldn't find Charlotta."

By now, Chris knew there couldn't be an ending to this story that wasn't going to turn his life upside down and ruin his birthday. The final conclusion hit like a sledgehammer. "Long story short, bitch went outside and fucked Dana in his truck. You gotta cut your losses with that bitch right now my nigga."

Chris knew Sergio wouldn't lie to him, but he loved Charlotta so much he wanted to give her the benefit of the doubt.

"How you know she fucked him?"

"'Cause we seen his fucking truck rocking back and forth when we went outside to look for the bitch. The bitch took five minutes to get dressed and get out the truck with all of us standing outside waiting on her. All my niggas saw that shit. Tamiko and all her girls was there. That shit was ridiculous."

Right then the tears started to stream down Chris's face, but this time Sergio was there to nip it in the bud. "Man fuck that bitch!" he screamed. "Don't sit hear shedding no tears over a bitch that don't give a flying fuck about you."

Chris was listening but he couldn't control it. He never could control his emotions and for the first time, he really wanted to. They didn't call him Cry Baby for nothing. As Sergio stared at him fiercely something in him grew stronger. Sergio's respect meant the world to him and he wasn't going to get it by sitting here boohooing like he was still ten years old. Chris wiped away his tears.

"I'll handle it," he said.

As if on cue, Tamiko pulled into the driveway with Charlotta riding shotgun. Sergio couldn't believe the nerve of this girl. She was about to come through and play this whole day out like nothing ever happened.

"This bitch got a lot of nerves," he mumbled.

When Charlotta saw Sergio's car outside of Chris's house she got nervous butterflies all through her stomach. She was wishing she'd listened to Tamiko and just stayed home, but regardless of what everyone else thought, she really did care about Chris. Her plan now was to lie her way back into his good graces. She knew staying home would only make her look guilty. Well, guiltier than she already looked. Tamiko blew her horn and waved Sergio over to the car. She was trying to keep him out of their business. Tamiko figured whatever was going to happen needed to happen without his interference. He walked over to her car with a look of disgust as Charlotta walked past him and up to the passenger side of his car.

"Get in for a minute," Tamiko said.

"Fuck that," Sergio refused as he leaned against her car anticipating fireworks. Charlotta could see the hurt in Chris's eyes. One glance was all it took to know that he knew everything.

"Happy Birthday Chris," she said flatly, handing him a shopping bag with a stolen outfit in it. He didn't reach out for it so she dropped the bag on the floor between his legs.

"I don't want it."

"Why not?"

"You know why."

"Can you get out of the car so we can talk?"

"What is it to talk about?"

"Whatever you feel we need to talk about."

Chris opened the car door and got out. This should be good, he thought. Charlotta began to walk toward his house.

"Not out here in front of everybody."

She knew she'd have a better chance if she got him away from Sergio. Sergio saw him following her into his house and shook his head in shame. He couldn't believe how weak Chris was for her. But Chris knew Sergio was right outside and today he was determined not to let him down. As they walked in and sat down, Chris just stared at Charlotta coldly.

"Okay, what did Sergio tell you?"

"You know what the fuck he told me."

"I know he told you I went to the club, and what else?"

"And you fucked Dana outside the club, in his truck."

Charlotta's eyes widened. This was the first time she'd ever heard someone say his name. Even in the midst of Tamiko's tongue lashing, she never said his name. So that was the infamous Dana Dane, she thought. She couldn't dwell on it right now.

"I didn't fuck that boy," she lied.

"First of, that nigga ain't hardly a boy. He old as hell!"

"Whatever, it don't matter 'cause I didn't fuck him."

"What the fuck was you doing in his truck then?"

"All we did was smoke some weed."

Chris didn't know enough about Dana to know that he didn't even smoke weed. He still knew it was a lie.

"You could've smoked some weed with Sergio. Why him?"

"I didn't know Sergio was even there."

"And that's why you thought you could do whatever you wanted to do."

"I didn't do shit!" she yelled. "What…got high with a nigga?"

"Whatever man, he ain't got no reason to lie to me."

"So you believe him over me?"

"Hell yeah!" They stared into each other's eyes angrily.

One-Mississippi. Two Mississippi.

"Fuck it then!" she spat.

"Right, so get out."

She couldn't believe he was putting her out. She stomped all the way to the door, mumbling and jerking her neck.

"Don't call me no more since you wanna believe other people."

"I'm not," Chris assured her.

"I'm serious this time."

"I am too…bye."

Charlotta slammed the door and then he heard car doors slamming and engines starting. He was glad everyone was leaving because right now he just wanted to be alone. He thought about his mother coming

home from the grocery store soon. He'd never really enjoy his birthday
when he was feeling this down and right now, he just didn't want to talk
to anyone. His mental screen painted a vivid picture of the scene in the
Bronco the night before. His version had Charlotta on top rodeo style.
Maybe because he knew she liked to be on top. He knew all the freaky
things she was capable of doing because she had done it with him on
several occasions.

The lump in his throat was too big to swallow. The swelling in his
eyes came too quickly to contain. He stood and began punching the
leather sofa he was sitting on. With each blow, he grew angrier. He was
punching Dana and Charlotta's no good asses. He stopped, realizing not
only was his hand hurting, but it wasn't making him feel any better
either. He wiped his face, grabbed his keys, and shot out the door. He
had no idea where he was going, but Chris knew he had to get away.
Away from anyone who might want to talk about what was wrong with
him.

****

Chris ended up at the liquor store trying to convince a crackhead to
go in the store and buy him a bottle of Cisco.

"What's in it for me?" the crackhead negotiated.

"Here," Chris responded, handing him a couple extra dollars.

The crackhead grinned and took off into the store. Chris looked
around to see if anybody was coming. He particularly didn't want to see
anybody from school. There was nobody around he knew, just a few
more crackheads, a drunk homeless dude, and an older man he only
knew by face. The older cat appeared to be hustling. An hour later, Chris
was still hanging out at the liquor store. With nowhere to go, he chose
the piss infested alley in the back of the liquor store to drink his sorrows
away.

Luckily, the cold air lessened the otherwise sickening stench of the
alley. He sat on an empty milk crate downing stiff shots from the neck

73

with only the homeless man to keep him company. The bum was holding a conversation with himself but every once in a while, he'd look over at Chris and say,

"You know what I'm saying blood?"

Chris ignored him and tried to stay a safe distance from the man who smelled worse than the alley itself. The Cisco took control of his thought process. His emotional rollercoaster had journeyed the whole spectrum. At that moment his mind was like a jam-packed freeway during rush hour traffic. Charlotta had belittled him again but at least this time he handled the situation like Sergio would have. He went into his pocket and pulled out his twenty-five semiautomatic pistol. He admired it for a second.

He thought about aiming it at the bum just to scare him away. The realization of the power he possessed with a gun in his hand started to register. Bullets hurt and killed, he thought. With his gun by his side, he could demand respect from people. Then he thought about Sergio. Sergio didn't need a gun to get his respect. Nobody would ever try and take his girl out in a parking lot to have sex with her. Then he thought about Dana and how much respect he had in the neighborhood. What made people like Sergio and Dana so much different from him?

He visualized all the people in his hood that he knew and respected because they didn't take shit from anybody, male or female. For the first time in his young life, Chris was contemplating serious changes. Changes that would turn him into someone he respected. The man he wanted to be sure wouldn't be in an alley in the middle of the day drinking and feeling sorry for himself over a girl. The man he wanted to be would know that there were plenty of fish in the sea and move on. Could he do it though, he wondered? Could he just up and change things like that?

"You know what I'm saying doe young blood?" the bum slurred.

Chris stood up and the alcohol went straight to his head until he was dizzy.

"Man get the fuck away from me," he shouted.

The bum looked at Chris and continued to mumble incoherently. Chris drew his weapon. "I'm not bullshitting with you!"

The bum wasn't as crazy as he pretended to be. Once he saw the pistol he quickly moved along down the alley. Chris put the gun back in his pocket and sat down the bottle with still a few swallows lingering. He tried to maintain his balance as he staggered the first few steps on his way out of the alley. When Chris made it up to the front he saw Melonhead pulling up in an STS Cadillac. He jumped out smoking a blunt and apparently he planned to take the lit marijuana in the store with him. That's the kind of thing gangsters did all the time. Fuck the rules, Chris thought. For some reason, Chris felt like he wanted to be acknowledged by Melonhead so he walked up and said,

"Let me hit that."

Melonhead paused.

"When you start smoking lil' nigga?"

"Today," he answered truthfully with his chest poked out.

"Here you go."

Melonhead passed him the blunt as he went inside the store. As Chris stood outside along with society's rejects, he took in all his surroundings along with a long pull from the blunt he'd just been handed. He knew the streets were the place he would have to earn his stripes and take his respect. He choked hard the second time he hit the weed and his mouth filled with saliva until he had to spit it out. The head rush he was feeling was amazing. He pulled on the blunt again but not as hard, as he continued to soak up his surroundings and what life meant to him at that very moment.

Chapter 9

For the two weeks following his birthday, Chris had been on punishment for a lot of things. Drinking, staying out until one in the morning, swearing under his breath. He didn't care because he was in the process of making changes that he knew everyone wasn't going to accept so easily, especially his mom. In his room, he did pushups, pull ups, and shadow boxed all day long. He was trying to build a hard body to match his new rock mentality through self-training. At night he would sit up in the dark and think about what he would do if someone was stupid enough to try him. He had seen Charlotta every day since his birthday, but he did not acknowledge her, nor did she acknowledge him. But Chris didn't acknowledge anyone anymore.

He didn't respond even when people spoke to him and if anyone even dared to call him Cry Baby, he just shot them a cold stare. Cry Baby was dead. He trained himself not to laugh or joke with anyone because he didn't want to give anyone a chance to insult him or play with him in a disrespectful manner. Even at home, he refused to watch comedic shows. Chris would only watch sports and gangster movies. The more he watched, the more he began to feel like a gangster. Sergio had supplied him with all the ammunition to load his mind with violent thoughts.

He watched VCR tapes of classic movies like King of New York, Scarface, and The Untouchables. While his mother was at work he studied the style, the mentality, and the viciousness of each character. He knew Al Capone was not just a fictional character made up in someone's mind, and he became fascinated with his real life story. He decided he needed a name change along with his new attitude. He decided Capone would be his new name. He would enforce this new name with aggression and it would begin the turning point of his social status in the hood. No more short end of the stick. No more living like the weak. He would live with power and aggression from here on out.

****

This would be the last time she loaned Charlotta some of her hard earned money, Evelyn promised herself. She knew Charlotta was only going to go hang out and do something stupid like have sex with grown men in the back of cars. Evelyn was the babysitter in her family and it kept her with some extra money in her pocket. Lately, Charlotta had been hitting her up for money on a regular basis. She also wasn't feeling all of her wild and loose behavior that seemed to be getting worse. It wasn't like Evelyn was a saint, but it seemed like the whole crew she was running with was becoming a little too…scandalous.

"Here," she said shoving Charlotta a twenty dollar bill.

"Don't act like that Ev."

"Whatever, I want my money back or a free outfit; one or the other; and I want it before the skating party at the end of this month."

"I'm gonna give you yo' money back bitch. Stop pressing me!"

"I'm not, but I already told you I'm saving up for this chain with the matching bracelet I saw at Eastland. All you trying to do is get your hair done so you can hit the club and chase dope boys."

Charlotta laughed at Evelyn and continued to be her usual sarcastic self.

"See, that's your problem; if you was chasing some dope boys you wouldn't have to save up for no punk ass chain and a bracelet. You could just ask for it like I do."

"Girl fuck these niggas, ain't no nigga about to be trying to regulate my life 'cause he done bought me a fucking chain. Every time you get something from a nigga he trying to control your every move. No thanks, I'm straight on that."

Charlotta just shook her head as if she felt sorry for her friend.

"So young, so naïve."

Evelyn mimicked her.

"So young, such a hoe."

Charlotta punched her in the arm and ran down the hall as the bell rang.

"What's up Ev?" she heard a familiar voice say.

She turned around to see Chris looking like he had a thugged out makeover. His pants were sagging, his shoes were untied, and his hat was backward and tilted to the left.

"What you still doing in the halls?" Chris said.

"Your punk ass ex was holding me up with her bullshit," she explained.

Chris brushed the thought of Charlotta out of his head and put his arm around Evelyn. She was surprised but didn't resist.

"Come on, let me walk you to class."

"Don't you gotta get to your own class?"

"Don't worry about that, come on."

As they walked quickly down the hall, Evelyn politely moved Chris's arm from around her shoulder.

"You look different Chris."

"Call me Capone."

"Ca who?"

"Capone. The only people who can call me Chris is the teachers."

Evelyn could smell the marijuana on his clothes and figured he was just tripping off the weed. She obliged anyway.

"Whatever…Capone."

After school, Sergio and Capone rode around smoking weed and kicking game about females and ordinary hood shit. Of course Sergio loved this new identity that had emerged. He had an inkling Charlotta had a lot to do with his dramatic turnaround. Sergio didn't know Capone's mind. He didn't know that the drastic changes in his way of thinking were not just the results of a bad relationship, but the after effects of everything that had ever gone wrong in his young life.

Especially the things that could not be avoided because of the way he was already perceived to be. Sergio still didn't want to be the one to totally corrupt Capone. After a few hours, Sergio took him home against his will.

"Ain't nothing out here in these streets man, for real."

"Man my mama ain't gone be home until eleven. Ain't shit to do at my crib."

Capone wanted to hang with Sergio and pick up on the things he couldn't learn at home or sitting in a classroom. Capone felt that after school was when the street lessons began and those were much more valuable at the present time.

"Yo' time will come bro and when it does, you'll be able to do whatever the fuck you want when you want, so don't rush it. Go fuck with some video games and do some shit a nigga yo' age supposed to do."

Sergio hit the streets at the tender age of thirteen. He was forced to act like an adult when he was still a child. He was trying to spare Capone the same journey. "You need a few dollars or something?" he asked.

"Naw, I'm good."

"Later."

Capone hopped out of the car and headed up the walkway but soon as Sergio was out of eyesight, he turned and headed away from the house. The streets were calling. He walked around the corner thinking he might run into Randy and Dink. Since his renewal, they seemed to treat him with respect, making them much more compatible as associates. Besides, they were young gangstas in training as well, but they were a couple seasons ahead of Capone. Just as he expected, they were standing on the corner drinking a forty ounce. There was another dude standing with them but Capone couldn't make out who it was yet. Once he got a little closer he could see it was pretty boy Jason, as people like to call him. He and Capone never cared much for each other, mainly because they were both going after Charlotta at the same time. Since Charlotta turned out to not be the prize that Capone thought she was, he held no grudges.

"What's up fellas?" he greeted.

"What's up Cry Baby?" Randy said testing the waters.

They slapped fives.

"Man I told y'all don't call me that shit. I ain't playing," Capone stated firmly.

They all laughed it off, but Randy could see it in his eye that Capone meant business. He apologized and they slapped fives again.

"You still a silly rabbit doe," Dink teased.

Capone hadn't heard that one in a while so he laughed it off. But after a quick chuckle, he got serious again.

"Naw just Capone though."

It seemed everyone was about to leave it alone and change the subject when Capone heard Jason's voice.

"Fuck you mean, just Capone? Nigga, you ain't no Capone! Capone was a gangsta nigga. Yo' name is Cry Baby Chris."

Capone knew this would happen eventually. Everyone wouldn't just warm up to the idea that he was different now. The transition would have some bumps and bruises. He was ready for those bumps and bruises and he certainly wasn't about to let pretty boy Jason get away with any more slick talk. Without hesitation, he punched Jason in the face with everything he had. Jason stumbled backward; his eyes bucked in disbelief.

Capone seized the opportunity to hit Jason with a quick three piece, but Jason took all three blows and retaliated with a blow to Capone's jaw. They locked up and began to only throw punches when one had a free hand to swing. Dink and Randy had no loyalty to either brawler;

they were just cheering on the continuation of the fight. Capone's lack of experience began to take its toll. The punch ration was starting to grow largely in Jason's favor. He hit Capone with an uppercut that sent him crashing to the ground.

Jason jumped on top of Capone to finish him off. Capone tried blocking the punching but was unsuccessful most of the time. Randy and Dink had seen enough and decided the fight was too one sided to continue watching and broke it up. Capone was so irate his entire body felt like one big burning flame. By the time he reached his feet, his gun was already in plain view for his target to see. He thumbed off the safety, aimed, and fired at Jason.

Bang! Bang! Bang! Bang!

Jason tried to run but the bullets lodged in his back and sent him crashing down hard on the sidewalk. Dink and Randy took off up the block in a race for an unknown destination. Capone quickly walked over to Jason lying on the sidewalk gasping for air.

Bang! Bang!

"Muthafucka!"

He finished him off with two to the head like mobsters do it. Capone took off in the opposite direction as Randy and Dink. As he ran, his body was in shock but his legs continued on.

Shit!" he whispered loudly, realizing his gun was out then tucking it in his jacket pocket. Putting his gun away was his first rational thought he'd had the entire time since he fired the first shot. The second coherent thought was making a turtle's pace stroll into his conscious mind. Maybe home wasn't the safest place to be at that moment. Police could be on the way to get him and take him away forever. He ran down the alley that led to his backyard and hopped the fence. He had to run in spurts now because he was too tired to keep up a steady pace.

He'd run some, then walk some; run some then walk some more until he reached Sergio's house. With no energy left to jump the fence, he grabbed the middle of the gate and did a cartwheel into the backyard. When he arrived at the front of the house he didn't see any cars, and that's when panic started to set in.

"Shit!" he yelled and ran to the backyard again.

He paced around with what seemed like hundreds of thoughts racing through his head. Hiding the gun was the one that stood out the most. He looked around and saw an empty dog house. He ran over and slid the gun underneath a filthy blanket inside the dog house. He could hear the sirens coming, making him more and more nervous as they grew closer. Standing in the backyard looking in all different directions wasn't going to make for a smooth getaway. Just then Sergio's Monte Carlo pulled in the driveway and he jumped out, moving hurry-scurry to his front door.

"Bro!" Capone shouted, running desperately to the front of the house.

Sergio was startled to see him but continued towards the front door searching for the right key. If Capone didn't know better he would have thought the police were after Sergio. Once inside Capone took a seat in the living room while Sergio unloaded pounds of weed from a garbage bag and a huge pistol from his waistline. "I'm in trouble bro," Capone confided.

"What happened?"

"I shot somebody."

Sergio paused.

"Who?"

"This nigga name Jason."

"I know 'em?"

"I think so. I'm not sure."

Sergio went back to work and Capone felt he was being a little too nonchalant about the whole thing. Maybe he'd react differently when he told him the worst part. "I think he dead."

"Huh?" Sergio's eyes widened.

"I think he dead," he repeated.

Just saying the words sent nervous jitters through his stomach. He jumped up and ran to the bathroom as he felt the bile rising in his throat. The vomit caught the toilet and the floor at the same time. While Capone was puking his guts out Sergio was trying to figure out how to get him somewhere safe. When he heard the dry heaving stop he entered the bathroom but kept his distance because of the smell.

"We gotta get you out of here."

"And go where?" Capone said struggling to breathe.

"Out the hood. You definitely can't stay around here. What makes you think he's dead? Lots of people survive being shot with a two-five."

"I know…but I hit him five or six times, twice in the back of his head."

Capone felt his stomach turning again but he had already hurled everything inside of him into the toilet.

"Yeah, you gotta go dog."

"Let me clean up real quick."

Capone splashed some water on his face and quickly rinsed his mouth with mouthwash. When he was finished, Sergio checked the windows to see if the coast was clear. Outside, Capone climbed in the backseat lying on the floor the way Sergio told him to do. They crept out of the neighborhood with ease and the next thing Capone heard was an unfamiliar female voice as she opened the car door and got in the front passenger seat. They rode until the sun went down then Sergio told him to get up off the floor. When Capone lifted his head up and looked around, he knew they were somewhere in the suburbs.

They pulled into a liquor store as Sergio gave the young lady some money and sent her inside. Afterward, they checked into the Red Roof Inn under the female's name which Capone still didn't know. Once inside, Sergio finally introduced her as Chocolate. Capone thought she probably got her name because of her smooth, dark skin. She had an hourglass figure and ass that would send some men into bankruptcy. He couldn't tell if her ponytail was her real hair but right now he couldn't care less. Sergio didn't mention anything about the shooting so he figured he should keep quiet as well.

The three of them sat around sipping gin and juice and smoking a blunt, watching television.

"Relax man," Sergio said after noticing that Capone still looked extremely nervous.

The more he thought about what he'd done the more gin he guzzled trying to forget. An hour passed before Capone joined in on the conversation that Chocolate and Sergio were having. When the movie they were watching ended, Sergio grabbed his car keys and headed for the door.

"I'll be back to get y'all in the morning."

Capone looked at Chocolate and she didn't look as confused as he felt. As Sergio closed the door behind him Chocolate took a sip of gin and a seductive smile eased on her face. She stared him straight in the eyes and began to undress until she was completely naked. She moved closer to him as he smashed a blunt tail into the ashtray. She nudged his shoulder with her palm.

"Lay down," she commanded.

She then unbuckled his belt and unzipped his pants. He was all stiff and ready. As she fingered his boxers and pulled out his penis, Capone felt all of his nervous tension releasing. As she took his rod into her mouth, Capone began to wonder if this was the last time he'd ever feel a woman's touch.

Chapter 10

18 months later

After a year in Alabama, Capone had been back in Detroit for almost six months. He was glad to get away from Sergio's aunt and crazy cousins. All they did was get drunk and fight almost every day. After a year down south, Capone felt like he could smash anybody in his weight class. He came back looking a lot different than people remembered him. He had long braids and tattoos now. The biggest tattoos were the two Glock pistols on his shoulder blades. Ironically, he had a tattooed tear under his right eye just to mock everyone that ever called him Cry Baby. They'd think twice about it from now on, no doubt.

He lived with Sergio in a plush apartment downtown surrounded by police whose headquarters were a stone toss away. The first thing Sergio did was get him a fake ID in case he came in contact with police. Homicide still watched and visited his mother's house from time to time, and that's the reason he'd only seen her once since he'd been back. Capone's relationship with his mother was almost non-existent. He had become everything she'd raised him not to be. It hurt him to know that he had disappointed her so much, but he was just doing what he felt was necessary to become a man. Growing up without his father, it seemed he had to find his own way to manhood.

During the first few months of Capone's return, he was hesitant to leave the house. He'd hang around Sergio's bachelor pad all day reading books he'd purchased to kill boredom, or do pushups and sit ups until he collapsed. He found himself with so much time on his hands he began to write his thoughts down in a journal. The journal became monotonous so he began to write poetry. At the moment he sat at the kitchen divider cutting up ounces of crack cocaine on the granite top. Sergio had diversified his hustle and was now a big dog in the game. Capone was beginning to help out more by breaking down rocks, bagging up weed, picking up money, and dropping off drugs.

Sergio supplied several crack houses in and out of his neighborhood. Capone was being schooled on how to keep an eye out for shady workers as well as how to talk in code on the phone. He had a reputation now as a shooter but the real gangstas in the hood couldn't care less, for they were all shooters as well. After counting and bagging enough crack to last the rest of the day, he washed his hands and rolled up a blunt.

Soon after, Sergio came in with a gang of shopping bags that appeared to be from a visit to Somerset Mall. Just another spur of the moment shopping spree, Capone thought. Sergio clapped and rubbed his hands together with a grin spreading across his face.

"Oh yeah, right on time."

Capone puffed and passed the weed.

"What's on the agenda?" he asked.

"You put that work together?"

"You know it."

"Well, we gotta fly to the hood and pick up some bread. Then I wanna swing by Chocolate's house and throw some shit on the stove. You know tomorrow is the first of the month right?"

"Yeah, I remember. That sounds like a plan; let's get to it I'm bored."

Sergio broke out in freestyle rap from nowhere.

/I got the plan nigga

You got the weed in yo' hand/

/So let's bounce to the hood

and get all the money we can/

/Fucking all the hoes with tight clothes and pretty feet/

/We some Detroit hustlers in the shit too deep/

Capone just stared unenthused.

"Yeah, whatever," he finally replied.

He wasn't impressed and had gotten quite used to Sergio's spontaneous freestyles.

The sun was blazing as Sergio pulled out of the parking lot in his white Cadillac Eldorado. He had a few cars now. Along with the Monte Carlo and Cadillac, he had a white Corvette with a black convertible top. White was now Sergio's favorite color and he had at least a hundred pairs of white sneakers to prove it.

"I should go jump in the 'Vette after we take care of this business, show them boys what my life like out here."

Capone just sat and stared out the window at the passing buildings. His silence wasn't unusual, but Sergio read something in his demeanor this day.

"What's on your mind bro?" he asked.

Capone hesitated trying to find the right words. He didn't want to sound ungrateful.

"You take good care of me bro, and you know I appreciate everything you do, but...sometimes I wish I could help out more."

Sergio looked at Capone with a puzzled stare. It didn't register how he could be unhappy.

"You do plenty dog, don't worry about that. Remember you got warrants, and just be glad you at a level of the game where the work is light and the chances is minimal. A lot of niggas wish they could start in the game where you at right now."

Sergio was speaking from experience. He knew what it took for Eastside hustlers with no plugs or handouts to come up. You either had to have one hell-of-a hustle hand or a mean trigger finger. Sergio was a natural born hustler that would shoot anything and anyone that tried to stop his cash flow. As he continued, Capone listened with honest ears.

He had a tremendous amount of respect for his big bro so he had no choice but to take his word as bond as he continued to search for his place in life.

****

Evelyn was tired…just plain tired of dealing with lames. She'd dated too many back to back to believe this was even her real life. After letting go of the last wanna be thug she dated briefly, she just decided to chill on dudes altogether for a while.

This was easier said than done since she was getting more attention from guys every day. She was blossoming into a gorgeous young lady with just enough curves to make the average player fiend with curiosity. She hadn't seen Charlotta in months and they barely talked on the phone anymore. Charlotta had hooked back up with Dana and was now his ride or die chick. Anything for a dollar, Evelyn thought. Meanwhile, she had taken a job at her uncle's dollar store and since she no longer had a social life, she decided she'd start babysitting again when she wasn't working at the store.

The last time she'd talked to Charlotta she was making drug runs back and forth to Minnesota for Dana. They were on different paths, to say the least. Evelyn just decided to block everyone out of mind while she focused her attention on school and securing a scholarship. In the fall, she planned to transfer to the School of Performing Arts.

Her eyes lit up when Capone and Sergio came strolling into the dollar store. It was her first time seeing Capone since he'd been back.

"What's up Ev," Capone and Sergio spoke simultaneously.

"What up y'all? Capone, come here nigga!" she said waving him over excitedly.

Evelyn thought the two of them looked like rappers as she came from behind the counter to give Capone a brief hug. She got a whiff of his Obsession cologne and grinned. It was her favorite.

"How you been?" she asked.

"I been good. How long you been working here?"

"I thought I told you she worked at the dollar store in the hood?" Sergio said as he went walking down the aisle.

"Naw, you didn't," Capone said trying to recall the conversation. "I would've stopped in before now if I knew you was here."

Evelyn and Capone had become good friends during Capone's relationship and break up with Charlotta. Out of pure loyalty, she always kept things on the up and up with Capone.

"You all buff now," Evelyn said squeezing his bicep.

"You all fine now," Capone said.

Evelyn blushed and decided to change the subject before the conversation became flirtatious.

"You seen Charlotta lately?"

"Un un, I ain't been trying to doe. I heard she back fucking with Dana."

"Yeah, I heard that too. Y'all still cool though right?"

"She…I mean, I wouldn't wanna hear she got hit by a truck or nothing. I ain't trying to get in touch or no shit like that either doe. It's all in the past."

Sergio slapped two boxes of baking soda and some sandwich bags on the counter.

"How much?"

"Four dollars," Evelyn replied.

"He gave Evelyn a ten and told her to keep the change as he headed for the exit. He saw the chemistry between Capone and Evelyn and decided to give them some privacy in case Capone wanted to put his bid in.

"I'll be in the car bro," Sergio said.

Evelyn stood there a minute taking in Capone's jewelry and all his tattoos. They were all alone in the store for the moment. Capone leaned on the counter right in front of the register.

"You and me still cool right?" he inquired.

"Yeah, of course."

"Good, 'cause I missed you."

Evelyn was taken aback by the revelation. Not so much the words, but the implications in Capone's eyes. She could see where this was leading and didn't want to go there.

"You didn't miss me, nigga."

"Oh, you think I'm bullshitting huh?"

"Yes, absolutely…bullshitter is smeared across your forehead right now."

They laughed at Evelyn's response but way louder and longer than necessary. It was a nervous tension releasing. Capone spotted a book on the counter titled Famous Black Poets. He zoomed in then grabbed the book off the counter.

"Let me see this."

"For what?" she asked surprised by his interest.

"This yo' book?"

"Yeah, I get bored just sitting here when no customers are coming so I'll read something to pass the time. You read poetry?"

"Hell yeah, I write too," he boasted.

"Yeah right, get up out of this store lying for no reason."

"I'm not lying. I swear on everything."

Just then they heard Sergio's horn blowing outside. He knew it was time to get going.

"Why don't you let me call you later on tonight," he chanced.

"I'll call you," Evelyn said.

She gave him a pen and showed him where he could write his number in the poetry book. He cracked a grin, not believing his game was finally tight enough to get Evelyn's attention.

"Call me tonight," he said.

This was such a bad idea, she thought to herself the moment Capone was gone. It would have been better to let him down easy and honestly. Now every time she opened the book, bam! There was Capone's number staring her in the face. It just reminded her of how good he smelled and how sweet he was back when he and Charlotta were an item. She shook it off. Mainly because Charlotta was still her friend, but besides that, dude was a gangster now and she didn't want any part of that lifestyle.

****

It was unusually hot for the middle of May. A fleet of cars lined one side of the street. A few Cadillacs, a couple of old schools, a Land Cruiser, and Charlotta's Camry. The bunch squatted under the street light focused on the ivory. It was one of those nights when all different crew members from all different cliques came together with one common goal; breaking up the dice game.

When headlights hit the corner, all the heads turned to get a glimpse of the oncoming car. Once they saw the white Corvette pulled to the end of the fleet of cars, most people went back to the dice game. Those who hadn't seen Sergio's new Corvette stood with their eyes glued to the car until he and Capone exited the vehicle. Capone spotted Charlotta immediately and couldn't help but notice how good she looked since he'd seen her last. She was thick like Tamiko in the ass department now, only hers was a little shapelier with a mean cuff. Her hair seemed to just grow longer and longer with age. Today it was in one big braid that hung down the middle of her back.

She wore heels and short shorts with a belly shirt that highlighted her small waist. She held a thick wad of cash in her hand as she shook the dice. The rumors were all through the hood that Charlotta was making good money with Dana. Capone had a nice buzz from smoking exotic weed and drinking Hennessy all day. He was feeling flirtatious as he gazed at Charlotta's ass bent over under the street light. Capone walked right up and slapped her on her left butt cheek. As she spun around to protest, he blew her a kiss.

She smiled salaciously and continued gambling. Capone and Sergio both pulled out bankrolls to let everyone know they didn't come to be spectators. Capone placed a side bet with Charlotta as he scanned over the crowd. Randy was there looking bigger and fatter than anyone ever imaged he'd grow to be. His hands and head were humongous.

Right next to Randy was Dink, looking scared to death of all the gangsters in his presence. As time went on he noticed Dink and Randy didn't seem as close as they used to be. Reason being, Dink was working for Dana now and Randy just couldn't respect the fact that he had stooped so low as to work for the same man that put a bullet in him just a couple years ago.

Eventually, Dink and Randy moved to opposite sides of each other and watched as Charlotta went on a winning streak. She'd hit her point four times in a row. Everyone was trying to bet big and fifties and hundreds covered the ground they encircled. Just then, a grass green Benz pulled up, not at the end of the fleet of cars, but on the grass. Things were about to get interesting as Melonhead and Nutty hopped out with enough swagger to loan a few guys some.

"Shoot this stack nigga!" Nutty yelled as he flashed a ridiculous wad of cash. He continued to boast and taunt. "What's happening? The real money getters here now. Ya'll niggas ain't got no real cash."

Sergio took offense to the statement immediately. He couldn't believe that Nutty had the audacity to stand there and front like he had more money than everybody, including him.

"Tell me what it is and we can bet it when it's my dice," Sergio replied.

Nutty seemed surprised that Sergio had to balls to call his bluff.

"Don't worry about how much it is. Shoot this stack big money boss hog," Nutty taunted.

Melonhead put his two cents in.

"Don't do it you gon' lose yo' shirt."

"Just tell me what it is. Whatever it is we can shoot it. You know I don't' give a fuck about no money; I'll go make some more. What's happening?" Sergio said putting the pressure back on Nutty.

The dice game had come to a halt with everyone waiting on Nutty's response. Nutty pushed his way to the middle of the circle looking as if he wished he'd never opened his big mouth.

"Who last on the dice? This nigga don't wanna do nothing," he said referring to Sergio.

Sergio shot him a condescending smirk. But Nutty was not finished grandstanding. When Charlotta finally did crap out it was Randy who had next on the dice.

"I got my backs," Charlotta said as she tossed a hundred dollar bill to the curb.

When Randy rolled a nine Nutty tried to place a five hundred dollar side bet with him.

"Naw man, I ain't trying to do all that. I'll bet you a hundred," Randy said.

Nutty took the bet, but Sergio knew that the only reason he even attempted that kind of bet with Randy was because Randy's money wasn't that long, but Sergio's was.

"I'll bet that five hundred he nine," Sergio said.

"Bet," Nutty said with no slick talk to add.

He had to take the bet. His pride and reputation was at stake. Charlotta felt like everyone was trying to steal the spotlight away from her and she didn't like it. She decided she had to boss up in order to take her shine back.

"Bet another five hundred he don't nine Sergio," she challenged.

Sergio looked at her like she'd gone mad.

"I don't discriminate against hoes. I'll take your money too, bet."

Charlotta had been called worse but she was still offended.

"Damn, why I gotta be a hoe?"

"I asked Capone that same shit just yesterday," Sergio shot back.

Everyone burst into laughter except Charlotta.

"That's why I'm 'bout to break yo' punk ass," she vowed.

Meanwhile, Randy was rolling everything but the right or the wrong number. He rolled so long Charlotta got nervous and started catching the dice. Finally, he rolled a nine and everyone that had bets against him let out a disappointed moan. Randy and Sergio snatched up all their winnings.

"Ha, haaaa! Let me get mines. Nobody move or I'm bussing heads," Sergio taunted all the losers.

As the game went on, the small betting baby ballers got knocked out of the game by the real ballers. The dice finally rolled around to Sergio.

"Who fading me?" he asked.

The only people still in the game were Melonhead, Nutty, Sergio, and Charlotta. Nutty stepped up.

"Go ahead, shoot," he said, dropping five hundred dollars down.

Sergio played with the dice a little, shook them hard, and rolled snake eyes. Nutty picked up the money.

"Bet that same five," Sergio said.

"Bet."

Sergio shook the dice and rolled a seven. He slid five hundred out of the pile and waited for Nutty.

"Let's go big money," he added.

"Let's go," Nutty said.

He shook the dice and rolled a ten and Nutty jumped all over what was considered to be a hard point to roll.

"Another five hundred you don't ten-four?"

"Bet," Sergio agreed.

He rolled a four on his first roll.

"Bet back?" he asked.

"Bet," Nutty agreed.

The crowd of onlookers were still placing tiny bets but enjoying the show. Sergio continued to roll fours until he had Nutty down several thousand. Melonhead tried to come to his rescue by making a thousand dollar wager against Sergio.

"Bet both, you niggas. I don't know who y'all think y'all fucking with. I been getting money since I was ten," Sergio exaggerated.

He continued taunting while Nutty began to catch the dice in fear for the first time. Sergio's continued slick talk only fueled Nutty's growing resentment. "I get money in my sleep; I don't know 'bout y'all," Sergio continued.

"Yeah, I bet you do by stepping on nigga's toes," Nutty accused.

Sergio held the dice.

"What? Who toes I stepped on, Nutty? If a nigga feel like that, he shoulda been stepped to me and said something."

"I'm saying something now nigga. You been stepping on my toes for years."

Sergio knew this had to have something to do with his rapid increase in coke clientele. He also knew he had violated back in the day, but couldn't see how he had stepped on any toes this time around.

"How Nutty? Explain to me how?"

"You know how nigga, but don't even worry about it. Shoot the dice."

"I ain't gon' worry about it," Sergio said in a matter of fact tone.

He shook the dice and rolled a ten. "Oh shit! Get money muthafuckas."

He snatched up all his winnings with a frown on his face. He was visibly upset now because of Nutty's accusations. He knew if Melonhead and Nutty were losing clientele it was because they were selling bullshit coke, not because he was stepping on any toes.

"You still shooting or you running," Nutty said.

"Scared niggas run, I don't. Drop it like it's hot."

They continued but Nutty's bankroll had dwindled down to a measly couple grand. Melonhead had decided to cut his losses.

"This gon' hurt 'em. Seven Mile!" Sergio shouted.

"Shut up and shoot," Nutty said.

"I tell y'all what fellas. Stooooop selling bullshit and y'all can get money like me."

By now Capone was just hugging his Glock and waiting for things to get out of hand the way they always did when too many gangsters crowded the same area at one time.

"Whatever, keep talking and I'ma shut all that shit down," Nutty warned.

Sergio was in disbelief. He knew he was going a little overboard with the trash talk, but only because Nutty had pissed him off. Now he was just talking crazy.

"You gon' what? Nigga you ain't gon' shut shit down. Play if you want to."

By now the dice were still in his hand. Resting.

"Like I said nigga, keep talking I'ma shut all that shit down and bring some order around this muthafucka. Fuck around and won't nobody be eating but us."

Sergio stood up and threw the dice down. Just then a white car bent the corner and pulled up on the crowd huddled under the streetlight. A voice came over the loudspeaker.

"Break this bullshit up before we take all you muthafuckas' money and haul your asses off to jail. Break it up right now!" the police demanded.

Half of the dudes in the circle had warrants and the other half didn't want the hassle. As everyone piled into their vehicles, Sergio and Nutty kept their eyes on each other. When Nutty pulled away from the sidewalk the look on his face said it all. As Sergio and Capone pulled off they made brief eye contact without saying a word. They knew the same thing Nutty knew. It wasn't over.

Chapter 11

It wasn't the last day of school, but it was the last day that most people showed up to get their report cards and say their goodbyes. The only reason you'd be in school after this day was if your parents forced you to go. Evelyn had cleaned out her locker and was coming out of the front doors of Pershing High School with some of her friends discussing summer plans.

Capone sat in the front of the school in Sergio's Corvette with the top down. She'd seen the car, but it hadn't registered that the car looked familiar until she heard the horn blowing. When she looked up, Capone was signaling her over to the car. She played it cool at first. She didn't want to seem too eager as if they had something going on when they didn't.

Secretly, she was dying to hop in the Corvette and ride home in style. When Capone blew the horn again she finally said her goodbyes and walked casually over to the car.

"Come on, get in," Capone said.

"You came up here to get me?" she asked looking half suspicious and half flattered.

"Yeah, why not?"

"I don't know, I'm just surprised."

She opened the car door and slid into the bucket seat. Capone made a U-turn and headed to Evelyn's house. She gave him the once-over, thinking to herself he looked sexy today. He wore a Detroit Piston's jersey with blue jeans and a red sweatband on his head. His neck held a gold link chain with a diamond encrusted cross. She knew the Corvette belonged to Sergio but couldn't help but think that Capone looked really, really good in it.

"So why you ain't call me yet?" Capone asked.

"Well, I…"

A horn blasted interrupting Evelyn's lie as they pulled to the stoplight. They both glanced over to see Tamiko and Charlotta giving them that 'we caught y'all' look.

"Don't y'all look cute together," Tamiko teased.

"Girrrl, don't say it like that; he 'bout to drop me off at home."

"Whaaaatever," Charlotta jumped in.

"Now bitch you already know, don't play."

"Where's my man at Capone? I haven't seen or heard from him since early yesterday," Tamiko said.

The question caught Capone off guard.

"I don't know. I didn't see him last night, but I thought he was at your house."

Tamiko was shaking her head.

"I know one thing, his ass better have his lies together when I see him."

Everyone couldn't help but laugh.

"Aw, you know it ain't like that," Capone said.

The light turned green and both cars pulled away slowly, yelling their last words out the window.

"Just tell him to call me when you see him."

"Okay." Capone said.

"Call me tonight," Charlotta added, but left no real indication of whom she was talking to. Neither wanted the awkward task of asking so they stared straight ahead at the road. Capone accelerated just enough to get some good space between the Corvette and Tamiko's car. He could see that Evelyn was uncomfortable.

"See, that right there is the reason I never called you. Don't get me wrong, you my nigga and all. But I don't like drama and I don't got time for it. You see how they was looking at us?"

"I understand," Capone said before a long pause. "I just wish I would have followed my first mind."

Evelyn glanced at him, but he wouldn't make eye contact.

"What do you mean?"

"Never mind, nothing," Capone said as he turned on Evelyn's street.

Now more than ever she felt the need to clarify things before the two of them went their separate ways. She didn't want to push Capone away, but she didn't want to lead him on either.

"Capone, we cool and hopefully we'll always be cool. I just don't want it to turn into something else that's all."

"I feel you," Capone said.

"Are you sure?"

"I gotta go find my brother," he said curtly.

As they slowly pulled in front of her house, Evelyn could feel his frustration.

"So you not gonna tell me what you mean by that?" she asked opening the car door.

"Mean by what?"

She got out and closed the door then leaned on it.

"When you said you should have followed your first mind?"

Capone stared straight ahead at the dashboard for several seconds before answering. He was deciding if he wanted to let the cat out of the bag.

"You remember Charlotta's fifteenth birthday party?"

"Un-huh."

"I came there that night with intentions to get at you. But you had so many dudes on you that night I just wound up getting at Charlotta."

There was a moment of silence.

"Hmmmp," was all she said.

"Hmmmp? I just shared my big secret with you and that's all you can say?"

Evelyn was smiling and blushing. She was also really confused.

"I don't know what else to say. I mean, I wish you would've followed your first mind too and maybe we wouldn't be in this situation now."

"Well, this ain't over," Capone said with confidence.

"Bye boy."

"Aye, you gotta admit though, we look good together in this drop top," he said coaxing a nod.

"We did…bye and thanks for the ride."

She stood on the sidewalk waving goodbye, hoping he'd get the hint and pull off. It was all she could do to keep from doing or saying the wrong thing. The kind of thing that would only make matters worse. As she thought back, she could see that Capone had been dropping subtle hints about his feelings for quite some time now. She knew he was not about to give up on her that easily, especially after the conversation they just had. A small part of her didn't want him to give up just yet.

****

It took three days for Sergio to get in touch with Tamiko, who had to get in touch with his lawyer and gather the bail money. She had been busy running around trying to find him instead of waiting by the phone for a call like he'd expected her to do. He was charged with possession of cocaine over fifty grams. The biggest problem was he wasn't in Wayne County.

Instead, he was cursing himself for being stupid enough to get caught with drugs in Oakland County where they'd give you the death penalty for such a crime if they could. He had several guys that he served weight to in Oakland County. He got pulled over in Pontiac and now his bond was set at twenty-five thousand dollars cash. That wouldn't be a problem except he'd just spent all his money on re-up. If his case was in Wayne County his bond would've been ten percent of that, but Oakland County was known for trying to make examples out of young black males with the guts to invade their suburbs with drugs that were already available, but for a much steeper price.

Sergio was feeling good now that he had talked to everyone he needed to talk to and things were set in motion. He knew it couldn't be too much longer for his release. Meanwhile, he and some other unlucky brother sat in the holding cell waiting to be escorted back to lock up.

Just out of boredom, they cracked jokes about the Caucasian male who had kept quiet about his rape charge until he was exposed in court. Most hustlers got way too much pussy to ever sympathize with a rapist. The jokes got boring after a while so Sergio put his disgust in a song.

/Yeah you took that pussy and now you gotta pay/

/You won't be going home 'til you old and gray/

/Sit yo' ass on that bench and don't look my way/

/or I'ma bite that ass 'til I get tooth decay/

The nervous white man just sat in the corner trying not to make eye contact and praying he made bail soon. When Sergio finally got back to lock up, he wasn't there ten minutes before he was called for a visit. He knew it was Tamiko. They sat opposite sides of the Plexiglas with just enough space at the bottom so that their voices could be heard clearly. Tamiko was looking extra sexy in a low cut blouse that Sergio had never seen.

He got an instant erection staring at her breast and thinking about the fact that it had been over a week since they'd had sex.

"I hit a lick on some clothes and some purses so I got some extra cash if you need it," Tamiko said.

"Naw, what I need you to do is give Capone that equipment to sell so he can get my bail money together.

"The lawn mower or the snow blower?"

"Both, the sooner the better."

"Okay."

"And make sure you let my lawyer know she's gotta be the one to post my bail."

"I already told her; she's waiting on us."

He sat back in the steel back chair for a few seconds.

"What?" Tamiko said, noticing him staring.

"Show me them titties real quick."

"What?"

"Let me get a tittie shot right quick."

"Hell naw, is you crazy?"

"Come on baby!" Sergio pleaded.

"Hell no! They got cameras everywhere in here just waiting for people to do some dumb shit and get put out."

"Just put 'em on the glass one time."

"No."

"Let me see a nipple at least."

"No Sergio."

"You on some bullshit!" he said, kicking the wall in frustration.

"And you just horny," she countered.

They stared into each other's eyes longing to be together. Their short time apart had heightened their appreciation for each other.

"Have I told you how much I love you lately?" Sergio said.

"Tell me again anyway."

"I love you more than anything in this world," he said staring into her slanted eyes.

He meant every word.

"Thank you for saying that. I really do need to hear it sometimes. I love you too baby."

****

Later that night Capone drove through the hood with the top up on the Corvette. It wasn't time to floss; he had way too much business to handle. The police had impounded Sergio's Cadillac and the Monte

Carlo hadn't been driven in so long it was in the garage on flat tires. First, he called a meeting with all the workers so he could make sure all of Sergio's spots were back up and running.

Then he made rounds to all the hoods he knew Sergio had weed clientele or other business going. He pulled up to the weed houses and blew the horn. He explained the situation to whoever was there to listen. He'd leave his number and tell them that he was holding it down for the meantime and that he was available 24/7. He drove through the city with a garbage bag full of marijuana and two Ziploc bags full of powder cocaine in the trunk. He hustled as hard as he knew how to but when he went home that night he was still disappointed in himself. It was still less than half of what Sergio needed to get out of jail. The next morning he got an early start in the hood.

He tried to stay on top of things the way he knew Sergio would. He went to Chocolate's house and the two of them cut and bagged some hard cocaine. When the workers were out, his pager went off and he'd shoot straight over with the re-up and collect the money. That afternoon he decided to swing by the dollar store to see if Evelyn was working.

He understood Evelyn's view on their relationship and was actually glad to see she lived by a set of principles, unlike Charlotta. But his gut told him that she was a girl worth the chase and he wasn't ready to stop his pursuit just yet. He pulled up at the dollar store and parallel parked out front. As he went for the door handle he stared straight at the faces of Melonhead and Nutty who had pulled up alongside him. They exchanged cold stares for a few seconds until Nutty pulled away slowly.

Capone sat back and took a deep breath. For a few seconds, he thought he was a dead man. He'd never had that feeling before and it scared him deeply. He felt the pounding in his chest as he placed his hand over his heart. He took another moment to gather his thoughts then got out of the car. When Capone stepped into the dollar store Evelyn was attending to a customer. His mind was somewhere else now.

Survival mode. He could see things coming to a boiling point. His Glock was on his hip and for the first time, he seriously contemplated killing Melonhead and Nutty. He tried to think about what Sergio would do if he were there.

"Come here," Evelyn said waving him over.

"What up?" he said.

"I just finished this poem I been writing and I want you to read it and tell me what you think."

She handed it over to him. It was titled The Stars, The Moon, and Other Shiny Things. As he read the poem the words didn't really translate to his brain. His mind was on murder and Evelyn could sense that he was tense about something. When he was done with his fraudulent examination he politely folded the paper, handed it back, and lied.

"I like it. I like it a lot."

"Do you? Don't just say you like it if you don't."

"Naw, it's good for real."

"So when you gonna let me read some of these alleged poems that you allegedly wrote?"

Capone kept watching his back to make sure no one was waiting for him outside.

"What's wrong?" Evelyn asked.

"Nothing, call me tonight and I'll read something to you."

"I'm a call you tonight at ten o'clock and you better be home."

"See you later."

Capone leaving so quickly was strange to Evelyn. He usually hung around for a while if no one was in the store. She knew something was bugging him and that gave her even more reason to call him tonight and see if she could get him to talk about it. Her attraction to Capone was rapidly affecting her judgment. He just seemed to be so different from the guys she dealt with in the past. He seemed…real.

After nightfall Capone's pager started blowing up. This time it wasn't the regular business code from one of the workers, instead, it was two numbers he'd never seen before with the emergency code 911 behind them. Capone called the first number back from his cell phone.

"Who dis?"

The dude yelled excitedly into the phone.

"Aye man, this Tre, some niggas just came through and shot up the spot dog. They had 'bout five guns dog just letting off like a muthafucka. Me and Red had to lay on the floor for like a half hour just to make sure they was gone, what the fuck man?"

"Is anybody hurt?"

"Naw man, ain't nobody hurt but I got my banger and I'm ready to go to war right now, what's up?"

"Stay right where you at I'ma call you right back."

"Aye man…"

Click.

Capone hung up and dialed the other number.

"Who dis?" he asked.

"Dog, this Black, somebody just firebombed the fucking crib nigga. I'm sitting in that bitch and all of sudden fucking cocktails just came flying through the windows. I got out the house before the fire spread, but the house is through. Somebody gotta tell me what the fuck is going on dog?"

"Where you at now?"

"I'm at my bitch house on Spring Garden."

Capone could hear a female voice in the background fussing about being disrespected.

"Stay right there."

Capone hung up the phone and sat down on the sofa at Chocolate's house.

"What's wrong?" she asked.

"I gotta go," he responded, not wanting to explain things to her.

This wasn't her area of the business. As he got up and headed for the door, he had no idea where he was going or what he was about to do. He pulled his gun out before he opened the door, anticipating an ambush. Once he was in the car alone he would be able to think clearly. What he was sure of was that the drama unfolding was definitely coming from Nutty and his crew. By now they had the knowledge of Sergio being in jail and probably thought it was the best time to launch an attack. Capone knew now more than ever that he needed to get Sergio out of jail ASAP.

Chapter 12

Capone's pager went off again and he recognized the number. It was a weed customer that usually bought a few pounds a week from Sergio. He couldn't think straight…so much was going on at once. He had to calm his nerves. He pulled over at the liquor store and called out to the dude that seemed permanently fixed to the parking lot. A few minutes later, the dude came out of the store clutching a pint of Remy Martin VSOP and the loose change in his other hand.

"Thanks my nigga," Capone said as he twisted and yanked off the cap as quickly as he could.

He took a big gulp and it burned like hell.

"Awe fuck!"

He grimaced and tried to shake it off as the burn opened his nasal passages and heated his esophagus. He sat in the parking lot drinking until he realized the Corvette was probably a target by now. He needed to switch up cars. His pager started going off again and again. He wanted to toss it out of the window, but he wouldn't let the confusion take over. He skidded out of the parking lot frustrated.

He needed a car and his frustrated mind was drawing blanks. He continued to drink.

"Charlotta!" he blurted out.

The name just popped into his head out of nowhere, but it made sense. He still knew her home number. It was forever etched in his brain like a serial number. He grabbed the phone and dialed her number praying she was home. A familiar voice answered the phone.

"You have reached my office after business hours…"

"Charlotta stop playing this Capone."

"Hey, what's up my nigga?" she said sounding overjoyed.

"How you doing?"

"I'm chillen, what's up with you?"

"I need a favor."

"That's just like a nigga to pop up when they need something, what?"

"I need to park Sergio's car in your garage and I need to borrow your car for a few hours."

"What you gonna do for me?"

"I'm serious right now."

"I'm serious too. You ain't called me in damn near two years and now when you do call out of the blue you wanna borrow my car?"

He wanted to tell her there was a very good reason he hadn't called her in two years. He was about to hang up on her, but he realized at that very moment, he needed her.

"So what do you want?"

"I'll tell you when you get here."

Click.

Capone was at her house in five minutes. He pulled all the way in the back of the house right in front of the garage. He popped the trunk and removed the money and the drugs from inside. Charlotta was standing in the door wearing a nightgown and some slippers. She reached for a hug and he hesitated before accepting her into his arms. She prolonged the embrace and even interlocked her fingers so he couldn't easily break her grip.

She smelled of sweet lotion and body spray. Just looking into her eyes brought back memories and mixed feelings.

"You missed me?" she asked.

"A little," he said trying to feed her narcissism.

"Good 'cause I missed you."

She finally let him go and they strolled into the living room. She went upstairs to get her car keys.

"You lucky I decided to come home early. I usually don't get in until after twelve."

She came downstairs and handed him the keys then followed Capone outside. He popped the trunk and stashed the money and drugs.

"Why you need my car anyway?"

"I gotta make some runs."

"Why you can't make runs in the car you was in?"

"I can't tell you all that. I just need a different car for a while."

She leaned on the driver side door so he couldn't open it.

"You really gonna owe me big for this."

"I know, whatever you want," he said slamming the trunk.

"For starters, I think you know what I want and I ain't about to beg for it like a ugly girl either."

"I'll be back tonight," he said just to get her off his back.

After he said it, he realized he couldn't think of a better way to end the night and get his mind off of his problems. She finally moved out of his way and headed back inside rubbing her exposed arms from the nippy night air.

"Don't play!" were her last words.

Once in the car, he pulled the pint bottle from his jacket. It was halfway gone, but he kept drinking to make sure he stayed calm. He was thinking much clearer now. He finally called the customer back who'd been paging him nonstop.

"Damn young dog, I thought you ain't want no money. I was about to call my other guy," the man said.

"I'm on my way right now give me twenty minutes."

He had to make the weed run. He had to get all the money from Sergio's workers and then get it all to Tamiko's house so she could take it to the lawyer. He was focused now, back on track. Still, he knew this was about to be an all-out war, something he knew nothing about dealing with. The thought made him unsettled and he reached for the drink again.

He thought about how Sergio would say he was too young and immature to handle this type of beef. He clutched his pistol in his lap trying to convince himself that he was a real killer. He'd done it before, he'd do it again.

The meeting with the weed customer went better than expected. The customer purchased the remainder of Capone's weed supply. Ten pounds to be exact. After taking care of that business, he linked up with all the workers who by now had formed a gun-toting goon squad ready to go to war. Capone began to feel a sense of power standing in a room full of soldiers he could command at his will. But once again, he wished Sergio was there to make the call.

If he took the wrong course of action, it could lead to being more costly than he was able to repay. The wrong course of action could also cost him his young life. He told the bloodthirsty soldiers to lay low and that Sergio would be home in the morning.

Chapter 13

On his way to Tamiko's house, Capone found himself swerving in and out of lanes. The liquor took control of his mind and body. With a pistol on his lap, locked and loaded, he felt safe. Tough even. The rapper Scarface's classic song "Jesse James" blasted through the speakers in Charlotta's Camry. He decided to stop by the house that had been shot up a few hours earlier and view the damage. He knew Sergio could always find another house, but this was the money spot.

Eight thousand dollars a day in crack rocks. When he hit the block all was still and the whole block had an empty feel to it. It was as if all the neighbors packed up to leave before the drama went any further. He sat parked directly in front of the house. He gawked from the passenger side at all the destroyed windows and golf ball sized bullet holes in the door. He checked in his rearview for cars and glanced around all sides for night crawlers and creepers.

As he felt the frustration rising again, he yanked the gear shift in drive and applied extreme force to the gas pedal. He hit Seven Mile and headed for Tamiko's house. Once in traffic, he eased up on the gas and maintained the speed limit in case police were lurking. The road was almost as quiet as the block he'd just left. There were a few cars in front of him, but none in the back.

He made a left on Conant as the street lights continued to shine on emptiness. Capone spotted the grass green Benz easing out into traffic. He let up off the accelerator slowly. He could only see one head inside the Benz. It was a head that wasn't big enough to be categorized as a melon, so it had to be Nutty driving. His mind began to race and his brain tunnels clogged.

He knew he didn't have time to rationalize and think it through. He viewed the quiet streets as a sign and the coincidence as an opportunity. I did it before. I'll do it again, he told himself. Here was the biggest of all of Sergio's problems right in front of him and he had a chance to do something about it. He ignored his heart pounding through his chest a thousand beats a minute. He saw the light turn yellow and then red before Nutty could catch it. Capone pushed the power button on the passenger side window. He crept up to the red light and crept up alongside the Benz. Got 'em!

Bang bang bang bang.

He stabbed off, running the red light, and jumped from the far left lane all the way to the far right. He bent the corner hard and went flying up the residential street doing seventy-five. He didn't yield at yield signs or stop at stop signs. He just drove. He knew Nutty was dead. He had seen the first two bullets enter his skull. He saw the look of disbelief when the barrel was staring him in the eye. Nutty attempted to block the first shot with his forearm but was no match for speeding lead. Capone had just killed another man.

He arrived at his apartment shortly after and he was half expecting to find flashing lights and his building swarming with police, but he found neither. He saw no one in the lobby, no one on the elevator, and no one in the hallway. He had already stopped by the Bell Isle Bridge and tossed the gun in the Detroit River. He had already cleaned the Camry of all the shell casings he found inside. Once he was in the apartment, he felt relieved.

He had committed a truly malicious act and had gotten away clean. Then he remembered he was already on the run for a murder. In his mind, he rationalized there was no difference in being convicted of one murder and ten because they both meant he'd go away to prison forever. The first thing he did after double locking the doors was go into Sergio's personal weed stash and grab enough weed to roll a fat blunt. He slid the lone blunt out of the box that rested on the coffee table then started breaking it down. He needed to calm down because, at the moment, there were no thoughts, only voices. Good and evil voices.

{Why did you do that?}

{I had to do it.}

{You're going to pay for that dearly.}

{I don't care.}

{Something terrible is going to happen to you.}

"So what, I don't give a fuck!" he said out loud.

{You just crossed a line there's no coming back from.}

He lit the blunt and pulled it hard. He coughed harder. The house phone rang but he ignored it. He was in the process of trying to bring himself back to reality and clear out the voices. As he paced around the room it felt like déjà-vu. The whole thing reminded him of being back in Sergio's backyard again with Jason around the corner laid out bleeding to death. The image of Jason stretched out on the sidewalk played across his mental screen like a home theater. He continued to pull on the weed harder and longer until he gagged. He saw Nutty's face again right before he pulled the trigger. Now Jason, then Nutty again.

"Fuck!" he shouted.

He felt like he was losing his mind. The phone rang again and it startled him, but it also brought him back to reality. He thought it might be the police so he ignored it. Alone in the apartment, he sat with everything off except one dim light. Then he got scared for some reason and turned that off also. The dark room went deathly silent. He flinched at every delusional squeak he heard. At the threat of noise, he'd run to the door and stick his ear to it.

When the blunt was gone he was ten times worse off than he was before he'd started smoking it. He cursed himself aloud for bringing about this self-induced paranoia. The phone rang again and he stood up ready to snatch the cord out and hurl it at the wall. Then he thought about all the people it could've been beside the police. It could be Tamiko calling about the money he never showed up with. Maybe it was Evelyn or Sergio. On the eighth ring, he finally answered.

"Hello?"

"Hey, what's going on?" Tamiko said.

"Oh, hey. Something came up, but I still got all the money and I'll bring it to you the first thing in the morning."

"Okay, is you alright? 'Cause you sound kinda different."

"Yeah, I'm straight. I'm just high."

"Damn, well, don't give me none of the shit you smoked."

"You right, I shouldn't be fucking with it either."

"Oh before I forget, Charlotta keeps calling me asking for this number. She claims you have her car."

"I do, I'm about to call her now," he explained.

"You backtracking now?" Tamiko pried.

"Naw, it ain't like that. I just had to take care of something."

"Mmmhmm. I'm telling you now she ain't changed one bit so you know what you working with if you decide to play in the sand again."

"Yeah, I know, but at least she hustles for her own money. I respect her hustle, but I'm cool on her."

"Okay, whatever. Do what you wanna do; just make sure you make it to my house in the morning so I can go get my baby."

"Okay, I'll be there."

"Bye."

He hung up and realized that for the first time since he'd been home his mind wasn't on the murder. Maybe that's all he needed was someone to talk to and get his mind off of things. He went to the refrigerator and grabbed a cold Budweiser. He wished Evelyn would call right now, but he knew she'd probably already called and wouldn't call back. He considered calling one of his other female friends but didn't want to be bothered with anyone he could think of.

Ironically, Charlotta was the only person he felt like he would be able to relax around on a night like this. They knew each other. He picked up the phone and dialed her number, knowing she was expecting his call.

"Heelloo!" she answered pissed off.

"What the hell wrong with you?"

"Nothing," she said as her tone relaxed after hearing his voice.

"You sure?"

"Yeah, but I thought you were trying to play me. I was getting tired of waiting for you to call."

"I wouldn't do you like that. Wouldn't want you out in the streets looking for me."

"Whatever nigga, so is you on your way to my house to bring me back my car?"

"Naw, I'm at home"

"Home? What the fuck you doing at home?"

"Calm yo' ass down."

"Calm down nothing. How you gonna go home with my car like I don't need my shit? I didn't say you could keep it overnight."

"I know, but I was thinking you could come get it and chill for a little while."

"And how am I supposed to get there, my looks?"

"You probably could, but I was thinking a cab. I'll give your money back."

"Maaan. Let me get a pen so I can write down the directions."

Capone finally turned on the television and some lights trying to relax before Charlotta arrived. He needed her just for tonight. Just to help keep away the voices. It was past late so he knew she'd be ready for whatever when she arrived. It had been a long time since Capone had traveled down this road but in the back of his mind, he knew one day he would.

****

Charlotta was having trouble getting past security without her ID She'd left in her purse which was in her car. She finally talked the guard into calling up to Capone's apartment to see if he was expecting someone. It made her feel special being invited to the apartment she'd heard so much about it from Tamiko.

She was pretty sure not many girls got to see this Bat Cave. She intended to present herself in a different light to Capone this time. She had long ago realized that Dana cared nothing about her. If he cared about her, he wouldn't continue to send her out of town with enough drugs to get her sent away for life. But money was money to Charlotta, and she refused to give in to fear of incarceration or anything else.

Charlotta felt Capone was the only guy she ever had a real connection with, even though she was too young and dumb to realize and appreciate it at the time. When Capone opened the door the first thing she noticed was his bright smile and how happy he looked to see her. She didn't even think he noticed her overnight bag as he grabbed her hand and pulled her inside. He complimented her on the Fendi jumpsuit she was wearing as she rushed off to the bathroom to change. Capone could see she hadn't changed much and wasn't wasting any time. She emerged in a pink camisole that came just below her butt cheeks. Her nails and toes were pink and she wore her hair bone straight with a part in the middle.

"You got some weed?" she asked.

"Yeah, ain't no more blunts though," he explained.

"I got one," Charlotta said as she reached in her Fendi night bag and rambled around until she found it.

He went to Sergio's stash and grabbed some more weed and when he came back, Charlotta sat with her legs crossed on the couch preparing the blunt.

"So what happened with Nutty and Sergio?" she asked.

"Nothing, Sergio went to jail before anything could happen."

"Well, I know something is about to go down. The hood just ain't big enough for all y'all no more."

Capone quickly changed the subject.

"How much that nigga paying you to take them bricks out of town?"

"He pays me well," she responded.

"How much?"

"Why?"

"I'm just asking," Capone said, but Charlotta wasn't just about to disclose that type of information willingly. She really didn't know what the going rate was of OT trips, and she didn't want people running around spreading rumors on how she was getting played.

"Fifty thousand," she blurted out jokingly.

"Yeah right, and all you driving is a Camry?" Capone said.

"Yeah, you know me, I'd have a fucking Porsche or something; coming through the hood real slow throwing up the peace sign like whaddup?"

As they giggled, the laughter was cut short by a jingle at the door. The knob turned as they watched in confusion as Sergio came through the door. He looked like he was breathing fire from his nostrils. He took one look at Charlotta and turned his nose up.

"What up bro, when you get out?" Capone said.

"About an hour ago."

"Damn my nigga, you pulling magic tricks around here and shit. We was coming to get you in the morning," Charlotta said.

"The fuck is she doing here?" Sergio responded.

"Man I gotta holla at you about some other shit right now."

Capone wasn't sure how much Sergio had learned in the hour he'd been out of jail, but from the look on his face, he knew a lot.

"I already know," Sergio said.

Capone still followed him into his bedroom and closed the door behind him.

"I don't think you know everything."

Sergio snorted as if he couldn't stand any more bad news at the moment.

"What's up?"

"Okay, you know who is responsible for all this shit right?"

"Yeah, I know. The whole fucking hood know."

"Well, I hope I did the right thing."

Right after he said it he realized he didn't care so much about what Sergio felt. Sergio had an airtight alibi for his whereabouts at the time of the murder. This was all his weight to hold if necessary. "I caught Nutty slipping so I got 'em," he explained.

"What you mean you got 'em?" Sergio said looking confused.

"I mean, I got 'em. He outta there. I got 'em right on Conant at the stop light and I left his ass right there."

Sergio's eyes grew big as bowling balls and then he burst into laughter as the realization kicked in. His laughter made Capone laugh as they slapped fives and Sergio pulled him in for a tight-grip hug.

"Did you make sure that bitch was dead?"

"Yeah, he dead," Capone assured him.

Sergio burst into another fit of laughter and once he stopped, he stood face to face with Capone staring like a proud father.

"Damn bro, when did you get this cold blooded?"

"I just did what I thought needed to be done."

"Well, you did good dog. Now you let me handle Melonhead bitch ass."

"Okay. How did you get out of jail without the money though?"

"Oh, I got tired of waiting so I called my connect and got the money from him. He's the one that hooked me up with the lawyer anyway so it was easy."

"Well, I got the money."

"Good, 'cause I wanna give it back first thing in the morning. Oh shit, you didn't do that shit in my Corvette did you?"

"Naw, I was in Charlotta car and nobody saw me."

"Cool cool." Sergio relaxed. "I know why Charlotta is here now but at the same time, I don't want the bitch sleeping here overnight, getting all comfortable and shit. Fuck her if you gon' fuck her and send her ass home."

"I got you."

They slapped fives again and went back into the living room where they found Charlotta on the house phone whispering. When she saw them come back in the room she reached out and handed the phone to Sergio.

"Who is that?" he asked.

"Who you think?" she snapped.

He snatched the phone from her knowing it was Tamiko. Charlotta rolled her eyes.

"Why you couldn't let me be the one to tell her with your big ass mouth?" Sergio said shooting daggers at Charlotta.

"Shut up nigga, you always whining."

Sergio shot Capone a dirty look.

"Hurry up dog," he told Capone.

Chapter 14

After only a few hours of sleep, Charlotta was awakened by a nauseated stomach as saliva filled her jaws. She jumped up, ran into the bathroom and slammed the door. She hugged the porcelain for dear life as last night's dinner debuted in the toilet.

"Are you okay in there?" her mother called out from the hall.

She tried to answer but was too busy puking.

"I'm okay Ma," she finally managed.

"You better not have no fucking morning sickness 'cause I'm telling you right now, I'm not raising no more kids."

Like you did such of a great job the first time, Charlotta thought. She ignored her mom's babbling. This wasn't the time to go back and forth about safe sex and being responsible for her actions. She just wanted the puking to stop. And who was her mother to judge anyway? When it was all over she sat on her knees trying to get some oxygen flowing into her lungs.

She rinsed her mouth and splashed some water on her face, wondering how the water to the face would help. She was out of the bathroom and halfway down the hall when nausea kicked in again.

"Awe shit!" she fumed, running back into the bathroom.

Later that day, Charlotta stopped by the pharmacy to get a pregnancy test. She ran into a baller in the parking lot and slid him her number. She was always on the lookout for a reserve. She didn't know what would happen with her and Capone, but she was still upset about being rushed out of the apartment after the wild and freaky sex they had. On the other hand, there was Dana who was becoming way too possessive for a dude that only gave her money when she was risking her freedom.

She arrived at Tamiko's house just in time to catch her leaving out.

"Wait a minute girl I need to use your bathroom," she said speeding up the walkway.

Tamiko turned and unlocked the door and held it open for her.

"How was your reunion?" she asked.

"It was perfect until yo' playa hating ass nigga came home trying to put me out," Charlotta said on her way to the bathroom.

"That's his crib bitch; he don't gotta be bothered with you if he don't want to. I wouldn't want you to be the first thing I see if I'm just getting out of jail either. Ugly ass," she added.

Charlotta was ignoring her and concentrating on peeing on the stick. Soon as she was done her late comeback was ready.

"You look just like me so maybe that's why he ain't been by here to see yo' ugly ass since he got out."

"Get it right, I'm the oldest so you look like me. And we got plans bitch for your information. I will be spending the whole day with my man as soon as I finish taking care of some business."

As Tamiko yelled from the living room, Charlotta tuned her out while she went over the possibilities. She knew if she was pregnant it was more than likely Dana's baby, and even if she was ready to have a baby so young it wouldn't be with him. She knew Dana was way too raw to make a good father.

"Damn, you fell in the toilet?"

"Wait a minute."

"Come on, I got things to do and I'm already running late."

The color started to form confirming what she already knew. She was pregnant.

"Charlotta!"

"Got dammit I'm coming out!" Charlotta yelled as she snatched the door open.

If there was anyone she was going to tell about her pregnancy it would be Tamiko, so she figured why wait. "I gotta make an appointment at the abortion clinic," she said.

She was so caught off guard Tamiko responded without thinking. "For what?"

"To set up a protest, what the hell you think? I'm pregnant."

"Don't tell me you let this nigga Dana get you pregnant?"

"Okay, if you don't ask, I won't tell."

Tamiko let her opinion form and settle for a minute. Now she was ready.

"You got to be the dumbest…"

"Look, I don't wanna hear that shit right now; what's done is done."

Tamiko grabbed her purse and headed to the door shaking her head.

"Sometimes I don't know why I even bother."

****

Sergio went crazy in the hood. Since Nutty's death, Melonhead had gone into hiding, but that didn't stop Sergio from burning down all their money spots in the hood. For one whole week, he patrolled the hood with soldiers packed in caravans and trucks. All his soldiers were willing to kill and die if need be. He told Capone to lay low, feeling that he'd already done enough. More importantly, if something were to happen to Capone, Sergio didn't think he could handle it.

His soldiers were expendable and if he lost a few in a war, so be it. Sergio took beef very seriously. He wasn't a guy that allowed his colleagues to play neutral. Anybody with business interests on either side had to choose a side or get dealt with. If he saw you in the streets he was checking for your status on the spot. You were with him or against him, plain and simple. Some cats tried to set up on the low while the beef was still cooking, but Sergio wasn't having it.

It got to a point where no one could hustle in the hood unless you were down with him. Sergio had officially taken over and most of the youngsters made the smart decision and fell in line. As the squad continued to patrol the hood relentlessly night after night, there was still no sign of Melonhead. After a few weeks, Sergio took comfort in the fact that Melonhead had gone into hiding. The hood was now his playground and therefore he got to decide who played in it.

****

Word was circulating on the street that Dana had got hot in Minnesota and was expected to be resurfacing in the hood to try and put some work down. Everyone always took it back to the hood when things got tight. Sergio ran into Dana at the gas station on Seven Mile and Ryan. Capone was the one who spotted Dana first pulling up in a black convertible Mustang 5.0 on gold Daytons. Dana had Dink riding in the passenger seat. Capone noticed that Dink was looking like he had finally made a come up. He could see the Rolex resting on Dink's wrist as he rubbed his chin. The Cuban link chain with diamonds outlining the circular charm didn't look bad either. Sergio decided to get with Dana and see exactly where his head was at.

He knew Dana was far from a punk, but if they were going to coincide in the hood they had to get some type of understanding about the order of things.

"Yo what's popping?" Dana said as they met up and slapped fives.

"You got the best hand getting that freeway money," Sergio said.

"I wish my nigga," Dana said.

"I heard shit got hot for you."

"Yeah, it's nothing to a boss. I raped the town and bounced," Dana said laughing.

"Fasho, a hustler gone get it regardless."

They slapped fives.

"Sup with all this beef shit I'm hearing?" Dana asked.

"Awe man, the beef is cooked, well-done cuz! You can hear a roach crawling around this bitch on the streets at night."

"Yeah, I never liked them bitch ass niggas anyway. I'm surprised they never found theyself at the barrow of my gun. But anyway, I been meaning to catch up with you on some money shit."

"Oh, what's happening?" Sergio asked.

A customer walked past and Dana held his tongue cautiously.

"Let's go jump in yo' ride and kick it," Dana suggested.

As they strolled towards Sergio's car, Dana said nothing. Sergio figured he didn't want any outsiders listening in on something that wasn't for their ears. He wondered to himself what was such a sensitive subject that had Dana acting all top secret. Capone went over to Dink who was sitting in the Mustang and engaged him in some hood small talk while he smoked up Dink's weed. The conversation was going nowhere but at least the weed was good. Dink went on and on about how good he was doing, even flashing his bankroll. When Capone started to ask questions about his hustle, Dink became secretive all of a sudden.

"I'm fucking with Dana nigga, that's all you need to know," he replied.

Capone decided to just shut up and finishing smoking while Dana and Sergio finished up their conversation. Capone knew he had changed a lot because he had no respect for Dink at all. What kind of nigga gets shot and ends up working for the same nigga that shot 'em? he thought.

"I'm out dog," Capone said as he saw Dana headed back to his car. He and Dana made eye contact but never bothered to speak. Capone brushed it off, knowing they never had a friendly history anyway. He couldn't take anything personal nowadays. He hopped back in the Corvette and they sped off.

"What was Dana talking about?" Capone asked.

"He was talking about us going in on a package together."

"What, some coke?"

"Naw, this counterfeit money bag; half a million dollars of it. He showed me some of that shit; it look real as fuck. I told him to give me a few days and I'ma get at him."

The first thing that popped into Capone's mind was the wad of money that Dink had just flashed on him. It was probably counterfeit money knowing Dink's fake ass. As they rode past the dollar store Capone remembered there was something he had to do.

"Hold on, go back to the dollar store."

Sergio grinned and gladly made a U-turn.

"Yeah, that's who the fuck you need to be checking for," he urged.

Capone jumped out and swaggered inside the dollar store excitedly. He slapped fives with Evelyn's uncle Craig, who was also the owner. Craig had gotten used to Capone hanging around the store now. He was always respectful of the fact that it was a place of business so Craig didn't mind. Capone walked behind the counter where Evelyn sat.

"What's up?" she asked.

"I got something for you," he said.

"Like what?"

He slid her a small square velvet box, and she shot him a look.

"What's this?"

"Open it."

She opened it and slapped her face as her eyes bucked.

"What the hell?"

"It's a ring," Capone said.

"I know it's a ring fool," Evelyn said, staring at the figure eight shaped ring covered in crushed diamonds.

Evelyn wanted to be morally stubborn but this time her material side got the best of her. It wasn't a super expensive ring, but it was beautiful and she wanted it. For the past few weeks, she and Capone's relationship had been growing more intense day by day. They really understood each other and they both knew it. The poetry was only a small part of what they shared.

They laughed at all the same things and saw life in a lot of the same ways. Evelyn knew in her heart it would be a long time before a guy like Capone came around again. She accepted the ring and planted a small lip gloss smudged kiss on his cheek. He didn't mind being at the stage they were at right now. He came a long way for this and it had taken his whole life to get here.

He knew his patience was gaining him major points. On the other hand, Capone knew he had to shake Charlotta once and for all. He had to play his cards right. One slip up and he could lose his chance with Evelyn for good.

"Call me tonight," he said as he turned to leave.

"Aight."

"Don't play!" he warned

"I'm not, I'ma call you."

"Aight."

Chapter 15

Sergio was feeling stupendous for two reasons. The first reason was the fact that the judge on his case had ordered all charges dropped after his probable cause hearing revealed that the search of his car was illegal. Not only did he get off scot free, but he also got his Eldorado back. The second thing was the counterfeit money scheme that he and Dana were working on had turned out to be a big pay day. He stashed the money at Tamiko's house and began to keep the bulk of his drugs at Chocolate's crib. He was making a lot of moves and up until now, Tamiko's house would've been the place to hit if he was being watched by grimy eyes. Once again he had to remind himself who was expendable and who wasn't.

In the meantime, he switched up his movements. He hated to think of Chocolate as a pawn, but the truth was if things were to ever get that crazy, he would much rather find her with a bullet in her head than Tamiko. He glanced at Tamiko in the passenger seat, looking as beautiful as ever as they drove back from court. He could tell she was just glad it was over.

"We should celebrate tonight," he suggested.

"Yeah, maybe we should. What you got in mind?"

"I don't know. Maybe we can start with a dinner, just me and you. Then we can get the crew together and go downtown."

"Sounds good to me. Can I bring Charlotta?"

Sergio sighed.

"You know what, I don't even care, fuck it."

"I don't know why she irritates you so much. If you stop being so mean to her y'all could get along a lot better."

"I said she can come, what else you want?" Sergio replied.

Tamiko ignored him and grabbed her cell phone and began to call her girls up.

****

Capone didn't go to court with Sergio because too many police would be swarming around. He knew Sergio understood. Capone woke up and jotted down a poem that came to him out of the blue. He named it "Black Hole" and promised to finish it later. That's how the poems he wrote always came to him, in spurts. He always had to run and jot it down on paper while it was on his mind. He never let anyone hear them except Evelyn.

Lately, his poems had become so dark and gloomy that if he shared the content it would only make her wonder what made him write such things. He contemplated keeping them to himself from now on. When Sergio turned his key in the door Capone tucked his notepad away quickly so he wouldn't have to explain to Sergio what he was doing. Poetry was his outlet and he used it to try and make sense of all the things that didn't make sense.

To him, it was a very private thing and something he just didn't want to share with Sergio.

"How did it go in court?" Capone asked.

"All charges dropped; nothing but a G thang."

"Oh shit! For real?" Capone leaped from the sofa and hugged Sergio, elated to hear such good news. "That's good as hell to hear man; that's some fasho good news."

"Hell yeah, we celebrating tonight too."

"I'm with that. I need to get out of this house anyway."

"I got a surprise for you," Sergio said pulling out the keys then tossing them to Capone.

"What's these for?"

"Those are the keys to Cadillac. It's yours now."

Capone couldn't believe it. Just like that he'd woke up and inherited a practically brand new car.

"Is you serious dog?"

"Come on man, you know I wouldn't play like that. Besides, I owe you more than that but hey, it's a start. Now you don't gotta sit around and wait on me when you wanna make a move.

"You don't owe me shit bro, but I really appreciate this man."

"Hey man don't feel no kinda way about it; it's nothing. We hustlers, we supposed to eat good, smoke good, ride good, fuck good, all that shit! Otherwise, what's the point?"

Capone nodded his head in agreement.

"So where we going tonight?"

"I was talking to my girl about it and she suggested we hit up Legends. I said fuck it, that sounds good."

"Oh, you bringing Tamiko?"

"Yeah, I gotta hang out with wifey tonight; she wouldn't have it any other way. We going to dinner first and then we gone split up around eight so she can get with her girls and meet us downtown. Matter of fact, you should call yo' girl Evelyn and see if she wanna hang out."

To Capone, that was the best idea Sergio ever had. This could make it official that they were dating and no longer trying to hide it...hopefully. He had been ducking Charlotta since the last time he'd slept with her. Not because he no longer cared for her, but because a part of him still did. He knew what was best for him and he'd been waiting years for this opportunity with Evelyn.

Maybe that would last for years like Sergio and Tamiko. He called Evelyn at the dollar store. The phone rang five times before a pickup.

"Craig's Dollar or Less," she answered.

"What up doe?"

"Hey, what's up?" Evelyn said recognizing his voice.

"You busy?"

"Not really, hold up," she said before moving around trying to straighten up the bad connection. "Hello? Hello?"

"Fix y'all raggedy ass phone," Capone teased.

"Shut up. How you know it ain't your raggedy ass phone?" she shot back.

He knew it wasn't but he decided he didn't want to go back and forth about it.

"Listen, we going to Legends tonight and I want you to come," he explained.

"For real? I been waiting on somebody to take me to Legends that could get me in. I heard that club was the shit, plus, I ain't been out all summer. But wait, who all going?"

"It's probably gonna be a lot of people. Sergio just beat his case so we kinda celebrating tonight. Tamiko and them gone be there too."

The phone went silent. For Evelyn, the fact that Tamiko would be there changed everything. Going out was one thing, but usually, wherever Tamiko was Charlotta wasn't far behind.

"I don't know about that one," she finally said.

"Come on now, you gotta get past this Charlotta shit."

"That's still my friend Capone, regardless of what it might look like to you."

He didn't know what else to say. Maybe this just wasn't going to work out the way he wanted it to.

"I got an idea. Let me call you right back," Evelyn said.

"Do that."

****

Evelyn looked at her watch and did something she hadn't done in a very long time. She called Charlotta.

"Talk quick," Charlotta answered.

"Hey girl, this Ev."

"Who?"

"Ev."

"Who?"

"Evelyn."

"Who?"

"Bitch stop playing, you knew who it was all along."

They both burst into laughter. It felt good to the both of them.

"Okay, are you shot or stranded, which one is it?"

"Neither, and it ain't like you ring my phone off the hook either."

"This is true," Charlotta agreed.

"Okay, so here's the thing. I know you know me and Capone are pretty cool now right?"

"Right."

"First of all, we ain't kicking it or nothing, we just friends. Anyway, he called me and asked if I wanna go to Legends tonight. He said a lot of people were going because Sergio just beat his case or whatever. I figured if you and Tamiko were going I could just roll with y'all so it won't be no confusion."

"I ain't heard shit about it," Charlotta informed.

"Oh, well he said Tamiko was going so I just assumed…"

"Oh, I'm going, believe that! I haven't been invited yet though so I'm about to call her ass right now and find out what's going on."

Charlotta was a little heated that she had to find out through Evelyn that Tamiko had planned a night out that she knew nothing about.

"So can you come and scoop me?" Evelyn said.

"I don't see why not," Charlotta said with a hint of disapproval.

"Okay, I'll see you later then. Bye."

****

Charlotta had borrowed the money for her abortion from Tamiko, but once she found out about the party, the money got spent on a fly black and red Gucci dress to match the black and red heels she had at home. She had to be fly tonight, just had to be. She was going to make it clear to Capone and Evelyn that she was, in fact, God's gift to the world, or at least Detroit. As she pulled up in front of Evelyn's house she blew the horn twice. Evelyn came out in record time in skin tight blue jeans and open toe heels. Charlotta thought Evelyn looked good but she couldn't compete with the hip hugger she was rocking. She gave Evelyn a once-over before they pulled off.

From Evelyn's house, they met up with Tamiko and her girls and all drove to Legends three cars deep. At the front entrance, Tamiko gave security an extra hundred for both Charlotta and Evelyn, who were under eighteen. Inside, the girls immediately caught the attention of all the hustlers, ballers, and gangsters that were hanging out at the hottest club in the city at the time. They heard a few cats calling out to them, but Tamiko kept everybody moving to where Sergio was in VIP. Sergio had two booths on lock and one of standby.

He had already ordered four bottles of champagne for each table. He and Capone sat in the first booth with three other crew members Charlotta knew by face but couldn't remember their names. As she looked around the room and saw that it was crawling with people associated with Sergio, she had to admit he was a boss. Tamiko playfully snapped her fingers so the gentleman could move and she could sit next to her man.

"Get up out my spot," she demanded.

Everyone began to spread out, mainly because they had noticed the girls Tamiko came in with and wanted to go and get their flirt on. Dudes began pairing off with girls and shooting their best game at them. Capone fingered for Evelyn to come and sit next to him, but she was standing right next to Charlotta who assumed the invitation was for her. He wound up with both Charlotta and Evelyn on opposite sides of him. Sergio shot Charlotta a dirty look then another one at Tamiko.

"Let's get some shots!" Tamiko said ignoring Sergio.

She ordered twenty-five shots of Tequila and told everyone there would be no chasing it with anything. Sergio's people seemed to be mixing it up well with Tamiko's girls at the other table. After several shots of Tequila and some champagne, everyone at Sergio's table had loosened up as well. Before long, Sergio and Charlotta turned into the comic relief with no holds barred.

"Hey, remember I used to have to check niggas in school about calling you Cry Baby?" Charlotta said to Capone.

Everyone laughed except Capone, but Sergio came to his rescue.

"Hold on, remember when Tamiko had to stop you from wearing them dirty ass clothes on your birthday? Tamiko was like, bitch you betta go put on something clean!"

"Stop lying!" Charlotta shouted.

"She said you snatched that shit right out the dirty clothes hamper and put it on," he continued.

"He lying y'all, he lying," Charlotta said laughing even though the joke was on her.

Although Sergio was making it up as he went along, Charlotta's jokes usually had some truth to them.

"So what Sergio, remember you used to wear that tight ass Starters jacket, looking gay? The Seahawks? That was before he had bread y'all; I swear this nigga was walking around tight as hell every day. Sleeves going up his forearms and shit, you remember that jacket, Tamiko?"

"Stop lying!" Sergio shouted.

"She ain't lying," Tamiko confirmed.

"Hell yeah, he used to rock that bitch with some ran down Adidas.

"Awe hell naw, you ain't never seen me with no ran down nothing. Matter of fact, I'll tell you what; them Air Max Capone bought you back in the day….shiiiid. You rocked them bitches for a year straight until they started leaning when you took 'em off. Tell me I'm lying?"

"You lying," Charlotta challenged.

"He ain't lying," Capone said.

Everyone was having a good laugh at Charlotta's and Sergio's expense. It was a beautiful night and everyone there was glad they had come out to celebrate with Sergio.

"Let's go mingle for a while Ev," Charlotta said.

"I'm straight," Evelyn responded.

"Damn, for real? You can't come downstairs and fuck with your girl?"

"Naw, you know it ain't like that. I'm just saying we chillen. I ain't trying to be bothered with a bunch of drunk ass niggas all up in my face," Evelyn explained.

"Hmmm. Except for that drunk ass nigga all up in your face now, huh?"

Evelyn knew she was referring to Capone who was feeling pretty good by now.

"Don't even play yourself bitch 'cause I came with you and I'm leaving with you soooo, what else you need to know," Evelyn snapped.

Just then Capone whispered something in Evelyn's ear and that was just about all Charlotta was gonna take from them tonight. Out of the millions of times they'd called each other every name in the book, Charlotta took offense tonight and used it as a platform for her grandstand.

"If I'm a bitch, I'm a down ass bitch and I rather be a down bitch than a creep hoe!"

Evelyn was dumbstruck. Charlotta had definitely crossed the line and everyone at the table was at a loss for words.

"Who you calling a creep hoe? Who a creep hoe?" Evelyn asked for clarification.

Charlotta just smacked her lips and rolled her eyes, knowing her comment was uncalled for.

"Bitch I ain't never fucked a nigga in the parking lot of a club since you wanna go there. That's what I call a creep hoe!

"Woah woah woah!" Sergio said trying to control the animosity that was quickly building before it escalated, but he was too late.

Charlotta reached across Capone, grabbed Evelyn by the collar and punched her in the face. Charlotta got two more blows in before Evelyn rose to her feet and responded with a wild swing that landed on Charlotta's eye. Tamiko saw that Charlotta was dazed and was about to interfere, but Sergio held her back. By then, Evelyn and Charlotta were locked in a double choke hold and Capone and a few others were trying to pull them apart. By the time security reached the mayhem, two buckets of ice were all over the floor and shot glasses were everywhere.

Charlotta was still heated and she had managed to get a hold to another bucket of ice, about to hurl it at Evelyn before security stopped her. She and Evelyn were the only ones asked to leave, and Evelyn knew she would kill Charlotta if she rode home in a car with her right now.

****

As crazy as it sounds the night couldn't have been going better for Capone. Charlotta had driven Evelyn right into his arms. Capone was her willing escort home but he felt like this might be his opportunity to take things to the next level. Evelyn vented her frustration as they drove through downtown Detroit with the music low.

"That's all right, that's all right; that bitch thinks she was mad, she gone really be now. Pish, trying to be real with muthafuckas," she finished, shaking her head in disappointment.

"Something told me she was gonna find a way to fuck shit up."

"Naw, she ain't fuck nothing up; the party still going. Only thing she did was give me a reason to do what I wanted to do anyway without feeling guilty about it."

Capone knew Evelyn was a little tipsy so he decided to take advantage of the opportunity in front of him.

"You know I don't gotta take you home this early. We can still hang out and enjoy the rest of the night."

"I don't care, my mama think I'm spending the night at Charlotta's house anyway. I'm with you now so whatever is cool with me."

She gave him a seductive glance and Capone knew right then this could be the night. He made a right turn and headed towards the apartment.

"You hungry?" Capone asked.

"Naw, I'm cool," Evelyn said taking off her heels and reclining in the soft leather seats. At this moment, her comfort level with Capone was at its peak. At the apartment, Capone grabbed a beer and offered her one but she refused, knowing she'd already had too much. As she relaxed on the sofa with her feet up watching television, Capone slid to the opposite end of the sofa and began massaging her feet.

"Wow, what a romantic," Evelyn said.

"Yeah, who woulda thought, huh?"

"This is really nice."

"I'm glad you like it."

Evelyn spun around and put her back to his chest.

"Massage right here," she said tapping her shoulder.

Capone obliged, giving her a shoulder and neck massage. She let out a moan that let him know it felt good. He kissed her neck while she rubbed her fingers across his face and then his pointed ears. He cupped her breast slowly from behind and she guided his fingertips to her nipples. Once he felt her nipples expanding he unbuttoned her shirt. Her breast and abs looked amazing as he kissed her collarbone and unhooked her bra.

Evelyn laid on her back and slid off her jeans to reveal pink lace panties. He carried her off into the bedroom. After stripping down to his birthday suit, Capone climbed in the bed with Evelyn and kissed her passionately. She stroked his rock hard penis while enjoying his tongue.

Finally, he removed her panties and kissed her stomach and inner thighs before going to taste her juice box. She moaned in ecstasy and stroked his braids.

Once inside her, she clung to him tightly as Capone grinded slowly, savoring every second inside her. He kissed her slowly and gave attention to every part of her body until she was quivering with pleasure. The sounds of her joyous and continuous moans excited him as he began to pound her fiercely until his climax.

They lay in each other's arms and Evelyn wondered was Charlotta the one who taught Capone to be such a tender lover. If so, maybe one day she would get to thank her. She smiled at the thought.

Chapter 16

So much time had passed since Charlotta had been to Minnesota. She had heard from Tamiko, who heard it from Sergio that the Minnesota thing was over. She was pissed at Dana for not telling her but figured she'd play nice until he paid for her abortion. She sat at home thinking about how to break the news to him that she was pregnant.

She figured she'd lie about the cost of the procedure and get some extra money out of him if she could. Once she got her story together, she made the call. Three rings before he picked up.

"What's popping?" Dana said.

"Hey boo, what you doing?"

"Chillen. What's up?"

"I miss you."

"Yeah right. What you want?"

Charlotta sighed. "Okay then, I'm pregnant, and I need some money for an abortion."

"Get it from your boy; that's who got you pregnant."

Charlotta shook her head in confusion.

"Fuck is you talking about, what boy?"

"Yo' boy Capone."

Click.

Dana hung up in Charlotta's face. She sat with the phone in her hand dazed and confused by the conversation she'd just had. She thought about who Dana could possibly be getting his information from. Dink and Randy came to mind first. "Rat bastards," she mumbled.

In truth, Charlotta hadn't seen or heard from Capone since the night at the club, and word on the streets was that he and Evelyn were an item now. She tried to convince herself that Evelyn was only getting her sloppy seconds so it didn't matter. She had to get focused on putting some money in her empty pockets. It was time to activate Plan B.

Charlotta hadn't done any boosting in the last two years but it was something that she always knew she could fall back on if needed. She drove to the mall and parked in front of Target. She headed inside, grabbed a shopping cart, then surveyed the area for floor walkers. She placed a big blue laundry hamper in her basket and headed for the children's clothes. Once there, she snuck around, sliding kids clothes in the basket and watching her back.

She stuffed the hamper with boys' and girls' outfits ages two to five because she could get more outfits that way. After she was sure she had at least twenty-five outfits she headed towards the cash register. Passing the household section, she tossed in some Tide and fabric softener just to make the cart look less suspicious. In the checkout line, she held a conversation with the cashier to keep from getting nervous and to keep the cashier's mind off of the clothes hamper. Once the cashier scanned the hamper without removing it from the cart, she knew she was home free. She paid for her items and walked away with a smile.

"Have a nice day," the cashier said.

"You too," Charlotta returned.

After that day, Charlotta decided to return to boosting full time until she could think of something better. She knew plenty of girls with small kids and the word of her prices spread quickly. When Target burned out she hit up K-Mart then another Target then another K-Mart. Charlotta still got a rush anytime she got away with stealing.

The money was okay but the rush was priceless. That was until the day she got swooped down on by the security guard at Target.

"Excuse me miss," she heard a voice call out from behind.

"Can I help you?" she asked after turning around to find store security.

She had her game face on, giving the security all kinds of attitude. Attitude usually helped her out of these situations. Security would get embarrassed and decide not to cause a scene on a hunch. But this was no hunch and this guy's mind was made up.

"Can you open your hamper for me please?" he asked.

"For what?" Charlotta challenged.

"Just open the hamper, ma'am."

"I ain't opening shit; what is you harassing me for?"

Another plain clothes security approached with a walkie-talkie. Charlotta felt like dashing through the aisle, bobbing, and weaving around customers until she reached the exit. She knew she'd never make it out of the parking lot so she slowly but surely began to admit defeat.

"Come with us please ma'am," the second security officer said.

He was a slim, hard-nosed white guy, forty at least. She could easily tell he was not about to be persuaded by her usual bullshit. The more he talked she began to believe he had to be a real cop at some point in his life.

"So what's it gonna be? We can do this the easy way or the hard way," he said, folding his arms waiting for a response.

"I was gonna pay for everything. I got the money right here, I swear. You can have it."

"Just follow me and we can discuss this privately without making a scene."

Charlotta followed both men through the store until they reached something that reminded her of an interrogation room.

"Have a seat, we've been expecting you," Hard Nose said.

"Listen, like I told you before, I was gonna pay for everything I have in my cart. Now maybe you thought I was stealing because I had stuff kinda hidden where you couldn't see it. Really, I just put the clothes in there so they wouldn't be all over the cart. I'm just a neat freak and I don't like stuff all over everywhere when I'm shopping, but I'll pay for everything."

When she was finished it was obvious that no one was convinced.

"Soooo this is really just a big misunderstanding?" Hard Nose said.

"Exactly, a misunderstanding. And if you could just tell me the total of all of my merchandise I'll pay for it right here right now, or I can take it to the register, however you wanna do it."

By now the other security guard had turned on a split screen monitor and was either fast forwarding or rewinding footage.

"You see this?" Hard Nose said.

Charlotta zoomed in to see herself with the same outfit and jacket she had on three days earlier when she came in to shoplift. She watched herself sliding clothes in the hamper she never paid for.

"Gotcha!"

"I paid for all that stuff!" she insisted as the real police entered the room with handcuffs out.

"Stand up and place your hands behind your back.

"Man fuck y'all!" she shouted out as she was taken into custody.

Chapter 17

Capone decided it was time for his mother to meet Evelyn. He figured he had put his mother through a lot over the past few years and Evelyn would be a welcomed change from all the negativity he had going on in his life. He treated them to Ponderosa which was his mom's favorite place to dine out. She loved the T-bone steak while Capone was more a fan of the buffet chicken. The three of them sat at the table all smiles and Capone felt good to be finally spending time with his mother.

"So Evelyn, Chris tells me you're a member of First Baptist Ministry."

Evelyn had to smile at the thought of the church she loved so much.

"Yeah, I'm not as active as I should be, but I make sure I have my butt in there every Sunday morning," Evelyn replied.

Sheila laughed out loud then caught herself.

"Amen. God is good."

"Yes, He is," Evelyn agreed.

"She going to college next year to Mama," Capone said.

"Really? What's your major?"

"I'm thinking it will be journalism, but I'm not really sure what I wanna do with my life so it could change."

"Well, you know God will guide you down the right path. You can't go wrong with him at the wheel."

"I know you're right and that's what I have to keep reminding myself of. I just have to pray on and leave it in God's hands."

Capone could tell his mother was thoroughly impressed. He'd never seen this look in her eyes when Charlotta was around and for all the looks of disappointment in her eyes he'd seen over the years, this was priceless. He couldn't have wished for a better start to his girl and his mother's relationship.

"Is Reverend Jones still the pastor over there at First Baptist? I ain't been there in years."

"Alright, that's enough with the religious talk," Capone interrupted.

"Boy don't tell me when it's enough, I'm the mama. Don't make me act a fool up in here to prove it," she threatened.

"Here's still there," Evelyn said giggling.

"Well, you need to have a talk with my son and get him together. He won't listen to me no more."

"I'm working on him," Evelyn said giving Shelia a wink.

Shelia and Evelyn chatted the entire evening away, letting Capone in on the conversation every once in a while. He didn't care. He was so happy they were getting along he just stuffed his face and let them enjoy each other's company. If he didn't know better, he'd swear they already knew each other.

Finally, he had done something good in his mother's eyes. Shelia made Evelyn promise to come and visit her church in the near future and Evelyn looked forward to it.

****

In a short time, Evelyn and Capone had developed a relationship that could carry a comfortable silence in each other's company. They could just chill in a room with each other and still be alone with their own thoughts. That was the mood as they chilled at the apartment that night. Capone was feeling as if he'd found his better half, even if he didn't feel he deserved such a blessing.

The way she brought things in his life together made him feel as if everything he'd been through in life up to that point was worth it. All the struggles in his childhood had made him stand up and fight for the things he wanted in life. It was the fighter in him that had been awarded the brand new car. It was the fighter in him that won his respect in the hood, and it was the fighter in him that had won Evelyn's heart. He'd always be a fighter now and forever.

Mary J Blige's hit song "My Life" blasted through the speakers as Evelyn relaxed on the sofa singing along. In that moment, the song seemed to speak to his inner being, defining feelings he could not express. It was consoling, uplifting, and blue all at the same time. As Evelyn and Mary continued to sing, the music reached deeper and deeper into his soul until his eyes began to tear up. For the first time in a long time, Capone felt Chris's presence. He excused himself and went to the bathroom to gain his composure. He stared into the mirror the way he used to years ago before he was Capone. He thought about how he and Evelyn were on different paths but seemed to be walking them together. He thought about how much he really wanted this life now that he had it. The murder case was heavy on his mind and he often wondered what would be his fate.

"What's wrong?" Evelyn said, startling him in the doorway.

"Nothing," he replied as he walked over to her and held her tight.

"It's something," she said, sensing his sadness.

Capone decided to open up to her. If he couldn't talk to his soul mate, then who could he talk to?"

"Do you ever think about the future?" he questioned.

"Of course, all the time."

"I mean, do you ever think about our future?"

Evelyn looked into his eyes.

"I think I know where this is going. Look, I knew about your situation beforehand and I had a choice not to get involved with you. I chose to get involved and now my heart is in it. I'm not gonna just get in the wind when things get rough."

"So what are you saying? Are you saying if I go to jail for twenty years you gonna try to still be my girl? That ain't what I want for you."

She placed a finger on his lips. "No. I'm saying I would never abandon you. I pray for you every night and I know that God hears me even if you don't believe."

"Evelyn, I understand all that but we gotta be realistic about this shit. I waited a long time to get with you, but I don't want you to feel obligated to stick around if I have to go away. I think we should enjoy the time we got together and when it's over, it's over."

"If you really feel like that then why let me meet your mother? Why convince me that you really wanted me in your life?"

"I do want you in my life, but I don't wanna set you up to be hurt."

Evelyn looked at Capone holding back tears. He kissed her before she could say anything else. She kissed him back like it was the last kiss they'd ever share. That night they made love like never before. All over the apartment, all night long.

****

The next morning Sergio came to pick Capone up in a sparkling white XK8. It seemed to Capone that Sergio was just getting money effortlessly at this point. They rode to the IHOP on Jefferson smoking on a blunt of exotic weed that Sergio had just copped. Since Capone had gotten serious with Evelyn, Sergio had practically moved out of his own apartment giving Capone more privacy than he expected.

Sergio spent most of his nights at Tamiko's house and never really came through except to change clothes or drop off shopping bags. Things were going great but lately, Capone had been thinking about orchestrating his own hustle. The money he made was more than enough to cover his modest living expenses and splurge on Evelyn whenever he had the urge. But lately, his mind was on becoming his own man and coming out of Sergio's shadow. The murder case was always lingering in the back of his mind and with it, the threat of his luck running out sooner than later.

"I got a question for you bro," Capone said.

"Shoot my nigga."

"What you think about me grabbing my own package and making my own move?"

"Come on man, you already know how I feel about that."

Sergio began to cough uncontrollably until he passed the blunt.

"I can't run forever bro; I need to stack some real cash. Plus, on some real shit, I gotta be my own man at some point. I appreciate everything you do, but I don't want nobody taking care of me when I could be taking care of myself."

Sergio being the older protective brother had never looked at things from the perspective that Capone had just presented. Every true hustler wanted to come from under the wing sooner or later and while Sergio didn't like the idea, he understood. Capone was tired of running his errands and being spoon fed. Sergio respected the fact that he was ready to start providing for himself and saving for his rainy days.

"Alright, I got something for you bro."

Capone just nodded as they pulled into the parking lot. They sprayed on some Hilfiger Cologne to mask the weed scent before getting out and heading inside. The wait wasn't long but if felt like forever for Capone who was high as a kite and could feel the glares from the goodie two shoes coming in from Sunday morning service. Ten minutes or so later they were seated at a table catty-corner to the front door. Sergio had requested a table where he could see the comings and goings. They both ordered blueberry pancakes while Sergio flirted with every pretty girl in the joint including the waitress.

"Yeah, this what a real nigga look like up close. Take it all in baby," Sergio said to a long hair girl with a nice, round bottom as she sashayed to her table giggling away.

Two beautiful Mexican ladies strolled by and made the mistake of glancing at Sergio. "Looking good, looking good. Que pasa!" he continued.

As Sergio continued blurting out random nonsense, Capone's eyes landed on a couple in the far right corner. He shoved Sergio's arm to get his attention.

"What up?"

"Look over there," Capone said pointing to the young Italian girl gazing into the black man's eyes.

The young woman was fine, but that's not what caught Sergio's eye. The big fella she was sitting with bared a striking resemblance to Melonhead. Then the big man let out a big hearty laugh and removed all doubt that it was him.

"Fat boy ain't left the country after all huh?"

Capone and Sergio carried pistols everywhere they went just in case of situations like this. If Sergio had reacted on his first instinct, he would've walked right over and put a bullet in Melonhead's brain. Instead, he held his composure. They weren't on the block so he had to adjust to his environment. When the food came they barely touched it. They sat across the room leering until the female got nervous and alerted her date that they were being watched.

When Melonhead got a glimpse of his stalkers he looked as if he'd seen a ghost. He took a second glance and saw Capone and Sergio waving at him. Melonhead got up and charged over to their table.

"I'm killing both of y'all niggas, y'all know that right?" he vowed as the girl tugged on his arm to get him to walk away.

"Not if we kill you first," Sergio said with a calm grin.

"Nigga who you think you fucking with?"

"You," Sergio said flatly.

"Oh yeah...Oh yeah?"

"Calm down homey, go back to your table, and enjoy your meal. This ain't the time or the place, but we'll meet up again."

"I'm killing both of y'all, believe that," Melonhead repeated before walking away.

Melonhead snatched up his lady friend and stormed out of the IHOP without another word.

Chapter 18

Charlotta had been fighting with her mother for the past week. Every day it was something new. She was tired of bailing her out of jail, she wasn't ready to be a grandmother, and she was tired of Charlotta coming and going as she pleased like she was grown. Those were the beefs on the surface. Underneath the surface, Charlotta knew the real problem was her mother wanted money and she simply didn't have it to give. The problem was, her mother was well aware of all of her wrong doings and she figured if she couldn't stop her she might as well benefit from it.

She told Charlotta that she needed to start paying rent, but of course, it would be a cold day in hell before that happened. The only place Charlotta would ever feel obligated to pay rent was her own place. Things finally came to a head and Charlotta was forced to move in with Tamiko until she could come up with something.

"Did I tell you about this new nigga I met?" Charlotta said.

"What new nigga?" Tamiko questioned.

"Some busta I met in the parking lot of Rite Aid the day I found out I was pregnant.

"Did you get an abortion yet?"

"Yeah bitch, shut up and let me finish telling you. So this nigga be talking all this shit about how he got a ten-inch dick and how he gon' do this and that. I'm like, I hope your pockets is as deep as your stroke 'cause right now that's all I care about. Fuck the ra ra!"

"You ain't tell him that," Tamiko challenged.

"Pish, you wanna bet? He one of them niggas you can talk to like that though."

Tamiko laughed.

"You silly. Guess who I seen yesterday though?"

"Who?"

"Dana. And he told me to tell you that you're cut off forever. Ha ha!"

"Girl, fuck Dana. He mad 'cause he think I'm fucking Capone and I'm not about to kiss his ass to make him think otherwise."

"That's where niggas got the game fucked up. The same thing you was doing another nigga can do better. Clown ass nigga don't care about no Capone. You know if his ass was still running out of town and he needed you to take penitentiary chances he'd be all up yo' ass right now. Now he wanna try and dog a bitch. I hate niggas!"

"Fuck that nigga; he ain't gon' stop my come up."

"I swear if I ever find out you back fucking with that nigga I'm a kick yo' ass myself."

"I don't know about all that," Charlotta disagreed.

She rolled her eyes wanting to say more, but Charlotta respected her cousin's opinion more than anyone on the face of the earth. She could talk all the trash she wanted, but Charlotta knew in her heart that if Dana called her for a road trip tonight she'd be on the first thing smoking. She couldn't afford to pass up on a money opportunity right now.

Sergio came from the bathroom and Charlotta cracked on him immediately.

"You must've had a whole lot of dirt to clean off the way you was chillen in that bathroom. First bath all week huh?"

"Shut yo' homeless ass up. First off, it took me thirty minutes just to clean off that dirt ring you left in the tub. Then I had to let the room air out for another ten minutes 'cause your funky ass feet was still lingering in the air.

"Shut yo' lying ass up. You ain't never smelled my feet. Tamiko tell this nigga he gotta bounce," Charlotta ordered.

"You'll bounce before he will sweetie," she corrected him.

Charlotta positioned herself against the doorway to Tamiko's bedroom while Sergio tossed on some crème colored slacks, a matching short sleeve shirt, and crème Maury gators. She was wishing she hadn't cracked on him without thinking because she was about to turn right around and ask for a favor.

"Bro I need a favor," she started.

Sergio grinned.

"Who you talking to?"

"I'm serious man; it's something in it for you too."

"Okay, now I'm listening."

"I need one of your lil' niggas to do an insurance job on my car."

"That's not a problem."

"Cool, how soon can you put it together?"

"I got a lot of shit to do today, so give me a couple days."

Just then Charlotta's pager went off and she recognized the number. It was LB, the new guy she'd been talking to. She grabbed the cordless phone and went into the kitchen for privacy. As LB answered the phone Charlotta wondered what made her call him back so quickly.

"What up doe?" LB said.

"Nothing much, what up with you?"

"I'm trying to hook up with your fine ass today."

"Well, I don't have any plans. What did you have in mind?"

"I was thinking we could hit the Taste Fest."

The Taste Fest was an annual food extravaganza hosted by local celebrities and radio personalities.

"I'm with that," Charlotta said.

"Then maybe we can head downtown and make a day of it."

"Okay."

"I can pick you up in about an hour if that's cool."

"Well, I'll just call you back in about an hour and we'll meet up somewhere."

Charlotta knew she wasn't allowed to bring anyone where Tamiko and Sergio laid their heads.

"Damn baby girl, you don't trust me or something?"

"Why should I? We just met. But that's not the issue. I'll explain when we know each other a little better."

"Alright…and hey…wear something sexy."

"Yeah, yeah."

Click.

****

Capone got Sergio to front him a kilo of coke. He drove all the way home with the brick on his lap wrapped in a Foot Locker bag. Once he entered the downtown area, he passed what seemed like millions of cop cars, but he stayed cool, calm, and collected. He kept the music low and made damn sure he obeyed all the traffic laws. Back at the apartment, he placed the package on the table. He stared at it awhile admiring the neatness of the wrapping.

He poked at the soft white substance inside. Capone had seen many kilos by this time but this one was special because it was his to work the best way he knew how to in order to come up. He retrieved a razor from his stash and split the duct tape down the middle. The strong, unmistakable scent of coke came rushing through his nostrils.

With coke this strong, it was no wonder Sergio was getting rich. He grabbed the triple beam scale and some Ziploc bags and began to break the work down into eighths of a kilo. When he was finished with that, he took two eighths and broke those down into ounces. This part of the job he was used to, but now he was becoming his own man responsible for his own success.

He was happy, but still a bit overwhelmed as he separated the work he planned to cook into crack from the coke he would sell in powder form. When he was done, he placed two eighths in the Foot Locker bag and stashed the rest. He didn't waste any time hitting the streets hard to get his clientele up.

See, he couldn't just go around selling drugs to the same people he had been serving all along. Those were Sergio's customers. He had to create his own clientele from scratch. He had a few people that were actually his people he had linked up with along the way, but for the most part, he was starting over. He knew there was no telling where he would run into a potential customer; the mall, the barbershop, the club...anywhere. The one big advantage he did have was that Sergio had decided to pass down all of his once clientele to Capone, knowing he no longer had the time or patience to deal with small weight. It was only three guys but they were consistent like clockwork, every two days, and Capone knew those sales would help him out way more than they did Sergio.

Things started off slow, but Capone expected that in the beginning. After he made a few sales he got tired of driving around all day and decided to swing by Randy's old blow spot to see if it was still up and running. He spotted Randy's Crown Victoria across the street from the house and he knew Randy was somewhere in the area. Capone parked a few houses from the spot then got out and knocked on the door. A dingy cat with matted braids and no shirt answered the door.

"What up cuz?"

"Randy in there?" Capone asked.

"Uuuuh," he looked around confused. "I think he went next door. Who is you?"

"Capone."

His eyes widened as if he knew the name well but not the face.

"Oh damn, let me call his phone. I know he ain't went far," the dingy dude said.

"Bet."

Moments later Randy came walking out of the house next door with a blunt in his hand, licking it and rolling it in one swift motion. The two greeted each other by slapping fives and a shoulder hug that signified they'd come a long way since middle school.

"What's popping my nigga?" Randy said.

"Not much, just stopping by to blow a blunt with you."

"You right on time then, 'cause this weed I'm smoking is straight garbage. I wanna go beat this nigga ass for selling me this shit."

Randy knocked on the door to his spot and gave away the blunt he'd just rolled. Capone always remembered Randy could roll a perfect blunt so he tossed him the weed and a fresh blunt.

"How's business?" Capone asked.

"You know the game homey, up and down."

"I hear that. What you should do is get you some of that cross addicted money."

"Crack?" Randy said with a smirk as he broke down the blunt.

"Hell yeah."

"Nigga you must got some coke."

"You know it. Dirt cheap too," Capone replied.

"I hate them damn crackheads man, they too hard headed. When blow heads come through, the money be right, they get what they came for, and be gone."

"Yeah, that's true, but I'm telling you, I think that's what you need to get; this bitch banging. If you got 'em both you ain't gon' have too many slow days."

"I hear you…I don't know though."

"Think about it, that slow roll might last longer but what did you really accomplish? Would you rather make a thousand dollars a day for six months or ten thousand a day for thirty days?"

Randy was just finishing up rolling the blunt. He lit it and took a long, hard pull as he pondered what Capone was saying. It made sense in a way. He couldn't get on his feet because he was spending more than he was making. He had workers to pay, three kids, and two baby mamas. At eighteen years old, life was stressful when it should be beautiful.

"I do feel what you saying dog; I just don't know if I'm ready to step out of my box. You know everything ain't for everybody," he explained, passing the blunt to Capone.

"You know what they say, chances make champions. But I didn't come through to twist your arm about that shit. I just stopped by to holla at you, but I'ma leave you my pager number in case you change your mind."

"Yeah, do that; you never know."

"Anyway, what's up with yo' boy Dink?"

"Awe man, I feed Dink with a long-handle spoon nowadays. Nigga just too soft for me. How you gon' be working for a nigga that shot you for no reason?"

Capone laughed and passed the weed. "Yeah, that's some dumb shit."

"You gotta be kidding me with that shit. We still kick it, but it ain't shit like it was."

They finished the blunt and slapped fives again saying their goodbyes. As Capone headed down the steps, he heard Randy call his name.

"What up?" he answered.

"I forgot to tell you. I think I seen Melonhead in the hood a couple days ago."

Capone scowled.

"Alright, good looking."

As Capone pulled away from Randy's spot he pulled his gun out and placed it on his lap. For a moment, he found himself getting upset about the fact that neither he nor Sergio had caught up with Melonhead yet. We should've just popped his ass at the IHOP, he thought. Now Melonhead was becoming what the mob would call a stone in their shoes.

He redirected his thoughts back to the money as he drove through the city, not exactly knowing who or what he was looking for. He stopped at Chocolate's house to smoke a blunt with her then he drove some more. He knew selling drugs could be easy at times but he never knew it could be so boring. He was used to making moves quickly and then going ahead with whatever else he had planned for the day. This independence he wanted so badly was a lot different.

****

The insurance job went off without a hitch. Charlotta got an eighteen thousand dollar check for burning her own car up. After looking out for Sergio, and the young thug that put in the work, she was still fifteen thousand dollars to the good. Of course, she bought a whole new wardrobe and started looking for a place to call her own. She had a little trouble finding an apartment because of her age, but she ended up renting a ranch style home from a slumlord that Sergio happened to know. Similar to the love-hate relationship George Jefferson had with Florence, Sergio had a little love for Charlotta mainly because she was Tamiko's closest cousin.

Her new guy LB was turning out to be a good thing. She still thought he was wack as hell, but he was already talking about cosigning for her a new car. A funny thing happened the last time they were together. Somehow the conversation landed on all the counterfeit money that had been floating around the city. From there, LB insinuated that he wanted to get his hands on some and Charlotta implied that she knew a guy.

Before the conversation was over they agreed to make it happen. So far, Charlotta had spent three thousand on clothes and seven thousand on her new place. Now she had her eyes on a purchasing a new vehicle and she knew this little lick could help her bounce back afterward. She called LB the next day to see if he had changed his mind about cosigning after sobering up.

"Hey what's good?" Charlotta said.

"Nothing much, just thinking about you," LB responded.

"You wanna go look at some cars today?"

"Yeah, we can do that," LB agreed.

"Alright, come scoop me."

Half an hour later, Charlotta spotted LB's big chubby frame sitting in an olive green Lincoln Continental outside her house. When she got in the car the first thing LB asked about was the counterfeit money.

"Oh shit, I forgot to call my people," she replied.

She pulled out her brand new cell phone and called Sergio. She was all prepared to talk in code using her new secret lingo she'd stolen from rapper Snoop Dog.

"Yo," Sergio answered.

"What's up my nigga? I got this kizzat, who tryna spezzend on that lizzoot."

"What?" Sergio replied.

"You heard me, nigga," Charlotta shouted, frustrated her code wasn't working.

"You been speaking on me?" Sergio asked.

"Come on now, you know me way better than that. It just came up in a random conversation and my guy said he had an outlet for it. I'm trying to help you out, but if you don't want my help—"

"Where you at now?" Sergio interrupted.

"I'm riding with ole boy now, you wanna speak to him?"

"Hell naw, call me when you get back home by yourself and I'll swing through."

"Alright, later."

Chapter 19

Charlotta strolled around the car lot matching wits with the bald head white man in a cheap suit. She'd come thinking she would be looking for a truck but changed her mind when she saw the red convertible Mustang. She acted out when the dealer spat out the asking price as if it was the most ridiculous thing she'd ever heard.

"Whoa, I mean does it grow wings or something? You asking way too much; this is a used car," she explained.

"Yeah it's used with under thirty-five thousand miles on it," he countered.

"Still, natural depreciation my friend," Charlotta shot back.

It was a term she'd learned watching a car show a few weeks back. It threw the salesman for a loop and he wondered did she know as much as she pretended.

"I'll knock off three hundred but that's the best I can do," he bargained.

"Three hundred dollars? Do I have to get into the insurance rate for a seventeen-year-old with this kinda car?"

Charlotta glance over at LB who obviously wasn't a negotiator. He could at least nod his head in agreement, she thought.

"Three hundred, that's it," he stated firmly.

"We can do this all day. I go low, you go high, but I know you don't really want me to walk off this lot with this money."

"Sweetheart, you have to understand where the bargaining ground is. There's only so much—"

"I guarantee you if I leave this lot and take a look around some other places I will find a convertible Mustang with low miles for the money I'm willing to spend."

She sounded like a seasoned veteran in the art of negotiating instead of a teenager. After a test drive, and a lot of flirting on Charlotta's part, she was able to get a thousand dollars knocked off the asking price. She thanked LB with a hug and a kiss and told him she'd be in touch later. It was time for her to show off her new whip. She went to the gas station in her hood that was always banging with people, whether they were buying anything or not. It looked like a club on the inside rather than a place of business.

The first person she spotted was Dink pulling up in his Cutlass with the music blasted, drowning out everything within the nearest block. She knew Dink always had a thing for her but was afraid to step on Dana's toes.

"Look at you, pulling up in a drop looking like a hood star," Dink said walking her way.

"Thank you, thank you. No pictures please," she joked.

Dink came up to the car and stared at Charlotta with lust in his eyes.

"So where you been hiding at?" he finally asked.

"I ain't hiding. I just moved into my new place so I just been getting settled in."

"Oh yeah, where you stay at now?"

"Pish, nigga you think I'm 'bout to tell you where I live?"

Dink leaned on the driver's side door too close for Charlotta's comfort. She pushed his elbow off.

"And get off my car," she ordered.

"Damn, it's like that? I was gon' come through and spend some of this money I'm getting," he replied pulling out a bankroll and flipping through it.

"I think I can afford you now; plus you and Dana don't fuck around no more, so what's up?" he continued.

Charlotta still had a couple thousand dollars of her money from the insurance job and today she was feeling too bossy to sit and listen to any more of Dink's bullshit.

"That shit probably counterfeit anyway while you trying to act all bossy and shit. You think I don't know what's going on out here in these streets?"

She pulled out her own bankroll and peeled off a hundred and tossed it at Dink's feet. "Go buy you some game clown," she said before peeling out of the station without the gas she'd come to get.

****

While Charlotta had decided to drop out of high school, Evelyn was in her senior year at the Detroit School of Performing Arts. She was still working at the dollar store after school, and with her studies, she didn't have much time for Capone. On the other hand, Capone was a busy man these days. He stayed on the go so much that it kind of worked out for the both of them, leaving no one feeling neglected. Every time they were together Evelyn made sure to put it on him good and make the best of their time together. Capone also did his part to make sure Evelyn was happy with the way things were going.

Knowing there was no telling how long their thing would last brought an unexpected passion to their dangerous romance. They would sex anywhere, from movie theaters, parks, and public restrooms. One time they even made love on the freeway on a late night when the road was deserted. Capone couldn't believe the daredevil that lay beneath the surface of Evelyn's sweet and innocent persona.

When he wasn't too busy, Capone would still pick her up from school and on this day, Evelyn stepped outside looking for her ride as promised the night before, but Capone was nowhere in sight. She heard a horn honking and she looked around until she spotted the sky-blue Toyota Corolla that the noise was coming from. She stopped mid-step trying to get a better look at the driver.

Once she was close enough to see the braids and his smooth almond skin, she knew it was Capone. She flashed a quick smile as she rushed to the car.

"Where is your car?" she asked once inside.

"Why, you don't like this one?"

"Not for you; this look like some bitch car. Who car is this?" she questioned.

"It's definitely not a bitch car," he said hopping out of the driver's seat and tossing her the keys.

Evelyn sat in the passenger seat processing it as he walked around and opened the car door.

"No you didn't," she said.

"Oh yeah I did," he shot back.

"OH NO YOU DIDN'T," she said right before she bailed from the car excitedly planting kisses on Capone's cheek.

"You like it?"

"Thank you so much baby I love it! I can't believe you," she said shaking her head.

"Did you peep the interior?"

"Yes I did, blue and gray my favorite colors. You are just too much," she said as she planted one last kiss on his cheek.

Evelyn finally settled down and got behind the wheel of her new car. She'd had her license for over a year now with only a little driving experience. She pulled off swerving a little just because she was so rusty behind the wheel.

Beep, beep.

She blew the horn at some friends from school who were standing at the bus stop. She wanted to make sure everyone saw her new spotless whip. Capone was thinking about Charlotta and how ungrateful she would have been if he would've bought her a Corolla. This girl was so much better for him in just about every way he could think of. If she wasn't his soul mate he didn't want to find the girl who was.

"So this is all mine huh?" Evelyn said.

"Yep."

"No car note?"

"Nope."

"I guess business is pretty good huh?" she said with a smirk.

"It's picking up."

That's all he would give her.

"Good. I hope you saving like you said you would."

"Why wouldn't I be?"

"I'm just saying. I'm very grateful for the car but don't buy me any more expensive gifts. You gotta save your money for the rainy days that's sure to come."

Capone stared at her for a while just wondering what he'd done to deserve such an angel.

"I hear you old wise one."

****

Sergio came through Charlotta's house that night to discuss the specifics of the transaction she was trying to put together. This LB cat wanted to put a large order in for a scam that was almost burned out. Sergio refused to do business with LB personally so if things went sour it would be all on Charlotta, not him. Once they got the numbers worked out Sergio left the counterfeit money with Charlotta for her to make the deal the next day.

"Be careful with this new nigga," Sergio said before leaving.

"Don't worry, I know what I'm doing."

"Okay... I just don't wanna see you get caught up."

"You don't think I can smell a cop. I'm already on probation; I'm not trying to get in no more shit."

"Okay, Miss-Know-It-All. Like I said, just be careful and know who you dealing with."

Sergio's cell phone rang.

"Yo what up?" he answered.

"Where you at bro?" Capone said.

"I'm at Charlotta's crib."

"Ask her if it's okay if I come through and holla at you real quick."

Sergio covered the speaker with his palm while he talked to Charlotta.

"Capone said can he come through? I was 'bout to leave but he wanna come holla at me about something real quick."

Charlotta shrugged.

"I don't care."

"Yeah, come through bro."

He gave Capone the directions and fifteen minutes later he looked out the window and saw the Eldorado pulling up. He met Capone at the door to make sure he watched his step because the rail was broken. Capone looked around thinking the house wasn't what he expected from Charlotta. The outside needed some work but once he stepped in he saw she had put a lot of work into the inside of the home. Charlotta's eye for detail and mixing color schemes allowed her to furnish the house and keep up her ghetto fabulous persona. All she couldn't pay for in cash she got from Rent-A-Center, including a big screen television.

Charlotta stood by silently in booty shorts and a tube top staring directly at Capone.

"So how you like my place?"

"I like it. It looks nice," he admitted.

"All for you Big Daddy," she teased, making Capone uncomfortable.

As Capone and Sergio began to talk, Charlotta got to cleaning, but all of a sudden following behind them dusting lamps and cleaning glass. It was clear she was eavesdropping so Sergio signaled for Capone to follow him outside. Charlotta rolled her eyes at them on the way out. They were in her house acting all secretive.

"I see you and Charlotta been getting along lately," Capone said.

"It's all about the money with me. Money will dead a lot of bullshit issues quick," Sergio chuckled.

"I heard that."

"Anyway, what's popping?"

"I got a big problem. I intended to get with you about it before now but it slipped my mind. Anyway, my license expires tomorrow and I need to get a new one."

"Awe man, that's all? I'll have you another in no time," Sergio assured him.

"No time like tomorrow? You know I can't drive without it."

Sergio pondered the question.

"It depends on how long it takes to track down my guy."

"Yeah, see, that's what I'm saying. Business is really picking up and I can't afford to shut down right now."

"Yeah, I feel you. I got an idea, though. Why don't you just post up at Charlotta's crib for a couple of days and have your people come to you? That will give me some time to take care of the ID situation."

"Charlotta though? I don't really want that bitch all in my business."

"Shit, you don't wanna stop yo' hustle either. Besides that, don't nobody even know where she lives besides us. At least that's what Tamiko tells me."

"Shit might work," Capone said thinking it over.

"Hell yeah, it'll work. I ain't never seen Charlotta chase a nigga the way she chase you. Throw her a couple of dollars and she'll be happy as hell just to have you around."

Sergio had come up with a simple solution to his problem, but in solving one, he very well could've been incurring another. He rationalized with himself for a minute. Money was the main motivation and he wasn't trying to have himself stagnated.

Things were finally going the way he pictured it years ago. Capone was becoming his own man and had gained his respect from his peers in the neighborhood. Earning that respect had cost him dearly but as of right now, he could live with it. However long or short this life turned out to be, he wouldn't trade it for anything in the world. He was now a full-fledged gangster who could survive on the mean streets of Detroit where wannabe gangster's died daily and even real G's sometimes didn't last. His clientele was increasing because of his diligence and dedication to putting in work like he was punching a clock.

Capone was never ever out of drugs and if he said he'd be there in twenty minutes, you could just about set your clock by him. Hustler's fucked with Capone because he was dependable and his product was A1. Randy finally decided to try his hand at the coke game and he quickly became one of Capone's best customers. Randy would re-up two and three times a week and once he saw that kind of flow, his mind was made up.

Capone walked into the house to have the conversation with Charlotta.

"Charlotta I need a favor," he started.

"Aww here we go with this bullshit again," she spat.

"Whatchu mean? You ain't even heard what I need yet."

"What Capone?" she asked faking disinterest.

"I just need some people to meet me over here tomorrow, and when I'm done I'll look out for you."

"I'm so sick of bailing y'all niggas out of situations I don't know what to do."

"What?"

"Y'all don't appreciate me," she whined.

"Yeah I do. I definitely appreciate you," Capone said as he eased up on her and wrapped his arms around her waist.

He knew if this was going to work he would have to play along with her games. He kissed what he knew to be her soft spot on her neck.

"What you think your bitch gon' say about you being at my house?"

"She don't gotta know nothing."

"Hmmpt...I guess."

****

Capone set up shop the next day at Charlotta's house. He brought with him his cell phone, a pager, and half a kilo of coke. Charlotta was in and out most of the day making her own moves with the counterfeit money she'd gotten from Sergio. Once LB saw the money in person he doubled his order. Sergio was downright paranoid of LB and he continued to tell Charlotta to be careful. She continued to assure him she had it all under control. Before long, Capone had Charlotta's house flooded with traffic.

Even after he got his license together he continued to use her house as a meeting spot. It was much safer than driving around with large amounts of drugs with no real stash in his Eldorado. This day he ran out of coke and had to make a run to Chocolate's house and back. By the time he made it back to Charlotta's, he had five cars outside waiting on him. If not for all the fancy cars outside with chrome wheels you'd think he was running a rock house.

He tossed the dope and a scale in a gym bag and went outside. He went from one car to the next making sales as quick as possible and stuffing the money in his jeans. He tried to keep it all separated until he had another chance to count it. If he was being watched at the moment he honestly didn't give a fuck. Charlotta pulled up and blew the horn at one of the cars blocking her driveway. She shot Capone an aggravated look and he quickly took control of the situation, clearing up the traffic at once.

"Dink been over here?" Charlotta asked as soon as she got out of her vehicle.

"Naw why?"

"I thought I just drove by him on the next block."

"It was probably one of my people with the same car," Capone surmised.

"Maybe…I just know I don't want that nigga over my house."

"What's up with you and Dink?"

"Ain't shit up with me and Dink punk ass. He wish it was something up. He been doing business with me on the counterfeit money thing, thinking it would get him closer to me I guess. But fuck that nigga; he ain't got shit coming this way."

"Yeah, that's how niggas is. It's the same way when a chick is selling weed or something. Every nigga who buying a lot of weed is probably trying to fuck. But at least you making money off his punk ass."

"I don't really understand why he would buy it from me when he could get it for cheaper from Dana but fuck it, he can keep playing hisself all he wants. But anyway, I see you got your clientele up," Charlotta smiled.

"Yeah, I got a good flow right now."

They both sat down in silence as the sun started to go down. This was a nice set up for Capone. He was glad Sergio suggested it.

Chapter 20

The next few days were a blur for Capone. He mostly remembered the part where he drove home every night high as a kite with a gym bag in the trunk full of small bills wrapped in rubber band stacks. Sergio was fronting him more work now that he saw that Capone could handle his own. He was up to a brick and a half, and the most tedious part of it all by far was counting all the small bills up after he was done. Thousands of dollars of singles, fives, and tens could become a headache no matter how much you loved making the money.

He began to notice how Charlotta had distanced herself from all of her male friends in order to appear as if she had no one in her life. Evelyn trusted Capone so she never questioned his whereabouts. She trusted him so much that he began to view her as either slightly gullible or sneaky in her own way. He told himself he trusted Evelyn, but he knew he'd never have the kind of trust she displayed. Not after what Charlotta had put him through.

Capone felt guilty about the situation even though he hadn't laid a hand on Charlotta since the night he hugged her and kissed her neck. Hustling so hard, it had been days since he'd had some time to spend with Evelyn. Although Charlotta had made no advances, just her presence was becoming more appealing day by day. Capone sat on the sofa counting money and smoking a blunt as Charlotta came from the bathroom wearing nothing but a towel. The towel was way too small to conceal all that it was intended to, making him leer until his dick got hard.

She came over and sat down next to him crossing her legs and making the towel loosen, almost becoming undone.

"Let me hit that," she said referring to the blunt.

The fact that Charlotta hadn't come on to him was making him want her even more. But right now, he was sure she knew what she was doing. She knew she was gorgeous and she knew how to get his attention when she really wanted it. He passed her the weed and glanced down at the towel that only really covered her breast at that point. He would definitely be able to see her vagina if she uncrossed her legs.

"Go put some clothes on," Capone said, not meaning a word of it.

"Close your eyes if you don't like what you see. This my house," she said making a valid point.

He knew if she made an advance right now, he wouldn't be strong enough to reject her. He actually wanted her to make a move as if the barely-there towel wasn't enough. "Let me give you a shotgun," Charlotta said in a nasal voice holding the smoke in her lungs.

It was as if she could smell the lust coming off of him. He glanced at her knowingly before he leaned in and she blew the marijuana smoke from her mouth to his. When she was done he met her lips with a kiss. Technically, Capone had made the first move, but after that, all his restraint flew out of the window. He snatched the loose towel from her upper body and began to kiss all over her soft, yellow skin. She rubbed his rock hard boner through his jeans and sucked on his ear the way she used to when they were a couple.

There was a sound of someone or something tampering with the front door right before...

Boom. Boom. Boom!

"Let me see your fucking hands right now!"

Police burst in like the SWAT team, guns drawn, yelling and screaming. By the third boom, Capone had already made it to the back of the house and into Charlotta's bedroom. Once he heard all the yelling inside, he dove straight through the bedroom window. Shattered glass came crashing down on his back as he landed in the backyard on all fours. He staggered to his feet as his gun fell from his waist onto the wet grass. He ran and leaped over the backyard fence then scrambled down the alley. As he ran for dear life he heard the engines gunning behind him and tires crunching the gravel.

He never looked back, but up ahead he saw the Crown Victoria pull in the alley to block his path. He continued to run straight towards the vehicle and as he approached, Capone attempted to flip over the hood of the vehicle.

Smack!

The driver kicked his door open just in time to make Capone do a cartwheel and come crashing down on the other side.

"Don't move muthafucka!" the cop said, with his gun to the back of Capone's head.

****

Back at Charlotta's house, police were a lot more lenient with her. They allowed her to get fully dressed before placing her in handcuffs and sitting her down on the couch in the living room. All she could think about was Sergio telling her to be careful. She was just waiting for LB to come through the door in full uniform, but the only familiar face she saw was Capone being dragged in looking wet, wild, and panting heavily.

They made eye contact and Charlotta's eyes bucked as she tried to talk with her eyes. He knew she was subliminally asking was there any drugs in the house. Capone shook his head signaling that there was nothing in the house. He'd sold the last of it over an hour ago, and only his lust had kept him from leaving to get more. Police sat Capone on the loveseat across from Charlotta, not allowing them to talk. For the first time, Capone noticed that some of the officers wore FBI jackets. He grew more nervous with every second that passed.

The guy who seemed to be in charge was a bald head Mexican named Rivera.

"Whose house is this?" Rivera asked.

"Who you looking for?" Charlotta fired back.

"We got who we're looking for. I'm sure of that."

Capone's head dropped as the cop who was dressed like SWAT came in waving the pistol he'd dropped in the backyard. A federal agent zoomed by with a video camera and disappeared into the back of the house.

"Can I ask y'all one question?" Charlotta said.

"Not until you answer mine. Whose house is this?"

"Okay, it's my house. Now, what is all this about?"

Capone sat bouncing one knee up and down nervously. He knew it was over for him but he wanted to tell Charlotta to shut up and be cool. Sergio had warned Capone about the feds and he knew they were nothing to play with.

"Y'all all up in my house, y'all better tell me something," Charlotta continued.

A female agent came over and put her in her place.

"Shut the fuck up, okay? You see this warrant? That means we're asking the questions here, okay?"

There was a total of nine law enforcement agents and officers in the house. At least five were federal agents. The feds moved swiftly through the house with a look of determination in their eyes. Rivera came back into the living room.

"What's your name again?" he asked pointing to Charlotta.

"Charlotta Luckett."

He turned to Capone.

"And what's your name?"

"My name is on my ID sir. Antonio Sanders," he replied.

Just then the female agent came out of the room carrying a duffle bag over her shoulder. She walked over to Rivera and unzipped the bag.

"How much we got there?" he asked.

"At least fifty grand. If we'd come a little earlier there probably was a lot more than this," she said.

"Anything else?"

"Not yet."

"Okay, I'll take this, you guys keep looking and see what you come up with."

Under the circumstance, Charlotta was uncharacteristically cool all of a sudden. Her face showed not a hint of fear and Capone had to wonder why.

"We gon' be straight my nigga," Charlotta assured him even though they were told not to talk.

"Anybody wanna explain this cash we just found? We know it's counterfeit, but anybody wanna own up to it? Make our job a little easier?"

"We ain't got nothing else to talk about. If we going to jail, take us to jail," Charlotta said.

"How about you Antonio? Is that how you feel too?"

Capone was visibly shaken now and his fingers were going numb because the handcuffs were way too tight. He didn't complain or respond to the questions he was being asked. He just sat there thinking about all the years in prison he was facing. He had an image flash in his head of him breaking down in the courtroom on sentencing day. Visions of him growing old in a cell with salt and pepper cornrows. It was just a matter of time before he got fingerprinted and it would all be over.

****

Sergio was distracted by a leaf stuck to his windshield wiper as he drove from his father's house. He had stopped by again to thank him for the huge favor. Sergio had just bought a home for him and Tamiko and his father was kind enough to put it in his name so it didn't get taken if anything happened to Sergio. The home was located in Grosse Pointe, a suburb right outside of Detroit. At this very moment, he was exiting the freeway and heading to his new pad worth a quarter million dollars and surrounded by homes worth a lot more. He was in a bit of a rush because he wanted to get there before the moving company arrived and started unloading things.

He and Tamiko had a lot of valuables and by her logic, the movers would handle things with a lot more care if a man was present during the unloading. He drove through the suburbs doing his regular Sergio stuff. He freestyled about how he had come up, smoking weed and dipping in and out of lanes like he was above the law. His speed increased as he got higher.

Before he knew it, he was doing sixty in a forty-five flying right past a police station. It was then he pressed on the brakes, realizing where he was at for the first time. When Sergio pulled in the driveway of his new home, he had to sit and take it all in for a minute. His house was a brick colonial style home with four bedrooms and two full bathrooms. It wasn't super fancy, but it was nice and roomy for a young couple with no kids. They planned to raise a family in this home one day. Despite Tamiko's disposition, she always believed she would be a great mother once their lives were more settled.

At this moment, Sergio was appreciating life more than he ever did. He was full of sunshine on this rainy day. Then he remembered all that he'd done and been through to make it to this point. He didn't know if he should thank God or Satan for his blessing. That thought ruined the moment so he snapped out of it, hopped out the Jag, and went inside. Once inside he could hear Tamiko's heels clunking across the hardwood floors in the still empty house.

"Tamiko, where you at?" he called out.

"I'm in my empty ass master bedroom," she shouted from upstairs.

He walked up the freshly varnished staircase, noticing how solid the steps were. Not a squeak. Tamiko stood in the middle of the master bedroom wearing a powder blue V-neck sweater and matching jeans.

"I think the bed should go right here," she said motioning to the wall opposite the window.

"I thought you said you wanted here?" he said pointing to the right side of the window.

"I changed my mind. I was thinking we could get one of those big wicker chairs to sit in the corner, another aquarium along this wall, and find a nice fern plant to sit in the corner."

She waited for him to say he liked her new ideas. Sergio walked closer, wrapped his arms around her waist, and pecked her lips.

"It's your house, do whatever you wanna do."

"I know it's my house, but since I'm allowing you to live in it rent-free, at least tell me what you think."

He was just about to tell her who wore the pants for real when his phone rang. His intentions were to turn his phone off until he was done with the whole moving process, but he decided to take this one call first.

"What up?"

"Dog, what the fuck is going on out here nigga? Fucking feds done ran up in two of my people's cribs looking for me about fucking counterfeit money," Dana shouted.

Sergio was shocked and confused.

"What?"

"Nigga you ain't deaf, you heard what the fuck I said."

"Dog, I don't know what's going on, but you better watch yo' tone," he warned.

"Nigga, I swear on everything, if I find out you been talking to them people, I'm banging yo' ass out. I don't care if the feds is listening.

"You don't care if the feds listening? Bitch ass nigga you calling me a rat?" Sergio snapped.

Tamiko stood in shock listening to one side of the confrontational phone call.

"I tell you what; just for calling my phone with this bullshit you better hope I don't see you before you see me."

Dana hung up before he could even finish the threat but he had to get the rest out for his own piece of mind.

"Bae who the fuck was that?" Tamiko asked.

"Dana bitch ass, talking about the feds ran in his people crib looking for him. The fuck that got to do with me? Hoe ass nigga better check his connect," Sergio fumed.

Sergio paced the floor for a minute breathing fire, then he took off towards the stairs.

"Just calm down," Tamiko called out as she followed behind him.

"Fuck that. That nigga was talking too crazy."

He stormed down the steps and all the way to the basement where the laundry closet was locked. He searched for his keys to unlock it. The AK-47 he'd stored just yesterday was inside. Tamiko trailed behind him trying to reason.

"Bae! Just stop and listen for a minute. You know this is not how you do things. You're upset and you about to go do something that's gon' get you hemmed up. We just got this house. The moving company is on the way with all our shit right now. This ain't the time to be running out the house to go be Billy Badass. 'Cause if something happens to you, I promise I'ma kill, somebody! Now whatever you feel like you need to do you can work it out later when you thinking straight."

She knew him better than his own mother, and she knew she was the only one that stood a chance at talking him down when he got heated. It was Tamiko's level head that balanced out the savage inside of him. He knew if something happened to him she'd go crazy and that's what he couldn't let happen. He continued to pace around the basement, but it was at a slower, more methodical rhythm now. Now it was like he was more strategizing than trying to keep from exploding.

He thought of Capone, knowing he was probably the only dude in the world he'd never have to worry about crossing him.

****

Evelyn sat in her bedroom, racking her brain with trigonometry. She had breezed through algebra and geometry but this was something different. She backed away from her desk when she felt a headache coming on. Her phone rang and she didn't really feel like being bothered, but she answered anyway thinking it might be Capone.

"Hello?" she answered sounding exhausted.

"It's over baby," Capone's cracking voice came through, forcing out words he could barely fix his mouth to say.

"What? Where you at?"

"It's all over. You gotta know where I am if I'm telling you this."

Evelyn took the phone from her ear and let out a long sigh as her heart sank. She placed the phone back to her ear.

"Tell me what happened."

"The feds ran up in Charlotta's house while I was there. They found a bunch of counterfeit money and I had burner on me of course."

Evelyn felt her whole body growing hot. Tears started streaming down her cheek as she began to sniffle.

"Is Charlotta in jail too?"

"Yeah, the feds took Charlotta, but I'm at 1300 Beaubien, police headquarters. They gonna find out I'm not who I say I am soon."

"Don't think about that right now," Evelyn said through a trembling voice.

She didn't want to think about it herself. "And don't talk to them about anything."

"You know I'm not gon' do that Evelyn. I just want to be realistic about things. We both knew this day was gonna come sooner or later."

Evelyn sniffed.

"What do you want me to do?"

"First I need you to call my mom and let her know I'm in jail. Then I need you to call my brother and tell him get everything out of the apartment just in case. Let him know what happened. Um…tell him to call his lawyer for me."

"I think I got the number around here somewhere. You left it here when he went to jail in Hazel Park."

"No, I need him to make the call."

"Okay. What about Charlotta? Do you want me to get Tamiko a message?"

It still hadn't registered that all this happened at Charlotta's house. Jealousy and suspicion wasn't on her radar in times like this.

"I'm sure Charlotta got in touch with somebody by now, but let him know she's gonna need a lawyer too. Real bad," he emphasized.

"Okay."

"There was a painful silence after that. They both knew this day would be heartbreaking but now that it was here, the pain was unbearable. Evelyn felt a tightening in her chest as if someone was squeezing her heart.

"I gotta go. I call you when I know something else," Capone said.

The sound of her constant sniffling had almost brought Capone himself to tears. He knew he had to be strong now. He had to be stronger than ever because the rest of his life depended on it. He needed Evelyn to be strong too, but he couldn't say it.

"Capone," Evelyn managed.

"Yeah."

"It's not over. You hear me?" It's not over."

"I love you Evelyn."

"I love you too."

"Bye."

"Bye."

Chapter 21

Charlotta was not talking at all. She kept giving Rivera the middle finger. This was the tenth time she'd been asked a question and she'd responded with either one or both of her middle fingers. She'd been in the interrogation room for almost an hour and it was going nowhere for federal agents hoping to flip Charlotta and gain access to her connect. Knowing the money trail would lead straight to Sergio and Dana, she refused to be a rat.

More than that, she just had a blind faith that the justice system favored the criminal.

"We know the money is not yours; just tell us whose it is and we can get this whole thing straightened out."

Rivera was trying to sound as compassionate as he could but Charlotta wasn't buying it. She gave another middle finger for her response. Rivera sighed and placed a small photo on the table. "Who is that? Do you know him?" he demanded.

She studied the picture all of two seconds and shoved it back in his direction.

"I ain't never seen that nigga in my life."

But she had seen him and knew him very well. The photo was an old county jail picture of Dana. It appeared to be at least five years old.

"So you're gonna take the rap for these bums? They don't care about you. You think they care about you? Let me tell you something sweetheart, anyone who cares about you is not gonna put you in this kinda position. Now think about that," he finished.

It didn't matter what he said; his persuasion was not going to work. No one had waved a grand prize in Charlotta's face to convince her to do the things she did. It was all her own will and if she went down for it, then so be it. She gave him the finger again.

"You keep sticking that little fucking finger up but let me tell you something; I'm here to help you help yourself. You don't want my help because you're young and stupid. But you know what, that's fine with me. All bets are off; now let's see who gets fucked."

Rivera bolted out of the room steaming mad, slamming doors behind him. As she sat there, the reality of her situation slowly sank in and she began to think about what it meant for her young life. She still felt in the depths of her soul that it just wasn't in the cards for her story to end this way. No way she was going to jail before she was eighteen years old.

****

Capone wouldn't say a word without a lawyer. Sergio had schooled him well about keeping his mouth shut when arrested. He didn't have any fingerprints on file because he'd never been arrested, but it didn't take long for homicide to breeze through their most wanted files and come up with his picture. They couldn't be positive without the prints, but they were pretty sure that he was the guy they'd been looking for the past three years.

First, he was visited by the feds who were still looking for information on Dana. The interview went nowhere and once they realized Capone was wanted for murder, they left him alone and decided to let homicide deal with him. Later on that day he got a visit from a bald head black man in his mid to late forties. He stood at the front of Capone's cell grinning like he'd just won the lotto.

Capone knew he had to be from homicide. Baldy called out Capone's real name to see if he'd flinch.

"You in some deep shit," Baldy said.

Capone held his composure but inside he was dying. Baldy left vowing his return. Capone waited for a visit from a lawyer but no one showed. He would harass the turnkey ever so often about a phone call or why his lawyer hadn't been to see him, as if it was somehow the turnkey's doing. He soon found out the turnkey was a real bitch and wouldn't be assisting him with any of his issues. He had been ignoring Capone the entire time and probably would continue to do so until his shift was over.

That night he did a thousand pushups in his cell just trying to keep his stress level down. The worst part of it all was not knowing what was about to happen. He eventually dozed off for a few hours but once he woke up he stayed up for the rest of the night.

****

The next day his attorney came to visit him. She was a brown skin woman who looked to be in her mid-thirties. She wore spiral locks and had a beautiful smile that made her eyes squint every time she showed her pearly whites. She sat erect in the visitor's booth dressed in a black business suit. Just seeing her there made Capone feel better. That fact that she was smiling made him feel like maybe his case wasn't so hopeless after all.

"How you doing Mr. Johnson?"

"Not good," Capone admitted.

"That's understandable, but that's why I'm here. My name is Dominique Morris and I'll be representing you in whatever charges are brought by the state. It appears for now that the feds won't be trying to tie you in with the female you were arrested with in the raid. As of right now, you're being charged with CCW, but I was made aware that there could be more charges coming. Have you spoken to anyone?"

"Un-unh," Capone replied.

"You haven't spoken to anyone about anything?"

"Nope."

"Good. Because if you did, now would be a good time to tell me."

"I just gave them the name on my ID. I haven't said nothing since then."

"Okay, well, we really can't do anything until you're formally charged with something besides the gun, but that's more than likely going to happen today. Once that happens, I can take look at the police report and we can go from there."

Capone just stared blankly off into space.

"Have you seen the girl, Charlotta?" he finally asked.

"No, I haven't seen her yet, but I will be representing her as well. So far all we know is she's being charged with possession of counterfeit currency."

Capone couldn't help but worry about Charlotta. Besides Evelyn, she was the only girl that ever really knew him. The only other girl he ever had a real bond with.

"She looking at some time huh?"

"With that amount of counterfeit currency found in her possession, she's looking at some kind of time."

"Damn," Capone said shaking his head.

"Do you have any other questions concerning your case?"

"Well, do you think I will be able to get a bond?"

"It's hard to say anything until we see what other charges, if any, are being brought forward. I wish I had more information, but I do know you're going to court for at least the gun charge tomorrow. Hopefully, by then, we'll find out a lot more. Try not to worry yourself too much while you wait. I know that's easy for me to say, but trust me, it never helps to stress yourself out."

Capone just nodded and with that said, Ms. Morris closed her briefcase and left. Later on that day, Baldy came back with the bad news. Capone was being charged with second-degree murder and felony firearm along with the CCW charge. For some reason, it all seemed like some kind of fantasy world until now. It was like he had been watching someone else's life on television and then all of sudden he was the main character in the movie.

He took a deep breath, then another one. There was nothing he could do to change the situation so all he could do is stand tall and handle it as it came. If he could make it through this without losing his sanity or self-respect, he could live with whatever the outcome would be. He did pushups again all night until he was tired enough to lay down and get some rest.

The next morning, Capone was already awake when he heard his name being called for court. When they cracked open his cell he was overjoyed just to get out of there. He was handcuffed to another prisoner and led through the back of the building to a police van. During the ride, the other prisoners discussed their crimes and criminal record. The jailhouse lawyers of the group gave out the odds of beating the case and how much time each charge carried.

Capone sat quietly with all these jail birds, none of which had brushed their teeth, wishing they would do the same. After bending a few corners they turned into the back of another building. Capone had no idea where he was at. He'd never been to any courthouse for any reason. Officers shuffled the prisoners out of the van and up against the wall. After identifying everyone for the third time they were led into a building and placed in a holding cell.

Capone sat on a wooden bench reading graffiti on the wall. The bench also had names carved in it. He wondered if Big Randy who had carved his name in the bench was the same Big Randy he went to school with. Forty-five minutes passed and just as he was about to doze off he heard the steel doors being unlocked.

"Alright everyone listen up. When you hear your name being called line up against this wall."

Capone was getting sick of this now. He was tired of answering to his fake name and he was sick and tired of lining up against walls. He was tired of listening to people tell him what to do every five minutes and if this was what he had to look forward to, he was realizing he could be royally fucked. He told himself if he had to line up against one more wall he was going to make a run for the back door. After everyone lined up against the wall with no one leaning on it or talking, they were ushered into a small room where they could now see the inside of the actual courtroom from.

"Who is that judge?" one concerned inmate asked.

"That's Ms. Thomas," another responded.

"I ain't up on her. She must be a new judge."

One by one they were called out to the courtroom. For the first time, Capone grew extremely nervous. He watched guys come back complaining about ridiculously high bonds and parole holds. One guy came back with good news. His bond was only five hundred dollars and he was certain he'd be getting out within a few hours. Capone was the last person to be called. He walked into the courtroom scanning the room for any friends or family.

He spotted Evelyn, Tamiko, and his mother all together in the third row. His lawyer Dominique waved him over and showed him where to stand as the charges were read.

"Speak up if she addresses you and don't say stuff like un hun."

"Okay," Capone agreed.

As the charges were being read, Capone didn't really hear anything but murder. He was light headed by the time his lawyer entered the not guilty plea. She squeezed his arm slightly in an attempt to console him. Before he was led out by the bailiff she told Capone she had some information concerning his case and she would be coming to visit him real soon.

****

Despite his efforts to find Dana, Sergio still ended up playing the cat and mouse game he was trying to avoid. With the feds on his trail, it was more than likely that Dana had left town. The whole situation had Sergio paranoid and feeling like he too may be on the hot sheet as well. He was feeling real bad about Capone being locked up and it was starting to show. Just last night he pounced on one of his workers over five hundred dollars when usually Sergio would've just docked his pay.

He began to snap at Tamiko over every little thing and she found herself leaving him at home alone and just trying to give him space. He couldn't stop thinking about how different life would be without his little brother on the streets to enjoy it all with him. He hoped Capone could handle the pressure of jail. He knew Capone had changed a lot since he was a kid, but he could never forget the young, soft kid who burst into tears every time things got too tough.

One thing he knew for sure was that this situation was going to mentally kill Capone or make him stronger. He opted to think positive, believing in his brother and that something good would come out of all his trials and tribulations. Sergio knew Tamiko was probably still upset with him so he called Evelyn to see what happened in court.

"Hello?"

"Ev?"

"Yeah, hey…I got some bad news."

"You didn't make it to court today?"

"Yeah I went to court, but they gave him a ridiculously high bond with him being on the Detroit's most wanted list and all that stuff. His bond is one hundred thousand dollars," she informed.

"Hmph," Sergio moaned.

Evelyn wondered what that meant. He wasn't saying anything.

"You still there?" she asked.

"Yeah, I'm waiting on you to give me the bad news."

"Oh, I thought the bond being so high would be the bad news."

"It is for them. They should've made it higher if they wanted to keep him in there. I just bought a house that set me back some, but I need my brother on these streets if they gon' let him out. Give me a week and I'll go get him," Sergio assured her.

"You will?" Evelyn said excitedly.

"Yeah, I'm gone get 'em out."

"Oh my God, I will be so happy to see my baby come home. You just don't know how much I been praying for him. I truly believe this is gonna work out for him in the long run."

"Let me know if you need anything. You know it's not a problem."

"I'll be okay. Thanks."

****

After talking to Sergio, Evelyn's spirit had been lifted. She no longer looked at the situation the same because just an hour ago, she was struggling to be positive about the grim look of things. Now she truly believed that Sergio would bring him home and his lawyer would somehow help him beat these cases, period.

Chapter 22

When Sergio got home he found Tamiko in the living room with her feet propped up on the ottoman indulging herself in a homemade pedicure. He walked over, leaned in, and planted a kiss on his lips.

"Don't let me find no toenail clippings on the floor around here, it's gon' be some trouble," he warned.

"Shut up. This my house, I ain't tryna hear that. Anything news on Capone?"

"Naw, I just got off the phone with Evelyn. Why you ain't call me after court?"

"Well, I was expecting you to call me, but when you didn't I figured you still had yo' lil' funky attitude."

"I thought you was mad at me 'cause I been tripping. That's why I didn't call," Sergio explained.

"At first I was, but then I realized how stressed out you been lately and I didn't wanna add to it by making home life fucked up too. So I just decided to give you a little space."

"Baby, I appreciate you for understanding me and knowing when to just fall back. You know I love you 'til death right?"

"You better."

Tamiko puckered her lips and closed her eyes waiting for another kiss and Sergio quickly obliged. She returned to her pedicure but not before having the last word. "I'm glad we made peace today 'cause I was on the verge of fucking you up."

They both burst into laughter but Sergio had to wonder was it really a joke. He headed into the kitchen and grabbed an unopened bottle of Remy Martin VSOP from the freezer. He filled his glass with cubes from the ice maker then cracked the seal and poured a stiff one. He came back in the living room and plopped down on the recliner.

"So when you going to get him out?" Tamiko asked.

"I need to get all this bread out the streets first. You know we just bought this house so I went all in on my last package. I'ma go get him in a week or so. His next court date won't be for another month. He'll be home way before then."

"Oh, before I forget, I ran into Randy at the mall. He said he needs you to call him it's important."

"Where's the number?"

"It's right here, hand me my purse."

After Tamiko gave him the number, Sergio went into the basement for some privacy.

"We need to talk homey," Randy stressed on the other end of the phone.

Sergio was a little confused. He and Randy had never done any business or had any ties except for the fact that he was a friend of Capone.

"About what?" Sergio asked.

"About roaches and rats, shit like that," Randy explained.

"Say no more. Take this number down and call me first thing in the morning."

"That's a bet."

****

Sergio and Randy met up the next day at the mall inside the food court. They ordered some Chinese food and settled in the back of the food court away from everyone.

"I think this nigga Dink is snitching on the whole hood," Randy started.

"What makes you say that?"

"Dig this man, you know me and Dink used to be tight like fucking Fruit of the Looms. I been stopped fucking with the nigga like that, but he still come around sometimes. Sometimes he comes to the spot bragging about how much money he getting with Dana or whatever. One day he came through with a ounce of dro to smoke on and he asked me to roll with him for a minute. I wasn't gonna fuck with him but he told me we could stop by his crib 'cause his sister was home. I always wanted to fuck Dink sister but he would always block me. Today he's offering up his sister, claiming she's older now and he ain't in her business no more. Anyway, I rode with the nigga and we smoking and drinking and kicking it. We wound up at his crib right?"

"I'm listening," Sergio said attentively.

"His sister ain't there when we get there so I'm ready to bounce, but I stick around and play a couple games of Madden and smoke another blunt. He asked me to go in the basement with him. I go down there with him and I see all these fucking uncut counterfeit bills drying all over the basement."

"Is this before or after I started fucking with it?"

"This is around the same time I saw you and you told me you had it, maybe a week or two before that. He showed me the briefcase with 'bout a hundred thousand in it. I'm like okay it's fake, so, big fucking deal. Plus it's not even yours, it's Dana's. I don't say shit though; I let him floss and tell him I'm about to bounce. His sister comes right when I'm about to leave so I stay for a while longer and get at her. I get her number and we start kicking it. Now, 'bout a month goes by and we still kicking it. She tells me that police ran up in Dink's crib. I asked what they find and she tells me they didn't find nothing but a money counter and some drug paraphernalia. But I'm knowing the whole time she just telling me what Dink told her. When he gets out, he starts calling me all of sudden trying to get me to buy some of this counterfeit shit from him."

I asked him about the raid and he tried to brush the shit off like it was nothing. But he moved out of the house like the same week he got out of jail and now all of sudden everybody getting hit."

Sergio searched Randy's eyes for the truth. Nothing in his eyes or body language led him to believe Randy wasn't speaking from the heart. The only thing Sergio was certain of was that Randy believed Dink was a snitch. Now Sergio just had to ask himself did he believe Dink could've been responsible for everything that had happened over the past week.

"So where Dink live at now?" Sergio asked.

"I don't know. He been real secretive about it, but I'm trying to get it out of his sister without sounding suspicious."

"Yeah, we definitely gonna need that info."

"Trust me I'm on it," Randy said.

Randy knew if he could get in good with Sergio, it could mean much bigger and better things for him. Sergio wanted to do a little more research on the charges that were brought up on Dink. He knew Dink was soft, but that didn't make him a snitch. He wanted to have something solid before he put that label on the man because once it was attached to your name, it was permanent.

****

The first thing Charlotta did was breathe deeply. She stood outside the federal courthouse looking for her mother who had just put her house up to make bail for Charlotta. She stood on the steps with her lawyer Dominique for almost an hour, but her mom was nowhere to be found.

"You want me to give you a lift?" Dominique asked.

"No, she will probably pull up as soon as I leave. I'm okay," Charlotta assured her.

"You sure? I don't mind."

"Yeah, go ahead, I'll be fine."

She didn't like Dominique that much. She found her to be a little too uppity for her taste. She stood on the steps another five minutes after her lawyer left and then she got pissed. She started walking up Lafayette mumbling to herself. Before she could reach the corner, Tamiko pulled alongside her in a white 540i she'd gotten for her birthday. She blew the horn at Charlotta who was off in her own world. Charlotta finally noticed her then ran to hop in.

"Where the fuck is my mama?"

"Why bitch, you ain't glad to see me? She just told me she had something to do and asked me to come get you."

"What the fuck she got to do that important? I just got out!"

"Yeah and if it wasn't for her yo' ass would still be sitting, so chill."

Just then Tamiko looked over at Charlotta's ungrateful ass for the first time. "Damn you a hot mess."

Charlotta's hair was everywhere and she felt like Pig Pen of Charlie Brown.

"Shut up and take me home so I can get my ass in the tub."

Charlotta fumbled with her ankle, moving the electronic tether the feds made her wear in order to make bail.

"You sure you wanna be at that house after everything that happened?

"Where else I'ma go? I sure as hell ain't about to be up in my mama house listening to her bullshit."

"Sergio said you could chill at our house for a while."

"I can't. I gotta stay where my tether is assigned to."

"Oh damn, you got a tether?"

"Hell yeah."

Charlotta was shocked to hear that Sergio had offered her a place to stay in her time of crisis. He probably just trying to make sure I didn't rat his ass out, she thought.

"Damn, did you get somebody to fix my door?"

"Yeah, Sergio sent somebody over there to fix it that same day."

"Tell him I said thanks for everything."

The first thing Charlotta noticed when she pulled up to her house was that her car was missing.

"Did one of y'all pick up my car?"

"No, you said leave it alone. I gave the spare key to your mama."

She didn't recall her mom telling her she was going to move the car. She couldn't think of a reasonable explanation for her car to be gone.

"That bitch talking about she got something to do, where the fuck is my car?"

"Calm down, maybe she came to get it and forgot to tell you."

Charlotta sprang from the car and ran into the house to call her mother. She didn't answer. Tamiko came in trying to help her figure things out. "I know my mama didn't get it. Somebody stole my shit!"

"You don't know that."

Tamiko was trying to think positive but she knew Charlotta didn't live in the best neighborhood. It was very likely that she was right. She didn't want to remind her it was her own fault after Tamiko had offered to get the car and put it somewhere safe.

"The fucking feds tore my house up!" Charlotta fumed as she moved about cleaning up.

Nothing was destroyed but their were clothes and small objects scattered everywhere. "If I beat this case I'm suing they ass," she continued.

Tamiko didn't think she'd beat it. She knew her cousin was looking at some time but she kept it to herself.

"Well, if you don't need nothing I'm going home. I'll call you tonight and check on you."

"Damn, you could at least help me clean up."

"Bitch you don't got nothing to do and nowhere to be. Clean yo' own house up."

With that, she eased her way out of the door before Charlotta talked her into helping. Later that day, Charlotta talked to her mom who just confirmed what she already knew. Her car had been stolen while she was in jail. After cleaning her house up, she got in the tub and put on her pajamas. Her curfew was six o'clock and it was already five-thirty. Her friend LB called but she didn't answer, not knowing who to trust at this point. Just as she began to get bored and stressed out, Sergio came through to check on her. When she let him in he was smoking a blunt and she was happier to see the blunt than Sergio.

"Damn, I need that in my life," she said reaching for the weed without permission.

"First thing a muthafucka do when they get out of jail is get high," Sergio chuckled.

"Whatever, my nerves is bad right now."

"You know they probably gon' make you do urine drops while you out on bond, right?"

"I don't give a fuck right now," she replied right before inhaling.

"Ain't you already on probation anyway? You know if your PO find out—"

"How she gon' find out? You gon' tell her?"

"Okay, smart ass, but if you get violated you looking at state and fed time."

"By the time my probation lien checks come up I'll be done with this shit. But let me ask you this, do you think I can beat this case?"

"That's what I came over here to talk to you about. First off, what exactly are you charged with?"

"Possession with intent to deliver, I mean distribute counterfeit currency."

She pulled on the blunt and searched his face for a reaction. She couldn't read him. She wished he'd say something.

"The lawyer said there's a confidential informant," she continued.

Sergio's eyes widened.

"You ever did any business with Dink?"

"Yeah, why?"

"The streets is saying he might be snitching. I'm checking into it now; I don't know nothing for sure yet."

"I gave him ten thousand like two days in a row."

"Randy gave me a whole run down on how he caught a fed case right before all this shit started happening. Feds is looking for Dana too. It don't take a genius to figure this shit out, but I don't understand why he put 'em on you."

"Right, because Dana alone should've been enough to get his ass out of the hot seat, but then again…I know why."

Charlotta thought back to that day at the gas station when she had stomped all over Dink's ego and pride. It was coming back to haunt her now.

"See, Dink always tried to fuck with me but I been hoeing that nigga forever, you know? I think I went too far with it and he been holding some type of eternal grudge. Plus, he knows he couldn't come at you like that when he was already plugged with the nigga who supposed to be the man. You would've peeped game immediately. But my dumb ass!"

She didn't even finish the sentence. She just shook her head wondering why she didn't see that trap.

"Don't worry about it now; it's too late to take it back. Just try not to get into any more trouble."

Charlotta paced the floor in silence for a moment. She'd almost smoked the whole blunt before handing it back to Sergio. She thought about Capone and realized she wasn't the only one in trouble.

"What's up with Capone?"

"They got him on a hundred thousand dollar bond right now, but he'll be out soon."

"That's my nigga regardless of whatever anybody thinks and I hope he don't think I had shit to do with that raid."

Sergio went into his pocket and pulled out a wad of cash and gave it to Charlotta. "That's three thousand. I feel kinda bad I got you mixed up in my shit, but you know how the game go. I'm gonna pay for your lawyer and hopefully, when it's all said and done, you'll be straight."

She gave him a hug.

"Thanks, I really appreciate this, but you still didn't answer my question."

"What?"

"Do you think I can beat this?"

Sergio sat down on the sofa.

"I'm gonna be honest with you. People don't beat the feds at their own game that often. Right now we just gotta wait this out and see what they tryna do."

"The lawyer said the more money you get caught with the more time they try to hit you with. I got caught with a hundred grand, plus they took all the money I had saved."

"Well, the only thing I can tell you is you got a damn good lawyer on your side and you got me."

"I hope that's enough. I'm not trying to go to jail."

"I told you I got you on this. Now let me ask you a question. Do you think you could get in touch with Dana if you had to?"

"I could reach out to one of his sisters, why?"

"I need to get a message to him before I wind up killing that crazy muthafucka. I need him to know that the snitch is in his circle, not mine."

It was the only thing that made sense. Sergio was more convinced the more he talked about it. It had to be Dink. He had a lot on his plate and everyone was counting on him. He didn't need any extra enemies and Charlotta wanted to help in any way she could.

"I'll see if I can find him or get the message to him."

Chapter 23

Capone got settled in at the Wayne County Jail southwest side. He'd gotten two visits since he made out his visiting list, one from his mom and one from Dominique, his lawyer. On the visit from his lawyer, he learned that Dink had recently made statements against him involving the homicide case. There wasn't much he could do with that information from where he sat, but he wanted to get it to Sergio as soon as his phone list was activated.

Meanwhile, he sat in a cell getting to know the guy that was sleeping over him every night in the top bunk. He was a young black man and a Muslim named Amin from the Joy Road area on the Westside of Detroit. They favored a lot in size, height, and skin color. Amin even wore cornrows. The biggest difference in their appearance was that Amin had light brown eyes and normal size ears. They sat up conversing until the wee hours of the morning just kicking it and developing a mutual respect for one another.

They discussed each other's cases without going into too much detail. Amin was facing a carjacking charge which carried a stiff penalty. He claimed he never carjacked anybody, but he did admit to snatching a dude out of his car and beating the shit out him over an unpaid debt. He claimed it was actually one of his friends that decided to jump in the car and pull off in it. Amin vowed he would never snitch so he sat in the county jail hoping he could beat the carjacking charge and just have the assault with great bodily harm to deal with.

"You know my sister used to try to kill me?" Amin blurted out.

He had a habit of blurting out random things that would cause for a full explanation. Capone thought he got a kick out it.

"What? What you mean?"

"Yeah, both of my sisters used to try to kill me. One night, I was sleep with my mouth wide open and my sister Re Re stuck a quarter in my mouth and started tickling my throat."

Capone burst into laughter at the thought of someone's own sister being that mischievous at a young age.

"I'm for real. I woke up and I couldn't talk."

"Then what happened?"

"I laid there choking and dying and shit while she ran and told my mama I was dying. My mama ran in and gave me the Heimlich maneuver and saved my fucking life," Amin explained shaking his head as he remembered the horrible incident.

"She probably wasn't trying to kill you dog. It sounds like a joke that got way out of hand."

"Naw bro! I'm telling you what I know. Another time when the kitchen caught on fire and she ran in my room yelling come here, look, look! She led me into the kitchen and then shoved me into the fire. I ran out of the kitchen and then she said stay here while I go next door and get Mama. I said I'm going with you, then she pushed me back into the kitchen and ran out of the house."

Capone couldn't believe what he was hearing. It was hilarious the way Amin was so animated when telling the story, but it was also scary to think your own sister could actually want you dead.

"Get the fuck outta here," Capone said still giggling.

"On my kids man. I was so young I didn't know no better so I just stayed there until my mom came and got me out."

"Why you think they wanted to kill you?"

"I don't know man but they wanted me dead! We all get along now, but back in the day…" Amin stopped and just shook his head.

Being cell mates with Amin made things a little easier. Some days he could actually forget about the time he was facing for a couple hours. Then there were days nothing and no one could lighten his mood. Some days he just felt like breaking down. When he talked to Sergio he had assured Capone that he'd be out in a week or less. That gave him hope knowing he would be back on the streets for however long or short that time would be.

"Johnson-visit," a deep voice yelled harshly over the intercom. Capone wondered who it could be as he hopped off the bunk and looked in the mirror. He had taken down his hair with intentions to get it braided but for now, he just had a big afro. He walked around Amin who was on the floor making salat, rubbed some lotion on his arms and face then headed out on the visit.

Evelyn was there waiting for him with the same sad look she'd been wearing for days. The same look he pictured her having every time they talked on the phone. She hated seeing him in there and she hated having to talk to him on the phone in there. The phone calls he made to Evelyn usually depressed Capone more than anything. When he sat down in front of the Plexiglas all he could think about is how he wished she'd fix her face.

"Hey," he spoke into the small ventilation hole.

"Hey, how are you?"

"I'll be better if you would give me smile," he replied.

"A what?"

"A smile. You don't gotta look so down; I'm the one in jail."

"Well, I'm sorry but this hurts so much to see you in here."

"I understand that but you know this is gonna be hard enough as it is. The only thing you can really do now is try to uplift my spirits. Take my mind off it for a minute, you know?"

"You're right, I'm sorry."

She blinked away the tears that were forming in her eyes and wiggled around in her chair in an attempt to perk up a little.

"Sergio keeps offering me money and stuff, but I keep telling him I'm okay. I live at home still so my mom makes sure I have everything I need."

"Yeah, but that's just how he is. I never told him about the money I have at your house, but he gotta know I'm not broke."

"Yeah, but like you said, that's just how he is. He told me you should be home by next week."

"I hope so. I feel like I'm going crazy in here. Everybody in here got a chip on they shoulder 'cause we all walking around not knowing what's about to happen to us."

"Have you been praying for your situation and talking to God about it like you said you would?"

"Yeah," he lied.

"What else you been doing?"

"Ain't much to do; guys watch TV and play cards or chess all day."

The truth was Capone was uncomfortable in this environment. He stayed in his cell to avoid the other inmates. Everyone in the county was always on edge and he wanted to avoid confrontation. Capone knew that he wasn't naturally aggressive, but rather used aggression as a survival tactic. Without all the liquor and weed in his system, he wasn't the gutsy killer that he was on the streets. There were no guns in the county and a lot of the dudes inside were older and twice his size. He was a little afraid.

"I went to church yesterday with your mom."

"Yeah? She came to see me yesterday and she didn't say anything about it."

"She probably wanted to let me tell you."

"That's crazy, you going to church with my mom and I still never even met yours."

"That is crazy," Evelyn chuckled.

She knew this day would come so she never tried to get her mom and Capone to meet, figuring she'd never give him a chance under the circumstance. Now it seemed like they would never meet.

"You wrote any poems lately?" he asked.

"Naw, I really haven't been in the mood."

"I wrote one last night called 'No Sunshine.'"

"That's the kind of stuff you don't need to be thinking about right now. I know what no sunshine means. You have to ask God for His help and His mercy. He is the only one that can help you right now. Not me, not Sergio, or nobody else. You need to go to God and sincerely ask for forgiveness if you haven't already." Evelyn was becoming emotional again because Capone seemed to be giving up before the fight of his life even began.

She knew he was never big on religion, but she knew that there was a believer deep down inside of him, and it was now or never if that believer was going to surface. Capone could see the disappointment in her eyes from him not having faith that there could be a positive outcome to his situation. He just couldn't front about the way he felt, not even for her. There was a brief silence as he thought about how all of this was affecting Evelyn. He didn't want her to suffer along with him for sins he had committed. Capone told Evelyn he loved her and finished up the visit before his time was up.

He went back to his cell to lie on his bunk, staring at the ceiling. For some reason, he began to think about his father. He wondered how much influence his father would've had on his life had he lived to raise him. He wondered would his father have turned his own life around and got back on track. Maybe not, he thought. He loved and respected his father most of his young life minus the abusiveness that came later. He was in deeper thought than he'd ever remembered being about his father when he heard something… a subtle voice inside his own head.

"You still have one father left."

He thought his mind had to be playing tricks on him because the voice came from inside his own head. He shook it off and laid down for a nap he felt was desperately need. Shortly after, Amin came in from making a phone call and prepared to make salat. As Amin kneeled down with his hands extended high in the air, Capone watched and thought how Amin looked at total peace every time he prayed. Seeing how Amin had such a close relationship with God and knowing that he probably had just as much if not more dirt under his belt, made Capone rethink what had just happened only minutes earlier.

It seemed everywhere he turned there was some reminder of the Higher Power he believed in but never got up the nerves to reach out to. Evelyn's words began to play in his head. Capone knew that his life was no longer in his own hands. As he contemplated what was about to happen, he began to believe that his fate would be better in the hand of that Higher Power than a judge and jury. That night, he waited for Amin to go to sleep and Capone did something he hadn't done in almost ten years. He got down on his knees and prayed.

It had been so long, he'd honestly forgotten how to pray. He had no idea where to start, but he tried his best to explain what he needed from God. He tried to explain how he'd gotten into this predicament in the first place. He told God that he believed that if he had been born different, better in some way, that none of this would've ever happened. As Amin lay sleep Capone prayed deeply, asking for forgiveness for all his sins, especially the murders.

From the minute he knelt down to his knees he felt as if he was doing the right thing. As he whispered aloud he began to feel a sense of hope replenishing him. He told God that if he could make all of this go away somehow, that he would make some significant changes in his life. When he was done, Capone felt as if a heavy weight had been lifted off of his shoulders. That night he slept better than he had in years.

****

Sergio had secured Capone's bail money and there was only one reason he wasn't out yet. Sergio wanted Capone's name clear of any involvement in what was about to go down. His alibi would be his brief stay in the county jail. Sergio had to question his own sanity with business being as good as it was; he was out trying to execute a murder he could've easily paid a soldier to do for peanuts. But for Sergio, this was way too important to put his trust in anyone but himself. There were too many lives at risk. His cell phone rang and he thought about ignoring it, but he knew Tamiko would only keep calling.

"Whassup bae?"

"Have you found her yet?"

"Who?"

"Charlotta with my damn car!"

"Oh, naw, I'm going to check for her in the hood as soon as I finish taking care of this business."

"Tell that bitch to bring me my car. She been gone all day and it's almost past her curfew."

Sergio looked at his watch and noticed that it was only 5:30 but it was almost nightfall. Just then he saw Randy and Dink pull into the gas station.

"I gotta go. I'll see you in a minute," he said ending the call with Tamiko.

Sergio hopped out of his Jaguar and pretended not to see them just as planned. Randy honked the horn on the stolen Chrysler LHS and Sergio turned and squinted his eyes peering inside the car. Randy rolled down the window and went straight into his rehearsed lines as if he was auditioning for a movie role.

"What up playboy? What you doing in these neck of the woods?"

"Oh shit, what up my nigga?" Sergio said in a surprised tone.

They slapped fives as if they'd been best friends forever.

"I got a weed house around here," Sergio continued. "I got ganz, rego, dro, quarters, halves, pounds, whatever a nigga need."

Randy's eyes lit up with false interest.

"You got a weed house around here? We was just about to go get some weed," he informed.

"Yeah, it's right down the street. I'll show it to you."

Instead of heading back to his car to lead the way, Sergio tapped on the back passenger window so he could be let inside the vehicle with Dink and Randy. Randy unlocked the doors and Sergio slid into the backseat right behind Dink who immediately grew nervous.

"Go straight up here and make a right," Sergio said.

"What's up Sergio?" Dink said curtly.

"What up Dink? Where you been at baby?"

"Chilling."

"Yeah, you been laying low. I ain't seen you in a minute."

"Yeah, I'm getting lazy man. I think I got some bitch pregnant," Dink said with a nervous giggle.

"Make a left up here."

They rode in silence for a while and Sergio stared at the back of Dink's head like it was a juicy hamburger. "What's up with your boy Dana?" he asked.

Dink paused before answering.

"I ain't seen him. I think he's out of town."

Sergio knew that was the wrong answer from Dink. The fact that he wouldn't acknowledge that Dana was on the run from the feds said it all. Randy wasn't playing hospitable anymore. He wore a face of stone as he glanced over at Dink. They hit a pothole that made everyone flinch at the sound of the car crashing deep into the pavement.

"Shit, I forgot all about that big ass pothole, my bad," Sergio said.

"Ain't shit," Randy replied.

Sergio looked at his watch. "So you say he out of town huh?"

"Yeah," Dink said as dry as possible.

Sergio looked at his watch again. It was 6:35 and his phone began to ring just like it was supposed to. On the other end was Charlotta pretending to be looking for Tamiko.

"I ain't seen her since this morning; I left out early," Sergio explained.

"You in the hood?" Charlotta asked.

"Naw, I'm at my new layout. I got the homies Dink and Randy with me."

On cue, Charlotta went into a rant about Dink and asked to speak with him. Dink declined, but Sergio insisted. By now, Dink could feel that something wasn't right. First, the questions about Dana and then Charlotta calls out of nowhere. Randy shut the music off so everyone could here whatever Charlotta was screaming into the phone.

"You a snitch bitch; I know you set me up!"

Click!

Dink quickly hung up the phone and handed it back to Sergio.

"Fuck her," he vented.

"What she say Dink?"

"Fuck Charlotta, she ain't talking about nothing."

When Dink realized he was now on a dead end street with almost no livable houses, he began to panic.

"I don't feel too good dog," Dink said as they pulled in front of a vacant house with all the windows boarded up. "I think I gotta throw up."

Dink tried to hit the automatic locks, but Randy quickly locked them back. Sergio grabbed Dink by the forehead and slammed the back of his neck against the headrest. At the same time his right hand swung around to Dink's throat as he sliced into his adam's-apple with a razor, slitting his throat from ear to ear. Dink's body slumped over into Randy's lap convulsing. Randy pulled away from the curb moving the car farther down the bend of the dead end street. Randy shoved Dink's still convulsing body to the floor as blood soaked his pants leg. He and Sergio hopped out of the car and Randy fired a couple of shots in Dink's skull to finish him off. Sergio stopped him after the second shot.

"Quiet remember?"

Randy nodded in agreement, but Sergio could tell his adrenaline was pumping. Sergio was glad to see he didn't have a fear of the moment that made some men freeze up. He knew he was gambling when he brought Randy along with him for such a high stakes situation, but he knew enough about the guy to make a solid judgment call. Dink laid motionless in the fetal position between the front driver and passenger side of the floor. Sergio popped the trunk and passed Randy a change of clothes. While Randy changed Sergio removed a small gasoline can from the trunk and began to pour gasoline on Dink and the car. He sat the can down and grabbed his own change of clothes and began to strip down.

When they were all done and all the bloody clothes were inside the stolen vehicle, Sergio poured the remainder of the gasoline inside the car and lit a match. Randy kicked the car door closed and they both fled as the fire spread amazingly fast. They had to walk several blocks to get back to the gas station Sergio was parked at. He took Randy home and was sure to drill him about what to say and what not to say if asked about Dink's whereabouts. He told Randy to call him in the morning and he'd toss him some change for his assistance.

****

The next morning Sergio woke up to the sound of his house phone ringing. It was Charlotta explaining that she'd made it home just before her curfew and didn't have time to drive to their house and then get dropped off back at home. Why she chose to wait until the next morning to call and explain that part was a mystery in itself. She asked

Sergio to relay her apology to Tamiko who was still sleeping, and tell her she was on her way with the car.

She had one last stop to make and that was to check on something concerning Dana, who she believed was back in town. Next, his pager went off and he remembered he was supposed to meet up with Randy in the hood. He jumped up and headed to the shower thinking about Dana. He wondered why he would come back if he had the feds looking for him. He knew Dana would never turn himself in and any reason he could think of to come back just seemed extremely stupid.

He hoped to get a call from Dana so they could have a one on one about what really transpired. After his shower, he got dressed and headed out without waking Tamiko. He knew once she woke, she would only start fussing about her car again. It was better for Charlotta to be the one to wake her up. On the freeway, Sergio called Randy and told him they could meet at Chocolate's house and gave him directions. He was starting to feel good about things again. Things could get back under control now that Dink was out of the way.

Now he could get Capone out of jail and get back to business. He started vibing to the beat and a freestyle came to him

"Snitches don't get stitches they die, niggas don't trust bitches they lie."

He thought he had enough skills to make an album one day if he really wanted to. He could call it Hood Chronicles or some shit like that. As he came up on the Charmers exit, he had to slow down to a snail's pace because of an accident on Harper and Charmers. Glass was all over the street and only one car at a time could get around it. When he arrived at Chocolate's house, Randy was already parked out front. He was surprised that Chocolate hadn't called him about the stranger parked out in front of her house.

"What up playboy?" Sergio greeted slapping fives.

"I'm chillen, what about you? You good?"

"Awe man, I never felt better," Sergio said smiling.

"Haha! I heard that."

Just then Chocolate snatched the door open and looked around outside suspiciously. Randy thought she looked mean.

"What's up baby? You missed me?" Sergio asked.

Chocolate gave him the middle finger and closed the door. He knew she was mad because it had been a while since he'd had sex with her. It was a big part of what kept her in line and when she wasn't getting it on a regular, she could be a bit more difficult to deal with. Sergio waved her off and went into the glove compartment of his Jaguar. He retrieved a white paper bag and handed it to Randy. A white BMW the spitting image of Tamiko's car bent the corner.

His first instinct was to hide, but then he remembered Charlotta had the car and it would've been impossible for Tamiko to get the car, drop off Charlotta, and make it to the hood that quick. It had to be Charlotta or a car that just happened to look exactly the same. As the car came cruising up the block, at no point did it appear that the driver had plans to stop or pull over. He knew Charlotta knew about Chocolate but she would never rat him out. As the car drove past he stood in shock of the blood splattered on the passenger side window. It was so much blood that he couldn't get a good look inside to see who was driving and if they were hurt.

Once the car passed, he glanced down at the license plate to make sure it wasn't Tamiko's car, but it was. His heart jumped into his throat as the car approached the corner and stopped at the stop sign. The passenger side door flew open and a body was shoved from the passenger side of the vehicle, crashing to the pavement violently.

By now Sergio had his gun out aimed at the car, but his eyes zoomed in on the stiff body lying in the street. He could easily make out that it was Charlotta. His mind went blank as he began firing shots at the BMW, but the driver quickly sped off. He continued to squeeze the trigger even though the car was out of sight. Randy jumped in his car and cranked the engine fast.

"'Bout to see if I can catch 'em," he said before speeding off.

Sergio ran down to the corner where Charlotta's body laid motionless. As he ran and got closer, he still couldn't believe his eyes; they had to be lying. As he slowly approached he could see at least one bullet hole in the side of her head. Once he was standing over her, he could now see the bullet hole in her forehead as well. He felt dizzy and the houses around him were spinning. He couldn't see straight as he knelt down over Charlotta's body babbling incoherently.

"I'm sorry I…what the fuuu… Charlotta! Charlotta!"

He tried to scoop her limp body from the ground but froze when he heard a familiar voice call out his name. He turned to see Chocolate running toward him with his AK-47 gripped tightly in her arms.

"Go put that up before the police show up! Somebody probably already called them."

He was back into the reality of the situation now. He realized he was holding a dead body in the middle of the street. As Chocolate ran back to the house, Randy pulled up to where Sergio was kneeled down over Charlotta's corpse.

"I couldn't catch that muthafucka! By the time I bent the first corner he was already gone."

"Just get out of here dog. I know police is on the way," he warned.

"You want me to call the ambulance?"

"Go knock on the door and tell Chocolate to call 'em."

Sergio knew the ambulance was just the next step in this process. Charlotta was already gone.

Chapter 24

Capone sat on his bunk with his feet hung over the side in Amin's face. They were kicking it about the future and how they were going to do things differently if given a second chance.

"Me, I'm going to fuck with my uncle when I get out. That nigga getting money," Amin said.

"Oh, fa real?"

"Hell yeah. He used to always tell me to stay away from them wild niggas I was running with. Now, look where I am because of one of them same niggas he warned me about."

"I hear you dog. When you see me out in them streets you'll see meet with one nigga and that's my brother. Other than that, I just be chillen with my girl, you know?"

"Yeah, but see the thing with me is, I need them niggas around to do what I was trying to do. Sometimes you need that united front, even if it's only a front. Like the way you be talking about your brother all the time. I'm sure he got a lot of soldiers around that just play that one position. Most of 'em probably don't know where that nigga live."

"Yeah, you right."

"See, most of the niggas I had around me was my soldiers in training. I knew half of them niggas wasn't cut from the same cloth as me, but I was trying to put them niggas on the payroll. I was trying to learn the game from my uncle and bring it back to the block and teach it to them. But everybody ain't soak it up the same, you feel me?"

Capone felt that Amin was a future boss. He had a lot of game about himself when he wasn't talking about something crazy and off the wall. The more Capone got to know him the more he came to like and respect him. Amin felt the same way about Capone but was still trying to feel him out. He wasn't big on trust and he was twice as skeptical towards people since his closest comrades had become MIA during his incarceration.

They sat quietly listening to the ruckus that had started in the dayroom. It sounded like Big Jake was trying to check somebody about turning the television.

"I hate that bitch ass nigga," Capone said.

When the mail came, Capone got letters from everyone. Randy, Tamiko, Chocolate, and of course Evelyn. Randy wrote just to tell Capone that if he wasn't out by the end of the week to put his name on the visitor's list and he would come and visit. He told Capone that not much had changed on the streets and not to stress about his situation. Tamiko and Chocolate sent cards with encouraging words and Tamiko put a hundred dollars of her own money in his account. He wondered to himself why she kept sending him money if he was supposed to be getting out.

Evelyn's letter was short and sweet with a poem attached. He checked the time by what was on television and figured Evelyn would be home by now. He wanted to hear her voice so he made his way to the phone while they were unoccupied.

"Aye homey," he heard a deep raspy voice call out.

He turned to see the so-called rock boss standing there.

"What's up?" Capone said.

"I was about to use that phone," Big Jake warned aggressively.

Capone knew that Big Jake had it in his mind that he ran the floor he happened to be stationed on. He thought quickly on how he should handle the situation. Technically, Big Jake was way out of line because there was another phone that wasn't being used at the time. On the other hand, Jake was 6'3 and 250 pounds.

"Shiiiid, it was open when I came over here though," Capone decided to say.

Big Jake stood there trying his best to look menacing. Capone never forgot what Sergio taught him about standing his ground the day he got his shoes took. He never forgot about Sergio scrapping it out with Melonhead and Nutty in a two on one. But more importantly, he had developed too much respect for himself to ever go backward.

"Say it again?" Big Jake asked if he didn't hear it correctly.

"I said wasn't nobody over here when I came to use it," Capone repeated.

They made fierce eye contact with each other for a few seconds then Capone turned and picked up the receiver preparing to dial out.

"I'ma let you slide this time young dog. Next time check with Big Jake to see if I'm floating around before you just hop on my phone. That's my phone I use," he explained.

Big Jake walked away after he felt he'd made his point. There were only two phones on the entire floor and Big Jake was claiming one of them. What he wanted to do was take the phone and bust Jake in the head with it, but he played it cool. He just knew, just like Jake knew, that people saw the exchange. It could have easily been avoided by Capone just choosing to use another phone, but that would've established him as weak. Big Jake never wanted or needed to use the phone. It was just one of the things he used to test people.

Since Capone refused to show weakness, he knew he had earned a measurable amount of respect from the other inmates. He grinned as he dialed Evelyn's number, knowing he would be tested again.

"Hello?" Evelyn answered sounding shaky.

"What's wrong with you?"

All the pain in her voice made every word shriek out barely comprehensible.

"Somebody killed Charlotta!" she cried.

She went into a wailing fit and Capone wondered did he hear her correctly. No way, he thought.

"What did you just say?"

"Charlotta is dead! Somebody killed her," she managed in between sobs.

Capone snatched the phone from his ear as he began to tear up almost instantly. He could still hear Evelyn boohooing through the speaker. He closed his eyes, took a deep breath, and swallowed hard. He was trying to keep his composure. At this very moment, he was close to losing control.

Capone knew falling apart in this environment was bad for one's health. He also knew falling apart would only increase the pain in his heart. He picked the phone back up and listened for Evelyn. She had gained control of herself and reduced her sobbing to light sniffles. He was in no mood to console her. He was just as hurt if not more.

"Tell me what happened."

"I don't know what happened."

"How did you find out?"

"It was on the news and then a girl from school called and told me."

"And what did she say?"

"All she knew was it happened on Spring Garden."

Spring Garden raised Capone's antennas because it was the street Chocolate lived on and he knew how much time Sergio spent on that block. But he couldn't figure out why Charlotta would be there if that's where she was found.

"I don't know if it's true but I also heard she was driving Tamiko's car when it happened. I haven't talked to her myself."

Just hearing Tamiko's name made Capone's soul cry inside just knowing the pain she was feeling at the moment. The two of them were like sisters.

"Who would want to kill Charlotta?" Evelyn asked.

"I don't even know. Nobody that I could think of, but you know she was out there in them streets fucking with some of everybody."

Capone and Evelyn were sensing the same thing but neither of them would say it. They were both thinking this might've had more to do with Sergio than Charlotta. They both held the phone in silence until the automated voice told them they only had a minute left.

"Call me back," Evelyn said.

"I can't talk right now."

"Call me back, Capone!"

"I'll call you later," he replied hanging up.

The next day, Evelyn came to visit Capone and he was cold and distant. She knew that Capone still had love in his heart for Charlotta because she was the only other girl he'd ever cared about. With she didn't know was that with Charlotta being so close to his inner circle, it was almost like losing a family member instead of an ex-girlfriend. Evelyn had been trying to muster up the strength to call some of Charlotta's family members, but like Capone, she wasn't up to it yet.

As she drove home, her somber mood was made even darker as she pulled over to let a speeding ambulance by. As the deafening sirens echoed into silence, she thought hard about the possibility that the ambulance was on the way to another Detroit homicide. Another life cut short in its prime due to senseless violence. She wondered how she ever let herself get mixed up with a guy like Capone. She thought about Dink who had just recently passed away and she had to just breathe deep.

She thought about all the people from her neighborhood that were in jail for murder and never coming home. She drove down Seven Mile glancing at the liquor stores that she'd watched alcoholics grow old and sickly standing in front of day after day and year after year. In a sense, she was starting to question if all of her focus on college and her future was all in vain. Maybe she'd never make it out of the hood either.

Maybe she'd just wake up on one day, walk outside, and die. Her mother had been to college, yet and still, it didn't allow her to live in an area that was free of crack houses and the threat of constant danger.

When Evelyn got home, she was glad no one was there because she had an enormous desire to be left alone. She strolled into the kitchen and slid a box of Pop Tarts off the shelf. She cut the ringer off on her phone and started chewing slowly, staring at the wall. At times like these, she had to write. It was the only thing that brought her clarity and peace of mind.

As thoughts came to her she stopped in mid-chew and went over to her desk to grab a pen and pad. As soon as she sat down, her thoughts spilled out on the paper.

Where I'm From: By Evelyn Hardy

Where I'm from, dreams are for dreamers and hope is almost always destroyed. Visionaries don't exist because visions are overshadowed by the need for instant gratification. Piss infested alleys, condemned buildings, and abandoned homes that all tell a similar tell. Right here lived a couple that dared to dream, but years later they too would succumb to all the evil of their environment. Around every corner is bad intentions. Every do right family filled with heartache and let down, while every do wrong family fills their homes with gifts. The eviction notice is surely on the way, where I'm from. Crime does pay where I'm from. The churches are empty but the liquor stores are packed with middle aged men baring pink lips and bloodshot eyes. Women with brown teeth and matted hair. You stink!

This whole place stinks, but all we need is to numb the pain one more day and then we'll get our shit together. Yeah right. All these sirens sounding and gunshots outside my window. Unpaid bills fill the garbage and only ice cold water resting in the refrigerator. Who am I to judge?

How dare you judge her for selling her body. How dare you judge him for renting it. Or him for selling poison to his people or them for purchasing it. Where the fuck are you from? Clearly not here and you say "no." Is everything really so black and white or can there be shades of gray? And is the grass really greener on the other side or are the weeds just hidden behind the picket fence? Is it really only predator and prey? Kill or be killed. The only thing I know for certain is that I will surely repeat the process if I do not dare to dream, starting right where I'm from.

Evelyn never really understood what triggered her to write the things she wrote. When things came over her she wrote them down. She read and re-read her work, not really understanding how she could write so passionately about a life not her own. Evelyn had been sheltered from the worst that Detroit had to offer. Her neighborhood wasn't the best or the worst, and she'd heard about a lot more than she had experienced firsthand. She was wise beyond her seventeen years and her surroundings were nurturing her poetic outlet and shoving her into adulthood at the same time.

The days leading up to Charlotta's funeral were rough on everyone that loved and knew her, but nobody took it worse than Tamiko, not even her own mother. Sergio was still blaming himself and Tamiko was just numb. Sergio remembered the last thing Charlotta had to say to him was that she was on her way to see Dana. He knew Dana was responsible for her death and he vowed that when he caught up with him, it would be the slowest, most painful death imaginable. There was no doubt in his mind who had killed Charlotta.

When questioned by the police about Charlotta's death, Sergio gave them nothing. This was something he needed to handle himself. As Sergio sprang from his long, hot shower, he heard Tamiko's voice on the phone.

"Okay, thank you," she said right before hanging up.

"Who was that?" he asked entering the room.

"That was the police telling me they found my car," she informed.

"Where at?"

"It was in a garage on Fairport and Gratiot. Somebody set the car and the garage on fire."

"When did they find it?"

"They say the fire was set last night about three in the morning."

Sergio finished putting lotion on his arms and legs then took a seat next to Tamiko.

"You okay?" he asked.

She sighed. "I'm better."

"You think you gonna be able to do this funeral tomorrow?"

"I have to. I don't really have a choice. Nobody in my family would understand if I didn't show up. Nobody knows what I'm going through, not even you."

He took a look at his girl laying there in deep thought, wishing he could do or say something to make her feel better. He got up and started to get dressed because he knew there was no use in trying.

"I love you," Sergio said as he planted a kiss on her forehead and one on her lips.

"I love you too," Tamiko returned as she watched him grab the keys to his rental car and get ready to head out.

Sergio knew she would probably start crying again the minute he left but he also knew she needed to be left alone. This was the first time Sergio had ever seen Tamiko this vulnerable and vice versa. Inside the rental car, he lit the cigarette he'd been thinking about the whole morning. He was trying to quit but decided right now wasn't a good time. Last night he was up all night trying to decide if he wanted to bail Capone out of jail or not.

He wanted to wait because of everything that was going on. Protecting the people he cared about was all that mattered now and with so many enemies, Sergio just didn't think putting Capone back on the streets now was a good idea. He knew if Capone got out today he would more than likely try and take matters into his own hands. Not only was

Dana a threat to all involved but Melonhead was still lurking around in the city somewhere. His mind was somewhere else when he pulled out of the driveway and he almost backed into an oncoming car. The driver banged the horn angrily to get Sergio's attention. Sergio shook his head and threw up an apologetic hand.

He drove down the street still going back and forth about whether to get Capone out of jail or not. Since he had to go downtown anyway to find something to wear to the funeral, he decided he'd stop and visit Capone just to see where his head was at. He would explain to him how important it was to keep a cool head once released. This case Capone was fighting was very serious and he couldn't afford to add to his troubles. Before heading downtown, Sergio stopped to pick up some money from Tre and Black, who now ran his weight houses on the east side.

He had six bulky bankrolls in his pockets and he considered taking some of the money to Chocolate's house instead of riding downtown with it. Just then he remembered he still had to pick up money on the westside so he decided to wait. He made it downtown a little after one o'clock and his first stop was an upscale clothing store called The Broadway. He'd decided to wear a suit to the funeral and The Broadway was known for the flyest tailor made pieces in the city at the time. After leaving The Broadway, he hit up City Boys to find a new pair of gators to match the suit.

They loved Sergio at City Boys and sometimes the manager would call Sergio when they got a fresh new selection of gators in. As soon as he stepped into the store, he spotted the shoes he wanted; ostrich and gator mixed with a tennis shoe grip. It came in three colors: crimson, teal, and light gray. As he joked and laughed with the sales clerk it took his mind off of his woes for a minute. Although his suit was gray he bought all the new flavors of gators and left his new cell number to give to the manager who wasn't around at the time.

"Tell that nigga I came through," Sergio said as he slapped fives with the sale clerk and headed for the exit.

There was a dude in a three piece suit Sergio hadn't paid much attention to until now. The dude had come in behind Sergio and now he was leaving out behind him. Sergio was fully conscious of the man's presence as he made his way to the rental car parked out front.

"Aye my man," Sergio heard a voice call out to him.

As he turned to acknowledge the stranger Sergio slipped his hand in his waist to reach for his weapon. He turned to see the man stalking towards him with his pistol already out, pointed directly at Sergio's chest. Sergio knew he was about to die but he refused to go out without a fight. As he tried to pull the gun from his waistline, the man fired shots into his stomach. Sergio stumbled a few steps and then crashed to the ground as his pistol went flying and flipping on the concrete.

As he lay on his back staring his killer in the eye, all he could think about was if it was his time he wasn't afraid. The gunman raised his pistol and aimed at Sergio's head this time.

"Bitch ass nigga," were the final three words Sergio managed before taking a final shot to the head.

The killer quickly fled the scene in a black Mercedes and seconds later a homeless man came along and grabbed Sergio's City Boy shopping bag off the ground. Within minutes, the police were all over the scene trying to move back the crowd quickly gathering outside of the store. It wasn't much later when an ambulance arrived on the scene, but it was too late. Sergio had died at the young age of twenty-two years old.

Chapter 25

Sergio's death was all over the five o' clock news but because Capone had been in court all day he was going through the long, tedious process of trying to make it back to his cell. This was his third preliminary hearing and the prosecutor still didn't have the missing statements that were supposed to be a part of his discovery package. Dominique moved for a dismissal but the prosecutor gave the judge an excuse about someone being on vacation and the judge allowed him another two weeks. Capone got back to his cell feeling starved since he hadn't eaten since the bologna sandwiches he had around noon.

He noticed Amin seemed anxious.

"Aye, I need to holla at you," Amin said.

All Capone could think about was the dinner cart bending the corner.

"Let me get something on my stomach first," Capone said, thinking Amin probably wanted to discuss his girl problems or something of that nature.

Capone walked away from him and headed towards the dayroom trying to be the first in line after he spotted the two trustees setting up dinner to serve. Capone grabbed his tray and took a seat in the dayroom right in front of the television. Amin pulled up right behind him.

"You want this shit?" Amin asked offering Capone his tray.

"Hell yeah, I ain't ate shit all day," Capone explained with his eyes bucked.

"I can't eat tuna fish. I'll throw up," Amin said.

Capone looked at him with a skeptical eye. To let Amin tell it, he couldn't eat any fish, fruits, or vegetables without hurling. Capone wondered how he was still alive but couldn't care less at the moment, just as long as he was handing over the tuna fish. Once Capone cleared the contents of Amin's tray on to his, he then changed the channel to check the six o' clock news. Big Jake had some choice words for Capone about changing the channel, but Capone just stared him down and turned his attention back to the news.

He knew Big Jake was an old head set in his ways so there wouldn't be much he could say to shut him up. Amin watched Capone closely as the story he'd saw on breaking news earlier was revisited. The street reporter stood out in front of the shoe store giving his account of what happened in dramatic fashion.

"This was a shocking and brazen homicide that took place right around the corner from police headquarters, with literally dozens of police officers swarming downtown. I can't...I don't understand how this could happen. But once again for our viewers who have just tuned in, a twenty-two-year-old man, who had been identified as Sergio Robinson, gunned down after leaving this very popular shoe store. He was rushed to the hospital but had already passed away upon arrival. Police say they have no motive or suspects at this time and they're asking the citizens to call if they have any information; as always you can remain anonymous."

By now the whole room was spinning around Capone's head and his blood was boiling to the point he thought he would throw up or pass out in a second. Amin's head dropped as his suspicions were confirmed. He knew by the look in Capone's eyes that it was his people who'd just been murdered.

"What the fuck!? What the fuck!?"

Capone slapped both of the trays in front of him off the table and the other inmates had to duck to keep from getting hit before they went crashing to the floor. Capone stormed over to the phone, not thinking clear enough to know who exactly he was about to call. He kept telling himself it wasn't true, but he knew it was. Someone had taken away his brother and his best friend. His hands shook uncontrollably as he dialed Evelyn's number. It seemed like the longest two minutes of his life as he waited for the automated system to connect him. Please try your call again later.

He slammed the phone down and picked it right back up to call Evelyn again. No answer. He tried Tamiko. No answer. He tried his mom, hoping she'd made it home from work. Nothing. He continued to tell himself, there was no way it was Sergio. He ran his fingers through his braids, pacing, on the verge of a breakdown. Inmates watched Capone from a distance, judging his body language and facial expression, putting the puzzle together for themselves.

Capone began to bang the phone against the receiver as hard as he could. He was trying to get the pain out any way he could. Amin was slow to approach as he made his way over to commiserate with him.

"Dog, I know you fucked up right now, but you gotta try to calm down before you be in the hole. If you go to the hole you won't be able to find out nothing," he warned.

Capone leaned against the wall and began to shed tears rapidly until he was interrupted by a raspy voice.

"I can't let you break my phone lil' nigga. I know you upset about some shit but I can't let you break my phone," Big Jake complained.

"What? Man fuck you; you betta get the fuck out my face with that shit," Capone lashed.

Capone wiped his tears away as his hurt turned to anger then rage.

"Oh fuck me? Fuck me lil' nigga?" Big Jake said approaching.

Capone didn't wait for him to make a move. With all the strength he had in him, Capone cocked back and punched Big Jake in the mouth. The punch stunned Big Jake and before he could respond Amin had socked him again before they both went into all-out attack mode like animals in the wilderness. They attacked so hard and fast Big Jake tried to back up and swing but lost his footing. As he went to the ground, no one called for CO's to come and stop the fight. Big Jake took a serious beating for a solid two minutes and when they finally let up, he had no choice but to surrender with a closed eye and swollen lip.

Capone really needed to let off some steam in that moment and he was just glad to have found a willing target. The other inmates stared in shock as the rock boss took his first L, walking away as some yelled out the CO's were coming. Everyone involved scurried off to their cells and pretended like the incident never happened.

****

The next day Capone got a visit from Randy. Capone's eyes were puffy from having cried a million tears the night before. Randy knew there wasn't much he could say, but he wanted to check on his friend anyway.

"Sup?" Randy said.

"Sup?" Capone responded.

"By the look on your face, I know you already heard."

"Yeah…what the streets saying though?"

"The streets ain't saying nothing, but from the last conversation I had with Sergio, I'm guessing it's the same reason Charlotta is gone."

Capone sighed and put his head down. He had a migraine headache and he knew it was either from lack of sleep or food, possibly both. He lifted his head up.

"You heard about Tamiko?" Randy asked.

Capone just stared at Randy with a blank look on his face. He didn't know what Randy was talking about, but he didn't think he wanted to know with the expression on Randy's face.

"What's wrong with Tamiko?" he decided to ask.

"She's in the hospital. When she heard about Sergio she had a nervous breakdown or something. You know she really fucked up right now, just like I know you is. I know Charlotta was your peoples and I know Sergio was like a brother."

Capone had tuned Randy out and could no longer hear the words, just noise in the faded background as he sat speechless on the verge of breaking down himself. Once again he had to end a visit before his time was up because he couldn't stand to sit and listen any longer.

"I appreciate you coming down but I gotta go cuz." Capone stood.

"Yeah, I know, but stay strong in here. You still got one manz out here if you don't got shit else," Randy assured him.

It was crazy how the two of them came to build such a strong bond, being that they'd got off to such a rotten start. But what was understood didn't need to be explained. Capone pounded his chest twice as he made his exit.

"One," Randy said as he returned the gesture.

"One."

****

When Evelyn found out that Tamiko was in the hospital, she told herself that she had to get down there to see her. She had to wait until the weekend because she got off work after visiting hours. Saturday morning she went to check on Tamiko. When she walked in the room Tamiko was sitting upright whiping yogurt from her johnny. She was startled when she spotted Evelyn in the doorway.

"Oooh shit, you scared me."

"Sorry," Evelyn said as she moved in for a hug with her arms extended wide.

Their embrace was long and tight. Evelyn could tell that Tamiko was happy she'd come to visit. There were lots of flowers from previous visitors.

"How you doing?" Evelyn asked.

"I'm okay now, but they don't wanna let me go. They keep giving me all these tests and shit like they really think I'm crazy. I've explained to them I just lost the two people in the world that meant the most to me. What the fuck did you expect?"

"They're just trying to help you get better."

"Anyway, how was Charlotta's funeral?" she asked since she was in the hospital the day of.

"It was beautiful, it really was. Your aunt gave a wonderful speech too. She had all these funny stories and it just reminded everybody of how fun it was to be around her, and she just had a way about herself that made it hard to stay mad at her."

Tears swelled in Evelyn's eyes at the thought of Charlotta really being gone forever.

"That was Charlotta," Tamiko added.

"Exactly, that was her. And when I went home it just made me think about her life and all the times we shared. I know the best way for me to get through it personally is to just focus on the good times."

When she finished Tamiko was smiling. It was the first time she'd smiled in days, but she was busy reminiscing on all the good times her and Charlotta shared. They had been through so much to be so young. It wasn't really until then that Tamiko realized not only was Charlotta her favorite cousin, she was also her best friend. The one person she could tell anything and the only female that always had her back.

"I'ma really miss that crazy bitch," Tamiko said still smiling.

"Yeah, I'm gon' miss her crazy ass too," Evelyn giggled. "You remember the time she beat up that lady security guard for accusing her of stealing at Toys R' Us?"

"Hell yeah, and I had to drive out of the parking lot with her laid down in the backseat so we didn't go to jail."

"Right! I was so mad at her. I was like Charlotta you make me sick. I didn't even get a chance to shop. I'm not fucking with you at the mall nooooo more!"

They shared a long, much-needed laugh and then Tamiko's face turned cold.

"I'm glad you here because I need to talk to you about something."

The furrow on Tamiko's forehead made Evelyn anxious and curious. "What is it?"

"Sergio had a lot of money put away that I never asked about because I never had to. I just always knew there was a lot more money than what we kept around the house. Well, yesterday I got a call from Sergio's dad and he told me that he has this money that he was told to give to me if something ever happened. There's a hundred and fifty thousand at his dad's house. I also know he had money at his mom's house and money in the streets but whatever is at his mom's house is hers to keep. The money in the streets is not theirs to keep, but the only person that can really collect it is Capone. We need to get him out of there as soon as possible."

"What do you need me to do?"

"I need you to get the money from Sergio's father so we can get Capone back on the streets where he needs to be. This can't happen like this."

Evelyn thought about the last statement Tamiko made. She quickly realized that Tamiko was looking for revenge, but who could blame her. There was only one person that would lay it all on the line to make sure justice was done. Evelyn was caught between a rock and a hard place. As much as she wanted Capone out of jail, she knew it could turn into more tragedy for all involved. It could mean more trouble with the law for Capone, and even worse, his freedom could be his demise.

But how could she look Tamiko in the eyes and explain her hesitation? She couldn't, so she made her decision and was ready to live with it.

"What do I do after I get the money?"

"Hand me a pen and my purse," Tamiko said as she pointed at the nightstand.

She withdrew a folded sheet of paper and a business card from her purse then copied the information on a separate sheet of paper. "This is

Sergio's dad, and this is the lawyer Dominique's number if you don't already have it. I'm gonna call his dad and let him know you're coming by to pick the money up. Then I need you to go to my house and get this money out of the safe."

"You want me to go to your house?"

"You're the only one I can trust to do this Ev. I'm gonna give you the keys and the combination to the safe. I need you to count all the money from the safe and the money from his dad, then call me and tell me what's what."

Evelyn was silent for a moment, feeling a little overwhelmed with responsibility.

"What's wrong?" Tamiko asked.

"Okay, I don't know if I feel comfortable going roaming around your house, especially not in no safe."

"Listen to you. That's why you're the only person I trust to do this. Who else would say some shit like that? I been knowing you since you were six years old Ev, and you're not a thief." She giggled.

"I know, it's just…"

"Come on Ev, do you want your man home or not?"

Evelyn sat in the chair next to the bed twirling her hair and feeling like she had no real say so in the matter. Tamiko fumbled through her purse for the keys.

"Here." She handed them over and Evelyn reluctantly took them. She stood to leave.

"What's the phone number to this room so I can call you tonight?"

"Give me the paper back."

Tamiko wrote down the room number and handed the paper back to her.

"I'm gonna need directions to your house."

"Okay, just call me, and I'll give you the combination to the safe once you're there."

"So how long you think you gonna be here?"

"They said a couple more days. I'll be home for Sergio's funeral."

Evelyn gave her another hug and headed for the door.

"Evelyn," Tamiko called out.

"Yeah?"

"You know this is how they both would want it, Charlotta and Sergio."

Evelyn knew she was referring to what was probably gonna happen once Capone got out. She couldn't think about that part and she couldn't make eye contact with Tamiko as she left the room.

"Yeah…I know," she said walking out.

****

As soon as she got home and put a bite to eat on her stomach, Evelyn made the call.

"Hello, how are you today sir?"

"I'm fine and you?"

"I'm fine too sir. My name is Evelyn and I'm a friend of Tamiko's. I'm sorry for your loss."

"Well, I appreciate you saying that, but my son lived and died the way he wanted to. It didn't make me love him any less, but he made his bed and now he has to lie in it."

Evelyn thought his response was a little cold but it wasn't for her to judge.

"Yes, I understand. I'm calling about some money you have for Tamiko. Did she call you about me?"

"Um, yeah, I've been expecting your call. You're coming by to pick it up right?"

"Yes, is it a good time for you?"

"Good as any."

"Okay, I just need the address and I'll be on my way."

As he called out the address she quickly jotted it down, said her goodbye, and headed out. The post-obit Evelyn seemed to be totally out of her element. In her life after death, she'd found all of her writing to be explicit and gloomy. Right now she was on her way to pick up drug money to bond her murderous boyfriend out of jail. It all began to weight heavy on her heart and she prayed for forgiveness as she drove.

****

Capone and Amin were closing in on fifteen hundred pushups.

"Come on man, let's go! All the way down," Amin ordered as he stood over Capone, whose body was dripping sweat.

"Forty-eight, forty-nine, fifty," Capone groaned and staggered to his feet, chest heaving and muscles extra tight.

"Feeling any better?" Amin asked.

"Hell naw!"

"Come on let's do some more then."

"Naw, I'm done."

"You gotta work that shit out dog. You can't let that stress and anger build up in you."

The truth was, the working out did alleviate some of the stress and anger that was building up in Capone, but he didn't want to admit it. He didn't feel like feeling better. It didn't make sense to try and feel better. He wanted to stay angry and one track minded.

****

Evelyn turned the key in the door and walked straight then turned left as directed. In the kitchen, she found the alarm system and punched in the code. Upstairs she fumbled around a bit before she found the dimmer knob at the front corridor. She stood at the portal of the master bedroom admiring the king size bed and satin sheets. On her way to the closet she was distracted again by Tamiko's massive perfume collection. Most of the bottles aligned along the mahogany dresser looked unused or rarely worn. She sprayed the Chanel in the air out of curiosity and

238

then got back to the task at hand. She called Tamiko at the hospital so she could get the combination to the safe.

Tamiko stayed on the phone while Evelyn removed the rug from the closet that revealed the floor safe. She carefully spun the knob on the safe making sure she stopped directly on each number. She heard the click and pulled the handle gently as the safe came open to reveal big wads of money wrapped in brown rubber bands. She told Tamiko she was in and agreed to call her when she was done counting it all. She grabbed an empty shopping bag and began to load all the stacks of cash in the bag.

Also inside the safe, she found a gold Cuban link chain with a diamond encrusted S and a bunch of naked pictured of Tamiko and Sergio in an unsealed envelope. After she was done she dumped all the money on the bed and took off all the rubber bands. She spent the next hour and a half counting and recounting the money. Fives, tens, fifties, and hundred dollar bills. Seventy-five thousand in all.

"Jesus!" she said massaging the soreness from her neck brought on by her sitting position.

By the time she finished counting the money she was tired and wanted a drink. She went downstairs and found the bar stocked with liquor. She grabbed the Alize knowing she couldn't handle anything stronger. She went to the kitchen and added a few ice cubes from the ice maker then took a seat in the living room. She relaxed in front of the big screen and took a time out before she called Tamiko back. She sat and watched The Cosby Show, sipping her drink until she began to doze off.

She was supposed to call Tamiko back but she didn't. She was supposed to call her mother to let her know where she was, but she didn't do that either. She fought off dream-land as long as she could but it was calling her name. She crashed right on the couch, knowing she'd have some explaining to do in the morning.

Chapter 26

"Man, don't you know Napolean introduced cannabis to the Europeans in the early eighteen hundreds?" Amin said in a matter of fact tone.

Capone gave him a cynical look.

"You got too much time on your hands dog."

"Hey, fuck you, reading is fundamental. I'm just saying if people was getting high two hundred years ago, what're the chances they gonna stop anytime soon?"

Capone was wondering how this conversation got into left field.

"I didn't say everybody was gonna stop. I said I'm gonna stop."

"No, you not. You not gon' stop," Amin challenged.

"How the hell you know?"

"Yeah, you'll stop when you change your lifestyle. But as long as you're knee deep in them streets, you gonna always be looking for that stress release. Now, if you would've never started drinking and smoking like my uncle, then you wouldn't have that dependency and the lifestyle wouldn't matter. But now, it's all become a part of the devil's system he uses to trap you and keep you from focusing on what's real."

Capone didn't feel like hearing Amin's shit today. He had too much on his mind. But he kept listening so he wouldn't have to think about all the things running through his head at the moment.

"So let me ask you this; if the weed is all a part of the devil's plan then why you fall into the trap every chance you get?"

"That's simple. I haven't decided to stand and fight that battle yet."

"Why not?"

"Because I haven't decided to change my lifestyle."

"So when do you think you'll be ready to stand up and fight?" Capone asked sarcastically.

He felt like Amin was so full of it right now he might as well feed into it with strong doubt and disapproval.

"I don't know; when the time comes I guess. You ever heard of the saying 'do as I say and not as I do'?"

"Yeah, so what?"

"Well, all it means is just because people don't always make the right choices don't mean they don't know what the right choice is."

They were both lying flat on their backs, legs crossed with their hands tucked behind their heads. The only difference was Capone was staring at the top of a double bunk and Amin was staring at the ceiling. After the incident with Big Jake, they both just decided to stay in their room and avoid conflict. Capone held no fear in his heart; only repressed anger and rage.

"When you pray five times a day, what do you pray for?" Capone asked.

"That's not for me. That's just me thanking Allah for my life and all the blessings along the way."

Capone wasn't a fan of God at all. The minute he decided to get down on his knees and pray, things got worse, ten times worse.

"I don't know man, sometimes I don't believe it is a God."

"Why you say that?"

"Shit, if it is, he must not care about me too much. Seems like he trying to take everything I care about away."

Amin let the thought settle for a brief moment before responding. He didn't want to seem insensitive to Capone's trials.

"I don't think that's the case, man."

"You don't understand. I only had one real nigga out here."

Amin could hear the pain in his voice. He understood Capone's loss but felt as if he was confused as to who was to blame.

"I know you told me a lot about Sergio…and Charlotta. And I don't wanna sound judgmental, 'cause you know I'm the last nigga to do that. But it don't sound like either one of them was living their lives in tune with the will of Allah. That means there could be a dozen reasons why their time was up. Honestly, for you to even think that Allah would be out to harm you on purpose is like a selfish thought."

Capone could see where the conversation was headed and he didn't want to continue it any longer. He got up and went into his locker then roamed through his mailbag until he came across the unopened letter from Charlotta. He never had the courage to open it until now. These were the last words she ever said to him and he never got a chance to respond. He sat down at the desk preparing to read the letter as if she was still with him.

"I just wanna put one more jewel in your head that my uncle told me," Amin interrupted.

"What's that?"

"How you react to a situation is more important than the situation itself."

Capone was so close to telling Amin to please shut the fuck up, but he knew his new-found friend was only trying to help.

"I feel you. Let me read this letter."

Dear Capone,

I hope this letter finds you holding up like the G I know you to be. In case you haven't heard, I'm out on a personal bond. The feds put a tether on my leg and I gotta go back to court in a few weeks. Sergio kept it real with me; he said I may have to do a little time but if I do I'll be straight while I'm gone and even straighter when I get out. You gotta take the good with the bad I guess. Just know this, they can't keep a real one down, so if you know this like I know, you'll be just fine.

I hate we got interrupted before I got a chance to put that thang on you foreal-foreal. But I been thinking, Evelyn is still my girl and even though you were mine first I think we need to stop that. It's just too shady. But then again, I don't know if I could ever resist you. Anyway, I believe you gonna come out of this a better person and if you have to go away we'll get through it together.

I was about to send you some money but Sergio and Charlotta both said they were sending you some so I decided to be the selfish bitch that I am and buy some shoes instead. I'm just playing. If you need anything let me know; I got you. Keep your head up and stay down.

Forever yours,

Charlotta

Capone stared at the letter intensely for all of sixty seconds. Amin thought he looked hypnotized. He couldn't explain to anybody what Charlotta was to him. She wasn't exactly a friend because she had done him wrong too many times. She wasn't exactly family because their sexual spark was still alive until her dying day. She was someone on the inside of his very tight circle and he now knew just how much he cared about her. He re-read the letter twice before putting it down.

"Damn," he said aloud.

"What's wrong bro?"

"I gotta get the fuck out of here."

All Capone could think about was payback. People had to pay dearly.

"I feel you dog. I'm just hoping they came come up with the surveillance tape from that gas station so I can prove to these crackers that I didn't take that car. That's all I…"

"Johnson?" a voice interrupted as a burly, bald dude stepped in front of the cell.

"What's up?" Capone said.

"Pack up, you made bail."

"Huh?" Capone wasn't sure he'd heard correctly.

"You heard me. Pack up," the deputy said.

"Get the fuck outta here," Amin said smiling, but shocked.

"I told you I was gon' bond out of this bitch."

"You got a bond reduction or something?"

"Hell naw, it was still a hundred thousand when I went to court."

Capone jumped up and began scurrying around as fast as he could. For the first time he felt a glimpse of hope. If he could've had one prayer in his whole life answered, it would've been this. He didn't know what his next move was but as long as it was out on the streets, he was ready.

"Aye write all your info down with a contact number so I can holla at you," Capone said to Amin who was already searching for a pen.

"Yeah, give me a number for you too so I can holla if something pop for me."

"I'll have to shoot you a number after I get out and get a new cell phone."

"Okay."

Capone tossed all his mail and legal paperwork in a brown paper bag and left everything else. He slapped fives with Amin and followed the deputy to the elevator. Capone met Dominique standing in the lobby looking in a rush as usual. She waved him over and gave him a quick hug. Evelyn, who was standing by, saw the embrace and didn't think it was really necessary.

"I'm glad you're out but listen, I've got a million things to do so Evelyn is gonna take you home and I need you to call me first thing in the morning."

"Okay," was all Capone could get out before his lawyer shot off.

Evelyn was headed towards him wearing a weak smile. He was expecting a lot more emotion from her.

"What's wrong with you? You don't look happy to see me."

"Boy shut up, I'm just tired," she said giving him a hug.

"Yeah, you look tired."

"You know how long I been down here sitting?"

"No."

"Six hours."

"Six hours?"

"Yeah, Dominique left twice and came back after shift change. Then they got you mixed up with another inmate with the same last name. It's just been a long day, let's go."

They walked through the revolving doors to freedom and Capone took in all the free air he could. He looked around at all the Wayne County deputies and Hall of Justice workers scampering by in their suits and uniforms.

"Your mom don't know you're out yet. I figured it would be a nice surprise plus I didn't want to say anything until I was sure you were getting out."

"She gonna be real surprised because I never told her I had a chance of getting out. Wait 'til she see me; she gon' be like what the hell?"

"Come on I parked over here."

The ride home was bittersweet for Evelyn. She was so glad to have Capone home with her but she had things on her mind that had to be discussed, things that she wasn't sure Capone would want to talk about. So much had happened in the last few weeks alone she could only imagine his mind state. She didn't want to lose him to the streets but felt there was very little she could say that would change his mind about his intentions. Nothing had really changed and just like before, she would have to enjoy the time they had together. She promised herself when the time was right she would say what she had to say.

They arrived at Capone's mother's house after a short, silent ride from the county.

"Oh my goodness!" Capone's mother squealed as she stood in the doorway in total disbelief.

"Hey Mama."

"When did you get out son?"

"Just now, we came straight here."

His mother hugged him so tightly they both stumbled over the threshold leading inside the house.

"But I thought your bond was a hundred thousand dollars?"

"It was," Capone replied holding the door open now for Evelyn.

"Tamiko put up the money," Evelyn explained.

"Where did she get that kind of money?"

"Sergio."

"Just like that huh?" Ms. Johnson said still staring at Capone.

"Where is Tamiko now?" Capone asked.

"She's still in the hospital. I'll take you to see her when you're ready."

"I'm ready now; just let me jump in the shower."

He took the bag with the new clothes and shoes Evelyn had bought for him and headed up the stairs. In his old room, everything was exactly the way he left it. He got nostalgic remembering how everything got started in that room. He never could've imagined how his life would change so fast. He shook it off before he started to get sidetracked. It was shower time and then he had to get to Tamiko.

****

Capone and Evelyn strolled in and Tamiko immediately opened her eyes as if she sensed their presence. A big smile spread across her face when she saw Capone closing in on her holding a bouquet of flowers. He sat the flowers on the nightstand and gave her a long hug.

"How you feeling?" Capone asked.

"Hostile, vicious, bitter," she admitted.

"Me too, but this shit ain't over."

"Evelyn, can you excuse us for a minute?" Tamiko asked.

She wasn't about to take any chances talking reckless around Evelyn. She trusted Capone with her life, but she knew Evelyn wasn't built like them, and she never pretended to be. Evelyn was more than happy to leave and actually glad she didn't have to hear anything she didn't want to hear. She figured the less she knew, the better. Tamiko shifted in the bed and stroked the hair from her face.

"Listen, you and I both know there are only two people who could've been responsible for this shit and that's Dana and or Melonhead. The one thing I know about the whole Melonhead situation is that he had gone into hiding. I don't even know what that whole beef was about, and I don't give a fuck what it was about. But I do know what the beef with Dana was about because I was right there when Sergio got the call from Dana."

"What he say?" Capone asked.

"Some bullshit about y'all was supposed to be snitching to the feds."

"What?" Capone said appalled.

"I know, like what the fuck is you talking about? I know my nigga was one hundred."

"Sergio told you that?"

"I was right there when them niggas was arguing on the phone. But then Sergio and Randy figured out that somebody was snitching and Sergio wanted to get the message to Dana about who it was. The next thing I know…" Her voice began to betray her as she thought about how graphic the scene of her cousin's murder must have been. She took her time. "The next thing I know, Sergio comes home and tells me somebody drove down the street and shoved my little cousin out of the passenger seat of my car with bullet holes in her head."

Capone took in what he was hearing, trying to make sense of it all.

"So, Charlotta was supposed to be delivering the message or something?" he asked trying to figure things out.

"I guess so. Sergio didn't really talk to me about shit after Charlotta died. He felt like it was his fault."

"Maybe Dana didn't believe Charlotta's story and thought it was a setup," Capone suggested.

"Dana is fucking crazy! Who knows why he does the shit he does? He could be in denial about having a snitch in his camp."

"You mean Dink?"

"Yes! That bitch was snitching on everybody and everything! I know Dana killed Charlotta. Melonhead would never be able to get in the car with my cousin."

Suddenly all the happiness that had come with being released had evaporated. He was expecting it to be like this. Short lived pleasure followed by intense pain. Then anger. There was a huge responsibly on his shoulders and he knew it. He was about to go to war with one of the hood's most notorious gangsters. Melonhead he knew he could handle, but Dana gave him serious doubt. There was a strong possibility he could die before his case ever made it to trial. But he knew it was time to leave any feelings of inadequacy behind in this room. Tamiko had faith in him. So much faith that she was willing to bet a hundred K that he would make things right.

He was determined not to let her down. He was determined not to let Sergio toss and turn in his grave because he didn't ride. He no longer cared about his own life, his own future. He only cared about the respect and redemption for himself and those that had fallen.

"As far as I'm concerned, everybody gotta go because I'm not about to be out here looking over my shoulders every day," Capone said.

"Exactly," Tamiko said nodding her head in agreement.

It felt good to the both of them to know that they were on the same page. Just then there was a knock on the door and they knew it was Evelyn.

"Come on," Capone said.

"You sure?"

"Yeah."

Evelyn came in nervously glancing around the room. She had to now pretend as if she didn't know murder was the topic of discussion while she was out of the room.

"Listen I really appreciate both of y'all, Ev. Thank you so much for getting my baby brother out of jail. I feel so much better now that I have him with me."

Tamiko grabbed Capone's hand.

"I want you to stay with me in my house while you're out on bond."

"You sure?" Capone asked.

"Of course I'm sure nigga. I need you there with me to keep me from going crazy without Sergio. Evelyn you know you're welcome at my house anytime and you can stay as long as you want. I got a couple extra rooms I'm really not doing shit with so…"

"Thanks," Evelyn said wondering was Tamiko offering her to move in or not.

Tamiko went on to explain the doctors still were not ready to release her but she would definitely make Sergio's funeral even if she had to check herself out of the hospital against their will. Capone didn't know if she was up to it but he knew she would not be denied the chance to say goodbye to the man that was her world. Today was the viewing of Sergio's body but Tamiko demanded that Capone not attend and she explained exactly why it wasn't a good idea.

****

On the drive home, Capone had the weirdest thought. He wondered was him being released from jail on a hundred thousand dollar bond a blessing from God; if so, he was about to give God a big slap in the face as a thank you. His mother had always warned him about having a devil's mentality. One thing he knew for sure was that he had to take advantage of his being on the streets right now. Capone wanted to spend his first night at home with his mother and Evelyn. It was complicated, to say the least, because even with everything that had happened, Capone and Evelyn were still months away from turning eighteen.

Evelyn had already put a huge strain on her relationship with her own mother and was beginning to see less of her. Sheila was not happy in going against her principles, but she wanted her son at home with her and she wanted him to be happy on this night. Capone and Evelyn made love as quietly as possible in the middle of the night and Evelyn quickly nodded off while Capone lay holding Evelyn in his arms plotting his next move.

The next morning, Sheila woke them both and told them she wanted everyone downstairs for a prayer session before she went to work. Sheila prayed that God's will be done and that whatever the outcome of Capone's trial he'd be made a stronger and better person. Capone prayed while incarcerated but now that he was back on the streets it felt awkward. The demons and angels were tugging at his arms again.

Chapter 27

Around nine o'clock the next morning Capone and Evelyn went to pick up Tamiko from the hospital. She had three hours to go home, shower, and get dressed before the funeral. Capone had learned a lot overnight. He learned that all of his stuff from the apartment was placed in a storage locker. He learned that all the money he'd saved hustling was still at Evelyn's house. She hadn't spent one dime of the eighteen thousand he'd left with her. It wasn't much, but he was damn sure glad to have it and knew he'd need it.

They arrived at Tamiko's house and she led Capone upstairs to the master bedroom. Evelyn stayed downstairs, becoming a little irritated with all the secrecy now.

"Take this," Tamiko said handing him a P-89 Ruger and a new fake identification card that made him twenty-one.

"I never seen this one," Capone said referring to the gun.

"He never took this one out of the house. I got some more stuff in the basement to give you later."

Tamiko flopped down on the bed and began to massage he temple.

"You okay?" Capone asked.

"Yeah, but...I can't lose you too so you really gotta be careful out there. I need you to really watch your back."

"I can take care of myself sis you know that. Plus you can't afford to worry about shit like that right now."

"Yeah, well, Sergio could handle himself too and look what happened."

"He always told me, win or lose you still gotta fight. Besides I don't think nobody is even expecting me to be on the streets. And if they do find out they probably won't see me as a threat now that Sergio is gone."

"You can't think like that though Capone. You gotta think like these muthafuckas and know that they will kill yo' ass in a heartbeat."

"Yeah, you right. I can't think like that."

"Hell naw, 'cause if they do consider you as a threat, by the time you realize it, it'll be too late."

Tamiko was definitely Sergio's girl and talking to her was like talking to him sometimes. They had already called Sergio's mom and set up a second viewing of the body just for Capone. It's cost them an extra fifteen hundred dollars but for Capone and Tamiko, the element of surprise was priceless. They strategized for another fifteen minutes before Capone and Evelyn left for his private viewing of the body. He wanted to be in and out of the funeral parlor at least an hour before the funeral started. The longer he was home without his name ringing in the streets, the more he could get done.

****

Sergio was dressed in a blue pin-striped suit and a blue tie. Capone stood over the casket thinking this was the first time he'd ever seen Sergio in a tie. The mortician had done a great job of making Sergio look like he was just in a deep sleep. This was already harder than Capone expected it to be, even though he expected it to be extremely hard. His chest began to tighten and he had to take long, deep breaths. This life was the one he had chosen for himself so he couldn't afford to feel sorry for himself or anyone else. He knew what Sergio would want so it just was what it was.

Still, it was the ultimate shock to his system to be standing over his brother's dead body. Capone felt as if he was all out of tears and had cashed in every emotion he had left in his feelings bank. There was nowhere to go from where he was mentally, neither up nor down. He began to speak to Sergio for last time face to face.

"You always told me you'd be dead, in jail or filthy rich by twenty-five. I never liked to hear you say that, but I'm sure you know I always looked up to you for the way you were always ready to deal with whatever life handed you. So now, I'm doing my best to handle this. A lot of people gonna miss you bro, but nobody more than me. I don't know if you can hear me or not but I'm feeling like we might meet up again sooner than later. I mean...I just don't fear the worse no more, you know? I don't know if that's a good or bad thing, but that's just how I feel dog. All I know is...I'm gonna hold you down until my last breath. I love you, man."

Capone left the funeral home feeling like his future was already written. No matter which way he was still headed to jail or the graveyard. It didn't matter anymore. Maybe this was all he was supposed to do with his life. Kill a few people, make a few dollars, and die before the age of eighteen. If that's all it was, he wouldn't be the first or the last. He thought about Jason, who he'd robbed of his life at such a tender age, as he drove around in Evelyn's Corolla thinking about his next move. He still had his Cadillac but didn't plan on driving it at all. His intention was to get a rental car from one of his clients that worked for a rental car company, but first he had to pay Chocolate a visit.

****

Chocolate's new house was much nicer than the old one. She had written him letters in the county with her new address and new phone number, explaining that her old house was too hot after everything that happened. This was the first time he'd ever called her since she changed her number, but when she didn't answer he decided to just drive to her house anyway. Halfway up the steps, he saw the front door swing open. Chocolate was startled by his presence.

Capone noticed she was dressed a little classy and upscale compared to her usual taste. Her eyes grew wide as she realized just who was standing on her porch.

"Oh shit! Come here, nigga!" Chocolate said as she reached out and snatched Capone into a bear hug. "When the fuck you get out?"

"Yesterday."

"Damn, I can't believe yo' ass is out! My nigga had told me he was gonna get you out, but then that shit happened and it was just like…" She threw her hands up in frustration.

"You gon' let me in?" Capone asked.

"Did you really just ask me that?" Chocolate said looking offended.

Capone stepped in and was glad to see the house wasn't lavishly decorated. It was pretty much the same stuff from the old house. He knew that more than likely there were drugs stashed at Chocolate's house the day Sergio was killed. He also knew that whatever she had left there was only one person that would be able to recover it, and that was him.

"I swear after everything that happened I just had to dip from the other crib."

"You did the right thing," Capone said.

Chocolate sat her keys down and headed for the kitchen.

"Where was you headed just now?" Capone asked.

"To the funeral," she called out from the kitchen.

Capone didn't think it was a good idea for Chocolate to go to Sergio's funeral, but he wasn't about to try and talk her out of it. She came back into the living room gripping a bottle of Remy Martin and two glasses.

"If you feeling like I'm feeling you might need a drink or two before you head to this funeral."

"I do need a drink, but I'm not going to the funeral."

"What?" Chocolate said giving him another look of disbelief.

"I'm not going. I said my goodbyes, but I don't want nobody to know I'm out right now."

"Oh, right. I was about to trip, but you right, and I'm glad to see you on point."

She poured herself a shot then Capone.

"I don't know how I'ma make it through this day." She snorted then tossed her shot back like a veteran.

"Better slow down," Capone said.

"Shit, this my third shot. Fuck what you talking."

"You know Tamiko is gonna be there, right?"

"No shit," Chocolate replied in a sarcastic manner. "I don't care. That was my nigga too. I'm gonna pay my respects, say my goodbyes, and that's it. Fuck all the drama. And I'm probably not gonna be the only one of his bitches there anyway."

"Well, just make sure you don't say nothing to Tamiko."

Chocolate paused on her way back to the kitchen. She spun around with her hands on her hips.

"Come on now, you know me way better than that."

She was right and Capone really didn't even know what made him say it. Chocolate had been the mistress for years and had never stepped out of line once when it came to Sergio's home life. She stayed in her place and Capone knew she had too much respect for Sergio to get foul at his funeral.

"A bitch just wanna say her goodbyes, you feel me?" she repeated.

She took another drink straight from the bottle before placing it back in the cabinet. Capone could see that Sergio's death was eating her up inside as well.

"Come here, Capone."

He quickly finished his drink and went to the kitchen where she stood waiting.

"What's up?"

"Grab that broom and follow me," she ordered as her heels clicked softly on the linoleum then loudly on the hardwood floors leading to the stairs.

The house was a little big for a single woman without kids, but Capone thought maybe she was planning for the future like Tamiko was when she settled on her house. In her bedroom, Chocolate pointed to a walk-in closet with a sliding door. Capone slid the door back and she pointed to a mini door inside the closet. It had to be a crawlspace.

"I'm already dressed so you know I'm not going in there," she warned.

"What's the broom for?" he asked.

"Spiders and spider webs. That's the other reason I'm not going in there."

She gestured for him to proceed. After unlatching the hook on the mini door, Capone squeezed himself into the crawlspace, leaving the broom behind.

"Keep going," Chocolate called out as he crawled on all fours over the wooden planks.

"I see it," Capone shouted as he accidentally ran his hand over a small bag folded face down.

****

Evelyn clung to Tamiko during and after the funeral. She was worried that something would jump off at the funeral and she'd be in harm's way. She had visions of gun-toting madmen coming to shoot up the casket like in the movies. In her lifetime, she'd seen a lot of crazy stuff on the ten o'clock news so she knew anything could happen. Maybe someone would find out Capone was home and come looking to finish him off before he got any bright ideas. But despite all her apprehension, everything went smoothly. Every seat in the house was full and Evelyn sat between Tamiko and Sergio's mom, who was holding up better than anyone expected.

Throughout the funeral, she had no massive breakdowns just silent tears. Tamiko held herself together like Evelyn knew she would. It wasn't like her to let people see her any other way. A lot of hustlers attended the funeral including Sergio's former employees. Tamiko gave them all blank stares as they offered their condolences. She was feeling everyone out because she didn't know who to trust anymore. Randy was the only one she allow herself to speak to.

She held a little sidebar with him and appointed Randy to gather certain individuals' contact information. Evelyn and Tamiko were leaving out when they were approached in the lobby by a group of unfamiliar faces wearing New York Yankee ball caps. Evelyn quickly grew nervous.

"Aye yo ma, can I get a quick minute with you?" the man out front asked.

"Who is you? I don't know none of y'all," Tamiko replied easing her hand in her purse.

"Chill ma, it ain't even like that word up," the spokesman for the group said.

Tamiko knew from the way this dude talked he couldn't be from Detroit.

"Straight up and down, Sergio was my man. We came from New York to pay our respects and I was told you were his wifey. I just wanted to offer my condolences and say I'm sorry for your loss."

The man went on to introduce himself as Block and he then rattled off the names of the rest of his crew. Tamiko tried not to be rude but she had to be cautious. She knew Sergio had ties to New York and she also knew that's where his drugs came from.

"Who told you who I was?" she inquired.

"Shorty right here," Block replied as he pointed a finger at Chocolate who was quick-stepping out the door.

"I don't know her either," she said.

"Well, that's neither here nor there. I know her from doing business in New York so she was the only familiar face I recognized."

Block paused and waited for Tamiko to speak. She quickly put the connection with the girl that was leaving and Sergio together but didn't let it bother her.

"Okay, well, you know my name is Tamiko and this is my friend Evelyn."

Evelyn waved but wasn't up for shaking any hands. She was too busy scoping out the ridiculous amount of diamonds that flooded Block's chain and watch. Block pulled out a thick sealed envelope from his right pocket with Tamiko's name on it.

"What's this?" she asked.

"Just a little something to help you get through the hard times."

Tamiko quickly slid the envelope inside her purse.

"Thank you."

"My number is inside. Like I said, that was my man's word up. If it happened to be me instead, I'm sure Sergio would've done the same thing for me. So just remember you always have friends on the east coast, you hear me?"

Tamiko nodded, and with that said, Block and his crew made their way to the exit. Tamiko and Evelyn trailed a safe distance behind them still being cautious. Evelyn could tell even Tamiko was a bit jarred by the whole encounter. Stranger from another state coming to bring her a gift?

"You think those were Sergio's friends for real?" Evelyn asked.

"Yes. I think I know who he is I just never met him in person."

They began to fill the sidewalk and for every step Tamiko and Evelyn took, it seemed they became more boxed in by friends and family. Some were busy pretending to be more grief stricken than they really were while others just mingled as if they were at a social event. Tamiko pointed out Sergio's mom talking to his dad, and Evelyn realized that was the first time she'd seen his mom. They were walking towards Sergio's parents when a voice called out.

"Tamiko!"

She turned to see a dark sedan right in front of the no parking sign on the street. The windows were tinted and only rolled down just enough to see the top of the guy's head in the passenger seat. Once again, Tamiko reached for her Glock tucked in her purse. The window came down a little more, revealing who was inside. It was a face she immediately recognized but gave her no comfort. It only made her want to pull out, aim, and fire.

"We should go," Evelyn said trying to pull Tamiko by the arm.

"Fuck that!" she spat as she yanked away and charged toward the sedan.

Tamiko was still undecided on whether to pull out and start dumping or play it cool and wait for the next words out of his mouth. Evelyn wasn't packing so she stayed a safe distance back in case guns started popping off.

"What the fuck you doing here?" Tamiko demanded.

Melonhead sat in the passenger seat of the sedan looking nervous.

"I just wanted to let you know I didn't have shit to do with that. I didn't pay for it and I didn't put in no work. I didn't have nothing to do with that shit and I'm not no pussy that would come here and say I didn't if I did."

Tamiko wore a confused scowl.

"So you think I'ma take your word for it just because you came to a funeral and said it wasn't you?"

"If I did it, I did it. But since I didn't, I'm trying to settle this shit once and for all. My beef was with Sergio, but he's no longer here, so people ain't gotta keep dying."

Tamiko was heated.

"See that's where you wrong. It's too late for that stop the violence shit nigga."

"You can be stubborn and stupid if you want, but…"

"Who the fuck is you calling stupid nigga?"

People could hear them arguing now and they were drawing attention because of the hostility in Tamiko's voice.

"I'm just saying, you got enough respect out here in the streets to put the word out and squash this shit."

"Put the word out to who?" she asked, but it was a rhetorical question.

"Who the fuck ever!" Melonhead said growing frustrated with Tamiko's stonewalling disposition.

A big body Benz pulled up alongside Melonhead but edged out in front of him to get a good look at Tamiko on the sidewalk.

"You good ma? Everything cool?" Block yelled from the driver seat.

"Yeah, I'm good, thanks," Tamiko replied.

She waved them goodbye and shot Melonhead a look that was cold as ice.

"You need to go," she warned.

Melonhead heeded the warning, rolled up the window, and pulled off slow. All of sudden Randy came from seemingly out of nowhere and began ushering both ladies to the parking lot.

"Where y'all parked at?" Randy said.

"Over here," Tamiko replied pointing her car out.

Randy used his large frame to move swiftly through the crowd until they were at Tamiko's Jaguar. Randy hadn't heard any of the conversation that had just transpired. He'd spotted Melonhead and was moving on the assumption that he was there to start trouble. Tamiko was glad to have him on her side.

"I'ma follow y'all to the freeway. I don't trust that muthafucka."

In the car, Evelyn continued to peek in the rearview mirror, even after they were long gone from the funeral home. This just wasn't the life she was used to. Looking over her shoulders, taking cover, being rushed away from the enemy.

"I can't live like this," she said as Tamiko changed lanes. Tamiko gave her a knowing glance but didn't comment. "I mean, how you deal with this shit after all these years?"

"Not good as you can tell from the hospital band I'm still wearing around my wrist."

"Yeah, but that was too much for anybody to have to deal with at one time. I'm talking about everything that led up to what happened. How did you even think straight on a daily basis not knowing if the man you love is gonna be dead or in jail before the day is over?"

"I don't know," Tamiko said as she pondered the question. "Maybe it's because I'm no angel myself. I knew Sergio's lifestyle was dangerous, but he'd been the same way all his life. That's who I fell in love with, so for me to think that his life was ever gonna change would be stupid on my part. If you think Capone is gonna change then the same goes for you."

Evelyn tried to make sense of what she was feeling as the two of them rode in silence for the rest of the ride. Her heart was with Capone but her mind was telling her to get out while she still could.

Chapter 28

At his next court date, Capone was presented with all the required paperwork to complete his discovery package and a trial date was set for three weeks later. Meanwhile, he went back to hustling. He relied heavily on Randy because that was the only way he could keep his face off the scene. Randy basically had total control over all of Sergio's territory and all his workers that were loyal enough to stick around and link up with Capone.

Capone let everyone know that it was his operation now but it still took some people longer than others to get used to the transition. Too many changes in command for some to soldiers to keep up, but Capone told people what they needed to know and nothing more. Some of the lowest guys on the totem pole didn't even know that Capone was out of jail. He spent most of his time between Evelyn, his mom's house, and Tamiko's. Evelyn hadn't been herself lately but Capone didn't have time to worry about it now. He was too busy working on a plan that would bring about the demise of all of his enemies.

Word on the streets was that Dana was still creeping in and out of town on the run from the feds. It was rumored that he was even riding around in the trunk of cars in order to keep his operation running. Capone knew it was only a matter of time before he got another out of town gig and then he'd be a ghost again. Time wasn't on his side. He tried to think positive as he drove in his rental car on the way to his lawyer's office.

"Come on in," Dominique said as she opened the door.

This was the first time Capone had ever come to her office. He was high as a kite and she could tell.

"Hello?" she said snapping him out of his daze.

"Huh?"

"I said how have you been?"

"Oh, I been...I been straight."

"I been straight," she mimicked, making fun of his super cool attitude.

It always seemed to her as if none of it made much difference to Capone one way or the other. He glanced around at all of her framed accomplishments that decorated the wall. He noticed the family photos on her desk as he stood in the middle of the floor.

"Have a seat; this won't take long. I just have a few things I wanna go over with you." She took a sip of her latte before she started. "As I told you before you have two associates that have been linked to your case by an eye witness from day one. One of those associates is dead now and the other is willing to take the stand in your defense. The prosecution doesn't have a strong case for murder one or two so I think if we can scare 'em a little then we might get a manslaughter plea offer and you'll be looking at about five years. Thing is, the witness for the prosecution is a very well-respected member of the community, and I'm just hoping she can't hurt our chances as much as they think she can.

"Yeah, but she's like seventy something years old. Nobody is gonna believe she can still see that good at her age," Capone said.

"She's sixty-five and she was only sixty-two at the time of the incident. The point is she's going to take the stand and say she saw you running down the streets with a gun in your hand seconds after the shooting. If we go to trial, that's gonna be hard to overcome, but I'm ready to fight if I have to."

Capone found out about the witness when he was in the county jail. When he got out, he had a long talk with Tamiko and she tried to convince him that he needed to kill the old lady. He'd kill ten gangsters to save his own life but Capone had limits. Limits that could cost him severely.

"The good thing is nobody is there to finger you as the trigger man. One guy is dead and the other is willing to say you weren't the shooter, but that's risky."

"Because Dink already made a statement saying I was?"

"Right, so that, along with an eye witness that's gonna be on the stand, is dangerous waters."

Dominique was blowing his high.

"You not making me feel real good about my chances right now."

"Well, that's not my job. My job is to represent you to the best of my ability but let me finish what I was saying. There is another angle to work here. You were in a fight so…in a scuffle anything could happen. Maybe Jason had a gun and it fell on the ground in the middle of the scuffle. Maybe someone that tried to break up the fight had a gun and it fell on the ground in the middle of all the commotion. You see where I'm going with this?"

"Hell yeah, but that still leaves me as the shooter."

"Yeah, but it's not premeditated and it's damn sure not intentional murder if we play our cards right."

"Yeah, that's true."

"I'm good at this and that's why Sergio retained me. The prosecutor knows if this goes to trial I'm going to pull out all stops. So when we go in that courtroom in a couple of weeks she's more than likely going to have an offer on the table. And it's gonna be an offer most people in your position could live with."

She paused for a moment. Capone could tell she wasn't finished so he waited patiently. "As good as I am, the one thing I won't do is guarantee a victory in a trial. Never have and never will."

Capone shook his head.

"I can't take a plea deal."

"Well, it's your decision."

Capone pulled out a wad of cash and sat it on her desk.

"It's all there," Capone said.

"Okay, let me get you a receipt."

She took out a pen and pad and began to write out a receipt. She tore off the top half and gave it to Capone.

"Okay, that squares us so don't get yourself in any more trouble before this is over."

"I'll try my best."

Capone couldn't help but think about what would happen if he were to get arrested on a drug charge while he was out on bond and how his girl would look at him. He had to be extra careful.

****

Evelyn had been keeping all kinds of secrets from her mom. If she knew anything truthful about Capone it was the fact that he spent a lot of money on her daughter. She was still lying about him having come into money from a lawsuit his family won, she was lying about him graduating school early and having several colleges looking at him, and she wouldn't dare tell her mother about the murder charge he was facing. Evelyn had created a whole other person to present to her mother when the time was right, but the fact was Capone had never been introduced to Evelyn's mom. There was never a good time. Since they'd been together Capone had been on the run from the law the entire time and now he was fighting for his freedom, but luckily, her uncle had assured her mom that Capone was a decent guy.

She knew once they were finally introduced Capone would make a good first impression because he really was a sweet guy at heart. His mom was a hardworking God-fearing woman, and she knew her mom and Sheila would really hit it off. But lately Evelyn hadn't been herself, and she was becoming isolated and jittery at home. Inside she was filled with guilt and growing tired of all the lies and pressure from her mom to meet Capone. She sat across from Capone at an upscale restaurant gazing at the menu, but food was the last thing on her mind.

"What's wrong?" Capone asked sensing the vibe.

"Nothing," she responded still staring blankly at the menu.

Capone had driven more than a couple of miles outside of the city so they could have a nice, quiet dinner, but this was too quiet.

"You ain't been yourself lately," he said.

"What do you mean?"

"Well, like, you didn't even tell me about the Detroit Free Press article. I had to find out through your uncle. You used to tell me everything and now something that big and you don't say nothing?"

With everything going on, Evelyn had completely forgotten about her accomplishment.

"When I called you to tell you about it, you said you was going to call me right back and you never did. I was going to tell you about it then," she explained.

"Well, we drove all the way here and you still didn't mention it."

Capone was feeling ignored and excluded. Evelyn had followed her liberal arts teacher's advice. After reading aloud a two-page presentation entitled "We Are the Future" her teacher suggested that she submit the work to the local newspaper. She told Evelyn she could make a few bucks and get her name out there at the same time. The Detroit Free Press liked the article and decided to print it. The editor also implied that he looked forward to receiving more "words of wisdom" from her. But Capone didn't know anything about any of it until he ran into Evelyn's uncle in the neighborhood.

"It's not like I was trying to hide it from you or nothing. I just forgot."

Capone sat back in his chair. Something was definitely wrong with Evelyn.

"Listen to what you saying; that don't even make sense. What is it you're not telling me Ev?"

Capone looked in her eye and he knew she was holding something back. She refused to hold her eyes on him because she knew he would read her like a book. The whole ride she'd been thinking things over. She wanted to wait until they left the restaurant so they didn't make a scene. Now she was wondering why she even agreed to come in the first place. The person Capone was forcing her to become was what weighed the heaviest on her mind and she just couldn't hold it in any longer.

"This…relationship isn't healthy for me. It never was. This whole lifestyle isn't healthy for me and now it's all just becoming too much. When I was at the funeral with Tamiko, I was scared for my life. Then all these dudes kept rolling up on us and I had no idea what was about to happen. I'm always scared when I'm with you because I don't know if I'm safe. All I know is people keep dying. They just keep dying and I don't wanna be next."

"So it's over?" he asked.

"Sometimes at night, I feel like I can't breathe. I have nightmares of something happening to you and I wake up crying."

"Okay, but why are you saying all of this now? If you were gonna leave you could've left me when I was in fucking jail!"

"But I didn't because I love you and I didn't wanna walk away from you when you needed me the most."

"I still need you now more than ever."

Evelyn shook her head.

"I know you always felt like Sergio and Tamiko were the perfect couple, but that's not me. I'm not that ride or die chick that's gonna stick with you through getting shot or going in and out of prison all your life. This is not the life I want for me and this is not the life I want for us."

"You picked a fine fucking time to tell me."

"Because you've been on the run for murder the entire time we've been dating. What would've been the point? I didn't know things would get this serious between us. I didn't know we would grow to feel this way about each other."

Capone poured himself another drink while Evelyn sat silently until she was ready to speak again. "We said in the beginning that we would just enjoy our time together and we did that. Now that you're about to go to trial, what happens if you beat the case? What are you gonna do then? Keep hustling? Shooting people?"

"Shhh!" Capone said looking around to see if anybody heard her.

"I'm sorry, but what are you going to do?"

Capone guzzled his champagne while he tried to think of what would be the best response. Anything positive he could think to say would be a bold face lie. Her truth had rendered him speechless. He never took the time to think about what would happen if Evelyn didn't want to live the life he lived. The only thing he knew for sure was that he didn't want to lose her. In that moment Capone realized he was successful at becoming the G he always wanted to be, but it was costing him everything.

"I know this ain't the life you wanted, Evelyn. I don't even know why I brought you into all this shit in the first place."

Evelyn listened and waited for the rest but it never came. She was hoping that Capone would say he was getting out of the game. She was hoping he would say that he loved her more than the streets and if he had to choose he was ready to make that choice. But all she heard was background voices of the conversations going on at the other tables.

"I'm ready to go!" she said.

The ride home was a cold one. The AC was on but the chill coming off Evelyn put the whole car on ice. Capone took advantage of the quiet time and analyzed the situation and all the what ifs. If he was lucky enough to stay alive and if he was lucky enough to stay free. Those two alone were two big what ifs. He knew Evelyn wasn't going inside with him so he pulled up out front of Tamiko's house and parked so Evelyn could get her car out of the driveway.

"You know Sergio used to always talk about investing his money in some businesses. Maybe when all of this is over I can go back to school and do something like that," Capone said.

"Maybe," Evelyn said unconvinced.

"You don't think I could? I'm serious."

"I believe you can do anything you put your mind to. I hope you are serious because I have been the biggest hypocrite running to church with your mom while looking the other way while you do all kinds of dirt. I can't go on like that; I refuse to."

"If that's how you feel, I guess my mom is a hypocrite too."

"That's different; your mom is always gonna love you no matter what."

Just then, Capone's cell phone rang and he found it between the seat and the console.

"Hello?"

"Aye where you at?" a familiar voice said.

"Who is this?" he said still trying to catch the voice.

"This Chocolate nigga, where the fuck you at?"

"At the crib, what up doe?"

"Guess who just walked in the Black Rose like shit is all good?"

"Who?"

"Bighead."

Capone paused. It didn't take him long to realize big head was code for Melonhead. He had to think quickly. Think, think, think.

"Who he with?"

"I only saw him and one more nigga. I don't know who the other nigga is."

"I'm on my way."

"Bet."

When Capone hung up the phone Evelyn's cold, blank stare had returned.

"I gotta go," Capone said.

Evelyn shoved the car door open without saying a word then slammed it shut. She knew something really bad was about to happen.

****

One the way to the club, Capone called Randy and told him he wanted to meet up at the gas station down the street from the club. He knew Randy had a brand new AK-47 just like the one he had because they had purchased them together. He filled Randy in on what was going down and Randy assured him he was on the way. He called Chocolate and told her to be ready to leave out behind Melonhead if he went towards the exit.

The club had an exit that let out on the side street that led to the freeway. Capone knew that by the club being on the westside, all the eastside club goers would be heading for the freeway once the club let out. Randy and Capone parked the car in an alley behind a garage. About forty-five minutes passed while they sat crouched down in the bushes of some involuntary co-conspirators house. Capone's legs were beginning to cramp and the night hawk was picking up from out of nowhere. Just then his cell phone rang and somehow he knew it was Chocolate before he even answered.

"Okay, I just left out behind them. They in the parking lot and they about to get in aaaaaa…green Tahoe."

"Okay, who's driving?"

"Melonhead got in on the passenger side."

"They pull out yet?"

"Hold on." There was a long pause. "He pulling out now."

"Is they headed towards the freeway?"

"Yeah, you should be able to see their headlights by now."

"Okay, I'm out," Capone said ending the call.

As soon as he hung up, he signaled for Randy to get in position on the opposite side of the street. Seconds later they could now see the headlights in plain view. The green Tahoe was the only car in the vicinity as it pulled up to the stop sign. Capone made eye contact with the driver as he moved in for the kill with no hesitation. The onslaught began from both sides as the driver tried to mash the gas, but his attempt was foiled by the downpour of bullets raining inside the truck.

Blocka! Blocka! Blocka! Blocka!

The choppas rang out over and over as the Tahoe slowed down and jumped the curb. Capone and Randy moved in to finish the job. As they continued to fire round after round, the bodies in the truck danced and bucked until they stopped shooting. They left both weapons at the crime scene and fled. Capone hit the auto locks and jumped behind the wheel and quickly darted out into traffic headed away from the scene of the crime. His phone began to ring and he knew who it was. He didn't want to answer. Had to concentrate on the road until they were safe. He wouldn't slow down until he was far away from the dead bodies. The phone continued to ring and he knew Chocolate wouldn't stop calling until he answered, so he did.

"I'm straight, I'm straight. I'll talk to you in a minute."

Chapter 29

As the days went by, Capone thought a lot more about Evelyn than he did the murders he and Randy had committed weeks before his trial was set to start. Evelyn wasn't returning his calls and it was killing him to know that he may have lost her forever. He knew that if he'd lost her he'd lost his soul mate. He tried to focus on the business that needed to be handled in the streets but his concentration just wasn't there. His trial date was closing in fast and it seemed like the more money he made the more problems he encountered.

His worker Tre had just been robbed and Tre swore he knew the guy that did it. Tre vowed revenge but it seemed more like he was expecting Randy and Capone to take action. Randy informed Capone that a couple other trusted soldiers had decided to run off with a package. Capone found himself drinking more than ever before. The trial along with trying to run Sergio's operation was becoming too big of a load for him to carry. Even with Randy's help, he still couldn't see how Sergio did it day in and day out. He needed a drink just to go to sleep at night.

He came in this night reeling from drinking three-quarters of a fifth of Remy Martin VSOP. He still had the bottle gripped tightly in his hand and a blunt dangling from his lips.

"Damn nigga, you need to slow the fuck down," Tamiko said.

"Naw, you need to speed up," Capone argued in a drunken slur.

"You really out here slipping like this shit is a game?"

"I'm tight," Capone spat in major denial.

"No, the fuck you ain't tight. You told me you were gonna be able to handle this shit. How you gonna handle anything when you running around here sloppy drunk? And if you still tripping off of the bitch Evelyn you need to let that shit go!"

Tamiko's harsh words were sobering. He had to catch himself because he was about to go off until he remembered that Tamiko was all he really had at this point. He just shot her a look that let her know she was the only one that could get away with such harsh words referring to the love of his life.

He had to remind himself that none of this was about him in the first place. It was about keeping promises to the loved ones he'd lost that could no longer fight for themselves. Capone sparked the blunt and took a seat next to Tamiko on the sofa.

"Do we got everything we need?" he asked.

"Yeah, we ready; that's why I need your head to be in the game right now. We need to do this now while the opportunity is here. But you gotta be at your best because if you not it's gonna cost you your life Capone, and I can't lose anybody else…I can't."

"I'll be ready. I haven't let you down yet and I'm not about to start now."

"Yeah, well, I hope not because like I said, you won't live to tell about it."

Capone took a long hit from the blunt and held it in his lungs as long as he could. He felt like his whole life came down to what happened in the next few days.

"You know I only get mad at you because I love you and I don't want nothing to happen to you that could be avoided. You the only brother I have," Tamiko said.

Capone sat the blunt down and laid down with the back of his head on Tamiko's lap and his arms folded.

"If I go to jail, you better write me."

"You ain't going to jail. If you do I'm breaking you out."

They both shared a moment of laughter and he glanced up at Tamiko as he was reminded of Charlotta. The statement about breaking him out sounded like something she would say.

"When all of this is over you think I should get out the game?" he asked.

"Nobody can make that decision for you. You gotta know what you want in this life and live with your decision. You know the game is live or die so..."

"Right."

"Speaking of live or die, you need to make a decision to go and whack that old bitch before she comes to court on your ass."

Capone knew that Tamiko's way made sense. The old lady really was a big part of the prosecution's case but there were two things stopping him from creeping on the old lady. One was the fact that he had so much on his plate he didn't wanna risk being charged with murder or attempted murder of a witness that was due to testify at his trial. The other thing that he just couldn't come out and tell Tamiko was that he just wasn't coldhearted enough to do it. He couldn't even send someone else to do it.

He just didn't have it in him, even though he knew he'd kill as many of his enemies in the street as he had to, he had limits to his thirst for blood. He questioned his ability to survive in the streets with such limited devotion. Later on that night, when Capone started to sober up some, he said a prayer that Evelyn taught him; a prayer for protection.

★★★★

Evenly couldn't stop thinking about Capone. No matter what she did to try and take her mind off of him, none of it worked. She wasn't even answering her phone at the moment fearing he was trying to call her from another number and she would hear his voice and miss him more. It was killing her to be away from him this long but she knew it was time for her to separate herself from the lifestyle and the person that brought it all about.

In her heart, she felt it was the right thing to do because, in reality, it was most likely that Capone was going to die or go to jail. Evelyn tried to turn her attention towards college and her future as a writer. It really was starting to feel like this was something she could do with her life, but first, he had to shake this funk of depression she was going through. As much as she knew she had to leave Capone and never look back, it still hurt...it hurt so bad.

*****

The three of them shared a common belief that had brought them together on this night with sinister plans. The belief that everybody—no matter how crazy or cold hearted—had somebody they cared about. Everything was riding on this belief if they were going to pull off the murder of a man that was thought by many to be untouchable. Randy was the one that found the house. He'd been there with Dink on more than one occasion. He remembered the street, but not the actual house so he staked out on the block for a couple of days before he finally caught Dana's sister pulling in the driveway.

It was around 10:30 when Felicia stood behind the door peering through the small glass window inside her door at the pretty young lady wearing a police badge and holding a single sheet of paper. She knew it had to have something to do with her brother before the woman said a single word.

She cracked the door open just enough to hear what the police officer had to say. Despite all of his attempts to hide his identity, everyone that went to school with Dana knew his real name.

"Detroit Police Department ma'am. Do you have a brother by the name of Danalon Giles?"

Felicia sighed as if she had been through all of this too many times.

"Yes I do, but he doesn't live here and I haven't seen him," she explained.

"We know he's not here ma'am; that's why we haven't executed this search warrant."

Tamiko waved her phony warrant at Felicia.

"So what is it that you want?" she wondered.

"Well, I was just hoping I could come in and ask you a few questions. It will only take about five minutes of your time."

"About what though? I already said I haven't seen him."

"Well, he's wanted for questioning in a homicide. If you could just give me a few minutes I promise I'll be on my way."

Felicia gave her a once-over. The casual clothing, the badge, the Glock stuffed in the holster. She looked the part but she seemed extremely young for a homicide detective. Dana always warned her about talking to police. Any information was too much information.

"Well, I don't have any information about his whereabouts or anything he's involved in so I don't think I can help you."

The door was already cracked open and Tamiko knew that's all she really needed.

"Yes I understand, but you're the only living relative on file and..."

Before Tamiko could finish her sentence, Randy and Capone emerged from the side of the porch and yanked the storm door open forcing their way inside. Felicia ran towards the back of the house screaming at the top of her lungs, but Randy hawked her down and brought her back to the living room dragging her by her hair. Capone locked the door while Tamiko pulled out her Glock and stood over a now kicking and screaming Felicia. Randy began smacking her repeatedly.

"Bitch shut the fuck up!"

"Who else is here?" Tamiko asked just to be certain.

"Nobody, I told you Dana is not here," she sobbed.

Capone moved swiftly through the house with a Mach-11, checking every room including the basement. Randy began to duct tape Felicia to her dining room chair.

"Please don't kill me!" she begged.

"You might as well cut that shit out right now. That begging and pleading ain't gon' get you nowhere with us," Tamiko warned.

"But I haven't done anything. I haven't even seen or talked to my brother in months."

Whack!

Tamiko knocked her upside the head with the gun.

"Don't say shit else unless I ask you something."

Felicia shrieked in pain and held her bleeding head with her hand until Randy snatched her hand behind her back and duct taped them both together. Capone came up from the basement and assured them that no else was in the house. He spotted the bleeding Felicia duct taped to the chair and his human nature was to feel guilty about what they were doing. He justified it all in his mind with Sergio and Charlotta's deaths. He was glad he was with two people that didn't have the same moral compass as he had. Two people that could give a fuck about Felicia's innocence.

"Okay, so if you do what we say then you might live. If not, then you're definitely about to die," Tamiko calmly explained.

"What do I have to do?" Felicia asked still sobbing.

"Where's your phone?"

Felicia signaled towards the living room and Capone went to retrieve it. He was amazed at how calm Tamiko was. It was as if she'd done this a thousand times before.

"This is what we need you to do; we need you to call your brother, and please don't lie and say you don't have a number for him because that would be your last words. When he answers, you tell him that somebody just came kicking on your door and you're scared for your life. You tell him that you don't want to sleep here tonight and that you want him to bring you money for a hotel and a gun."

Tamiko's voice was calm and soothing, making Felicia feel that if she cooperated she had a chance to make it out of this alive, but then again, this was the same girl that had just slapped her with a pistol, so it was hard to trust her words.

"What if he's out of town?" Felicia asked.

"We wouldn't be here if he was out of town; now make the call," she ordered.

"How can I call if I'm tied up?"

"Just give us the number. Randy, you dial."

As Felicia called out the number, Capone went from room to room peeking out the blinds.

"Make it sound real, Felicia; your life depends on it. Well, I guess it is real ain't it?" Tamiko giggled.

It was almost like she was enjoying herself as Randy dialed the number and waited for Dana to pick up. Once Randy heard Dana's voice he put the phone to Felicia's ear. She did just as she was told and her voice trembled with fear as Tamiko pointed the gun at her head. They could hear Dana's voice screaming into the phone but couldn't decipher his words. Felicia hung up the phone praying her one and only brother would come and save her. There was nothing left to do but wait.

Two hours passed before the before the three of them began to get edgy. Even Tamiko had begun to pace the floor and peek out the window every two minutes. Felicia stared at Randy off and on until she remembered where she knew him from. Randy knew that she'd probably realized who he was or at least where she'd seen him before. It didn't matter to him because he was surely going to kill her right along with her brother. The initial shock of the situation had worn off of Capone and he was now in full attack mode, ready for murder and mayhem. He had two clips for his Mach-11 plus Randy and Tamiko had plenty ammunition as well. His main concern was Tamiko.

He couldn't let anything happen to her. The phone rang and at first, nobody said anything, and then they realized it could be Dana so Tamiko instructed Randy to give Felicia the phone.

"Un un…no because I can't find it. Yes, I'm still here Dana but I'm scared. Please hurry!" Felicia said before the call ended.

She hated walking her brother into an ambush but she wasn't willing to die for his sins.

"What he say?" Tamiko asked.

"He asked where my gun is and why I didn't use it when they started kicking on my door."

"You got a gun in the house?" Capone asked.

"And don't lie!" Tamiko added.

Felicia nodded, not wanting them to find it later and kill her for lying.

"Where?" Tamiko asked

"In my bedroom."

"Where?" Tamiko asked.

"On the top shelf in the closet."

Capone went to retrieve it. The gun was a small chrome .380, just the kind of gun he expected to find. He slipped it into his back pocket. By now, three hours had passed and panic started to set in. Maybe Dana didn't care about his sister as much as they'd thought. Maybe he was completely heartless.

"You think we should have her call him again?" he suggested.

"Naw, he'll be here," Tamiko replied.

You could hear a pin drop as they all sat still, each individual mind racing at its own pace. Tears would trickle down Felicia's face ever so often as she contemplated her fate. Randy scooted the chair he was sitting in right next to her as he anticipated blowing her brains out right in front of Dana. All of a sudden there was a loud crash of fire bombs flying through the windows one by by one. Everyone scattered except Felicia who was bound to a chair. The third firebomb came right through the front window just missing Tamiko's face as she ducked in the nick of time. She had to stick her hands in the broken glass to break her fall and when she rose up she was bleeding. The fourth bomb sounded like it shattered the bathroom window.

No one was expecting Dana to attack his own sister's house with her inside. Capone stayed low expecting bullets to follow the fire bombs, but the only shots he heard were coming from inside the house. Tamiko was firing shots out the front window at someone. She fired round after round and Randy backed her up as she ran out of bullets and reloaded. Capone jumped to his feet and ran to the front to back Randy up. He let off twenty rounds from the Mach-11 and when he stopped they all went and took cover.

The fire spread quickly in the living room and now it was hard to see any of their targets from the blazing picture window. Shots rang out in twos from outside as the smoke increased the already blurred vision of everyone inside. Capone grabbed Tamiko by the arm and ran towards the back of the house. His adrenaline was pumping and there was no real thought process to his movement. He saw the bathroom on fire but the curtain that started it had fallen to the floor. Without hesitation, Capone dove straight through the bathroom window. His gun fell from his hand and bounced around on the concrete.

He jumped to his feet and grabbed the gun as Tamiko climbed out of the window behind him. As he went to help her she landed on her feet and they could hear footsteps running towards the back of the house. Two masked men emerged from the side of the house and Tamiko didn't have time to do anything but duck as Capone emptied his clip cutting down both would be assassins in the backyard. Tamiko wasn't able to remove the gun from her holster in time. Capone looked down and realized she was hit.

As she lay on her back holding her leg with one hand, he reached down and grabbed her, trying desperately to pull her to her feet. The flames from the house were visible in every room now.

"Where you hit at?" Capone asked but didn't hear the answer because more gunfire erupted. This time it was coming from the front of the house again.

Afraid for his own life, he took cover while Tamiko crawled to the bushes. Knowing she was hidden, he began to creep down the side of the house back towards the front. He could feel the flames coming from the house hotter than hell. As the wood began to burn and crackle, Capone used the brick masonry of the front porch as a shield. There were no shots being fired now, just the sound of burning wood. He peeked out and spotted two dead bodies on the front lawn and neither were Randy.

"Capone!" he heard Tamiko yell out.

It sounded like she was still in the bushes. He turned to run back to her but as soon as he made the first step he felt the burning sensation in his lower back as he spun around and went crashing to the ground. Lying on his back he saw Dana raise the gun and point it at his face. He raised his hand to cover his face as the shot went flying through his hand and exited from his elbow. The second shot grazed his head and he knew it was over for him. As more shots came he didn't feel the pain of any more bullets piercing his skin. He figured this part of death must not be that painful. With blood in his eyes blurring his vision, he saw Dana's body drop right in front of him.

He saw Dana get two more shots to the head and then Tamiko came into his vision. Debris fell from the still burning house and smoke began to clog his lungs. He coughed up a thick glob of blood and the cough was so strong it lifted him up and turned him on his side. He felt

Tamiko and Randy pulling him up from the ground as he began to pass out. Capone knew he was about to die.

Unconscious, Capone did not see any bright lights or vast blue skies. He could feel his body floating on air. He quickly put things together and realized he had to be on his way to either heaven or hell. He didn't feel the inner peace he'd heard about so he knew something was wrong. As far as he could tell there was just a mass of dark nothingness. He felt a strong presence near and when he turned his back to look at who was approaching, Satan appeared in the distance and motioned him to come closer. As he turned back in the opposite direction he now saw Jesus perched high on the only cloud in sight.

But Jesus didn't motion for him to come closer, he just sat and watched. Capone was petrified and he did not want to go with Satan. Satan would surely take him straight to hell. Never in his life had he considered that hell was a real place waiting for sinners. He wished he could go with Jesus instead. He wished Jesus would signal for him but every time he looked back, he saw Jesus just watching and Satan still signaling for him to come join him. He finally turned back to Jesus.

"Can I go with you? Please, can I go with you?"

Jesus did not reply and Capone was so afraid to turn back and look in the opposite direction knowing Satan was still waiting...lurking. He could feel the evil grin on his face without seeing him. "Please let me go with you!" he begged.

****

Evelyn had just begun indulging in a big bowl of cookies and cream ice cream. She had been eating a lot since the break-up with Capone. He hadn't called her nor was the break-up official, but her mind was made up. Her ringer to her private line had been off for days so she decided to turn it back on. Five minutes later her phone rang. She stalled at first but felt it in the pit of her stomach that she needed to answer the phone.

"Evelyn?" a voice ruefully called out.

"Yeah?'"

"This Tamiko."

She was obviously sobbing and Evelyn was afraid to ask why so instead she just held the phone.

"Are you there?" Tamiko asked.

"Yeah, I'm still here."

"Capone just got shot and he's at the hospital all by himself because we couldn't stay. Please go be with him; he needs you there."

"Oh my God, what hospital?" she asked, voice trembling with fear.

"St. Johns, please hurry he really needs you."

Evelyn hung up the phone and grabbed her car keys and ran out of the bedroom. Skipping several steps on the way downstairs, she blew past her mom before she could see the panic and tears in her eyes. As soon as she pulled out of the driveway, Evelyn gunned the Corolla at top speed praying for Capone's life as well as her own safety. At the stop light, she tried calling Sheila but got no answer.

****

Capone came to and found his eye being held open by a thumb and index finger. Blinded by the light from the ophthalmoscope, he forced his other eye open. Lots of people were in the room and most were wearing surgical masks. There was a tall white man holding a hand full of bloody surgical cotton. He couldn't see the tubes jammed in his nose and mouth but he could feel them.

Pain riveted through his entire body and he could feel someone poking on nerves on the inside of his hand. The heart monitor made a strange sound and he passed out again.

****

Evelyn arrived at the hospital to find Sheila already there praying. She rushed over to Sheila and hugged her tightly.

"What they saying?" she asked.

"Nothing yet, he's still in surgery."

Evelyn began fanning her forehead and refused to sit down.

"Oh my God, my heart is beating so fast," she said.

"Evelyn, please tell me what happened to my son."

"I honestly don't know Ms. Johnson. I was at home when Tamiko called my crying, saying that he had been shot. I jumped in my car and drove straight here."

"Yeah, she's the one that called me too, but when I tried to call her back and get some information about what happened she said she had to go and hung up in my face."

"She knows what happened; it's all her fault! Whatever happened it's all her fault!" Evelyn shouted before bursting into tears.

Sheila tried comforting her and the two continued to pray and console each other throughout the night. The police finally showed up asking questions about what happened to Capone. Who was he last seen with? Did he have any enemies? The usual drill. By that time, Evelyn had calmed down and she chose not to reveal her suspicions to the police about Tamiko's involvement.

"Are you hungry?" Sheila asked.

"No, I'm okay. I need to call home though, and my cell phone isn't working in here. Do you have any change for the payphone?"

Sheila dug down in the bottom of her purse and found two quarters. Evelyn checked her watch and couldn't believe it was two in the morning. She made her way to the payphone trying to massage the stiffness out of her neck as a result of sitting in the same spot the last four hours. Just as she pushed the second quarter into the slot, Tamiko and Randy came into her view. Tamiko was wearing a turtleneck, but the bulge around the neck area indicated she was concealing some sort of bandage. Randy was walking with a slight limp. Evelyn slammed the phone down and went to confront them.

"Somebody tell me what the fuck happened," she shouted losing her cool.

Sheila went to try and calm her but then she spotted the doctor approaching from the corner of her eye.

"Excuse me, Ms. Johnson," he called out.

Evelyn and Sheila turned to see the surgeon patiently waiting to get everyone's attention.

"Is everyone here for Chris Johnson?" he asked, gesturing to everyone standing near.

"Yes!" they all confirmed simultaneously.

"The good news is he's gonna make it, but he's still in pretty bad shape."

"What do you mean?" Sheila asked.

"He's got some kidney and lung damage along with some bullet fragments in some pretty dangerous areas. Chris was shot five times. Twice in the back, the shoulder, the hand, and he was also grazed in the head."

"Oh my God!" Sheila shrieked.

"He's out like a light right now, but I'm going to allow each of you five minutes to visit him one at a time. No touching and definitely do not wake him."

Everyone agreed and the doctor told Sheila to follow him while everyone else stayed behind in the waiting room.

Chapter 30

Capone woke up the next morning and Tamiko was the only one there. She stared at him intensely waiting to see if he would talk. He tried to remove the breathing tube from his mouth but his right shoulder stabbed with pain.

"How you feeling?" Tamiko asked.

He successfully removed the tube with his left hand.

"We got 'em right?" he spoke groggily.

"Yeah, we got 'em," Tamiko smiled shaking her head.

She couldn't believe after nearly losing his life, that was his only concern.

"Where is Randy? And what's wrong with your neck?"

"He's around. We both caught some flesh wounds but we'll be okay," she assured him.

Tamiko placed the breathing tube back in his mouth seeing he was growing short of breath. "Don't try to do much talking. I just had to be here to see you when you woke up. Your mom and Evelyn were here all night and they'll be back around three o' clock."

Capone signaled for Tamiko to remove to tube again but the nurse came in and caught her in the act.

"Don't do that!" the nurse said angrily.

"He was trying to tell me something."

"He's not supposed to be talking; he's supposed to be resting."

Tamiko waved her off and as soon as the nurse left out, she took the tube out again.

"I saw, Jesus," Capone blurted out.

"Okay, baby I think you need to go back to sleep and get some more rest," Tamiko said.

"I'm serious."

The nurse came back and caught Tamiko red handed with the tube in her hand for the second time.

"Didn't I just tell you, never mind you gotta go."

"Okay, I'm leaving just let me tell him one more thing."

"You got one minute," she said as she checked Capone's blood pressure.

After removing the cuff she left the two of them alone to wrap it up.

"One minute," she called out from the hallway.

"That shit was all over the news man. We killed five muthafuckas and we all lived to tell about it," Tamiko said.

Capone smiled at Tamiko knowingly. They both knew they'd be legends in the hood from this point on.

"For Sergio and Charlotta," Capone said.

"For Sergio and Charlotta," Tamiko replied.

She kissed his forehead and prepared to leave before she was thrown out.

****

Over the next few days, Capone was so doped up he slept the hours away, waking up for visits, and falling asleep shortly. On the fourth day, Capone woke up to a room full of police officers who insisted he be handcuffed to the bed. At first, he was extremely confused until the lead homicide detective informed him that he was a suspect in the five homicides that had been plastered all over the news for the past week. One of the bullets removed from Capone's body matched a gun found at the crime scene, linking him directly to the murders.

He wasn't well enough to be taken into custody but a police officer was placed outside of his room to assure he wasn't going anywhere. Tamiko and Randy disappeared into thin air and Evelyn came to visit him one last time and assured him she wouldn't be back. Dominique came to visit as soon as she got word of the new charges, but there wasn't much she could do. She gave it to Capone pretty straight telling him based on what evidence police claim to have he was more than likely "fucked."

She still agreed to represent him on the new charges as well as the preexisting murder charge with the understanding that there was really nothing she could do for him. Capone's short life was seemingly over before he'd reached his eighteenth birthday. It all hit like a ton of bricks and he was now realizing just how much he'd screwed his life up. In his mind, he would've much rather died by Dana's gun than for his life to end like this. Dominique was able to postpone his previously set court date until he was healthy enough to stand trial.

He went from the hospital straight to a holding cell downtown at police headquarters. Capone did the only thing he could do in this situation; he prayed. He prayed for a miracle and begged God like never before. He vowed to change his ways if he could just get a second chance at life. Every night he thought about committing suicide and taking the easy way out. He didn't believe he could go through with it so he continued to pray, but his prayers would not be answered. Capone was charged with five counts of felony murder along with the now reduced manslaughter charge in the shooting death of Jason.

In court, Dominique argued that the evidence showed multiple shooters on the scene and none of which were on trial except Capone. The prosecutor presented fingerprint evidence as proof that it was Dana's gun that shot Capone, once again placing him at the scene. In the end, the prosecution dropped four of the murder charges due to lack of evidence, but Capone was convicted of Dana's murder and sentenced to life in prison. He was also convicted of killing Jason and received another ten years for manslaughter.

Capone threw away his gangster nickname as soon as he hit quarantine. Being a gangster had destroyed his life and he knew the only possible way to save it was to change his ways. He continued to pray for another opportunity and he had to believe that he would get it. If he stopped believing, there would be nothing left to do but to go through with the suicide. He made promises to God he wasn't even sure he could keep but he felt as if he had to make them. On the bus ride to a level four prison, he heard stories that sent chills through his body about prison life. Stories of dudes being raped and stabbed in the showers. Stories of twenty-two hour lock down and Nazi police who were hell bent on abusing anyone that showed signs of weakness.

As he walked across the prison yard with his blankets and sheets in his hand, he spotted big, burly dudes with tattoos everywhere and mean scowls on their faces. Everyone seemed to have a bad attitude; every guard and every inmate. Right then Chris knew there was no way in hell he could do this time alone. He would have to let Capone back in to do it with him.

Stay Tuned!

Index

Facebook: Author King Benjamin

Twitter: @kbwordplayz

Instagram Author King Benjamin

Check out more from King Benjamin

Roxanne

Gank Masterz

More Than I Can Bare

Wash You off My Skin

Record Label Romance

Don't wait for the next release through word of mouth. Subscribe to Kingbenjaminpresents.com today.